ONLY YOURS

SUSAN MALLERY

WHEELER
CHIVERS

GALE
CENGAGE Learning™

This Large Print edition is published by Thorndike Press, Waterville, Maine USA and by AudioGo Ltd, Bath, England.
Copyright © 2011 by Susan Macias Redmond.
The moral right of the author has been asserted.
Wheeler Publishing, a part of Gale, Cengage Learning.

Wheeler Publishing Large Print Hardcover.
The text of this Large Print edition is unabridged.
Other aspects of the book may vary from the original edition.
Set in 16 pt. Plantin.

LIBRARY OF CONGRESS CATALOGING-IN-PUBLICATION DATA

Mallery, Susan.
  Only yours / by Susan Mallery. — Large print ed.
    p. cm. — (Wheeler Publishing large print hardcover)
    ISBN-13: 978-1-4104-3890-4 (hardcover)
    ISBN-10: 1-4104-3890-2 (hardcover)
    1. Large type books. I. Title.
  PS3613.A453O56 2011
  813'.6—dc23   2011027690

BRITISH LIBRARY CATALOGUING-IN-PUBLICATION DATA AVAILABLE
Published in the U.S. in 2011 by arrangement with Harlequin Books S.A.
Published in the U.K. in 2012 by arrangement with Harlequin Enterprises II B.V.
U.K. Hardcover: 978 1 445 86564 5 (Chivers Large Print)
U.K. Softcover: 978 1 445 86565 2 (Camden Large Print)

Printed and bound in Great Britain by the MPG Books Group
1 2 3 4 5 6 7 15 14 13 12 11

To Kristy Lorimer.
A dark, mysterious stranger,
an adorable if slightly
off-center heroine and
a goofy dog named Fluffy. All for you.

CHAPTER ONE

Montana Hendrix's perfectly good morning was thwarted by a hot dog, a four-year-old boy and a Lab and golden retriever mix named Fluffy.

Things had started out well enough. Montana had been determined to get the nearly a year old dog into a therapy-dog training program. Sure, Fluffy was exuberant and clumsy, with a habit of eating anything and simply being too happy, but she had a huge heart. If she was, in simple terms, a screwup, Montana refused to hold that against her. Montana knew what it was like to fail to meet her potential, to always feel she wasn't good enough. She'd made a career out of it. Fluffy was not going to suffer the way she had. And even if she was projecting a little too much on to an innocent dog, well, sometimes that happened.

So there she was, on a beautiful Fool's Gold summer morning, walking Fluffy . . .

7

or, rather, being walked by Fluffy.

"Think calm," Montana, holding firmly on to the leash, told the dog. "Therapy dogs are calm. Therapy dogs understand restraint."

Fluffy gave her a doggie grin, then nearly knocked over a trash can with a sweep of her ever-moving tail. *Restraint* wasn't in Fluffy's vocabulary. She was barely calm in her sleep.

Later Montana would tell herself she should have seen it coming. This particular morning was the first weekend after school had let out and there was a festival to celebrate. Street vendors had been setting up for days. Although it was early, the smell of hot dogs and barbecue filled the air. The sidewalks were crowded and Fluffy kept pulling toward the children playing in the park. Her expression was clear — she wanted to be playing, too.

Up ahead, a mother paid for a hot dog. Her young son took it eagerly, but before he took a bite, he spotted Fluffy. The boy grinned at Fluffy and held out the food. At that exact moment, Montana was distracted by the latest display in Morgan's Bookstore and accidentally loosened her grip. Fluffy lunged, the leash slipped and that was when the trouble started.

Offering a hot dog from a distance might have seemed like a good idea . . . until a ninety-pound dog came barreling toward the little boy. He shrieked, dropped the hot dog and ran behind his mother. The poor woman had missed the beginning of the encounter. All she saw was a crazy-looking dog headed right for her and her son. She screamed.

Montana started after Fluffy, yelling for her to stop. But it was as effective as telling the earth to slow down its rotation.

The mother scooped up her little boy and ducked behind a lemonade stand. Fluffy picked up the hot dog without breaking stride and swallowed it in one gulp, then kept on going. Apparently freedom called.

Montana hurried after her, the new summer sandals she'd bought the week before cutting into her feet. She knew she had to get Fluffy. The dog was sweet, but not very well trained. Montana's boss, Max Thurman, had made it clear that Fluffy was not therapy-dog material. If word of today's disaster reached him, he would insist the dog leave the program. Montana couldn't stand for that to happen.

Fluffy was a lot faster than she was and quickly ran out of sight. Montana followed the sound of shrieks and screams, making her way through the streets of the town, dodging a peanut cart and narrowly missing a close encounter with two guys on bikes. She turned a corner just in time to see a tail disappearing through the automatic doors of a tall building.

"No," Montana breathed, staring up at the hospital. "Not there. Anywhere but there."

She raced forward, inwardly cringing at the thought of what Fluffy could do in a place like that. Big puppy feet on slippery floors were not a happy combination. She ran up the six steps leading to the entrance and dashed inside only to find a trail of havoc marking the way.

A supply cart was pushed against the wall. Linens spilled onto the floor. A little girl in a wheelchair grinned and pointed down the hall.

Montana got to the bank of elevators only to find several people willing to tell her that yes, a dog had gotten on. She watched the light panel to see an elevator had stopped on the fourth floor, then jumped in the next one and rode up.

The doors opened to the sound of screams. A chair lay on its side. More linens were scattered on the floor, along with a couple of charts. Up ahead double doors marked the entrance to the burn unit. Various signs explained what could and couldn't enter that part of the hospital. A joyous bark told her Fluffy had violated every single posted rule.

Not knowing what else to do, Montana followed the sound and pushed through the doors. Up ahead several nurses were trying to corral the happy dog while Fluffy did her best to lick all of them at the same time. When Montana called her, the dog turned and raced toward her. Just as a doctor walked out of a nearby room.

Fluffy did her best to stop. Montana saw her puppy paws scramble as the dog tried to slow. But she couldn't get traction on the floor. She started to slide, her butt went down, her front paws braced and then she was zipping along in a sitting position. She plowed directly into the doctor, sending him tumbling into Montana.

The doctor was about six inches taller and a whole lot heavier than Montana. His shoulder hit her chest, knocking the air out of her. They sailed across the floor, flying a few feet before stopping against the very hard floor, his body slamming into hers.

Montana lay there, dazed. She couldn't breathe. All she felt was dead weight on top of her and a warm tongue licking her bare ankle.

The man got off her and knelt beside her. "Are you hurt?" he demanded.

She shook her head, then managed to gasp in air. Fluffy moved closer and sat down, looking calm and well behaved. A trick Montana wasn't going to fall for.

The man reached for her. He ran his large, long-fingered hands up and down her legs and arms, then felt the back of her head. His touch was impersonal, but it was the most action she'd had in months. Before she could figure out if she liked it, she looked at his face.

He was the most beautiful man she'd ever seen. Eyes the color of green smoke, fringed by dark lashes. A perfect mouth, with a strong jaw. His cheekbone —

"She's fine," he said, turning to speak with someone behind him.

When he shifted his head she saw the other side of his face. Thick red scars grew from his shirt collar, along the side of his neck to his left jaw and cheek. They spiraled, creating an angry pattern that looked painful and pulled his skin.

She had a feeling her shock showed, but he didn't seem to notice. Instead he grabbed her hand and pulled her to her feet.

"Dizzy?" he asked curtly.

"No," she managed, now that she could breathe again.

"Good." He moved closer. "What the hell is wrong with you? What kind of irresponsible idiot allows something like this to happen? You should be arrested and charged with attempted murder. Do you know what kind of germs that dog has? That you have? This is a burn unit. These patients are vulnerable to infection. They are suffering with a level of pain you can't begin to imagine."

She took a step back. "I'm sorry," she began.

"Do you think anyone here gives a damn about you being sorry? Your thoughtlessness is criminal."

She could feel his rage in every word. Even more scary than what he was saying was the way he was saying it. Not with a loud voice and a lot of energy, but with a coldness that left her feeling small and stupid.

"I didn't —"

"Think," he interrupted. "Yes, that much is clear. I doubt you think much about anything. Now, get out."

Embarrassment gripped her. She was aware of the other staff members hovering

13

close by, listening.

Montana knew that Fluffy's running through the hospital was a bad thing. But it wasn't as if she'd planned the event.

"It was an accident," she said, raising her chin.

"That's not an excuse."

"I suppose you've never made a mistake."

His gray-green eyes flashed with derision. "Have you ever had a burn? Touched a hot pan or the burner on a stove? Do you remember what that felt like? Imagine that over a significant part of your body. The healing process is slow and what we do here to help it along is excruciating. On this ward, an infection kills. So any mistakes I've made have no bearing on this discussion."

There was no point in telling him that the work she did was important. She often came to the hospital with therapy dogs. Those therapy dogs helped patients heal, especially children. But she suspected this particular man wouldn't care about that.

"You're right," she said slowly. "There's no excuse for what happened here today. I'm sorry."

His mouth twisted. "Get out."

His complete dismissal stunned her. "Excuse me?"

"Are you deaf? Get out. Go away. Take

14

your damn dog with you and don't come back."

Montana was willing to admit fault and take the blame, but to have her apology ignored was just plain rude. Being a screwup didn't mean she was a bad person.

"You're a doctor?" she asked, even though she already knew the answer to the question.

The man's eyes narrowed. "Yes."

"You might want to take that stick out of your ass. It'll make it easier to pretend to be human, which will probably help your patients."

With that she grabbed Fluffy's leash, ignored the fact that the dog was licking the doctor's hand and walked out of the burn unit, her head held high.

On her way back to the kennel, she kept a firm grip on Fluffy, but no amount of holding could erase the fact that they'd both messed up big-time. Montana loved her job. It had taken her a long time to find out what she was supposed to do with her life. She loved training the dogs, and working with kids at the hospital and older folks at the nursing home. She'd started a reading program at all five local elementary schools.

She could lose everything because of what had happened today. If the administrator called Max and insisted Montana not be allowed back in the hospital, her boss would fire her. A fair amount of the therapy work took place there. If she couldn't go to the hospital, she wasn't much use to him. And then what?

She knew she only had herself to blame. Max had made it clear Fluffy wasn't going to be successful in the program, but Montana had wanted to give the dog another chance.

All her life Montana had been different. On her good days, she told herself she was a little flaky. On her bad days, well, the words were a lot worse than that.

Regardless of the label, it appeared that nothing had changed. She was still incapable of getting anything right.

Order was restored on the burn ward in a matter of minutes. Simon Bradley dismissed the intruder from his mind and continued his rounds. His last patient of the morning was the most worrisome. Nine-year-old Kalinda Riley had been brought in two days before when the family's gas barbecue had exploded. Kalinda was the only one hurt.

She'd been burned over forty percent of her body. He'd performed surgery yesterday. If she survived, it would be the first operation of many. For the rest of her life, her existence would be defined by her burns. He should know.

Her parents were devastated and frightened. They wanted answers and he had none to give them. The next few weeks would decide if the little girl lived or died. He didn't like to guess or assume, but he also couldn't escape the heaviness in his chest.

"Dr. Bradley."

He smiled at Kalinda's mother. Mrs. Riley was not yet thirty and probably pretty when she wasn't pale with worry and fear. Kalinda was her only child.

"She's been quiet," the mother continued. "We're keeping her sedated as she heals."

"There was a dog here before."

Simon tensed. "It won't happen again."

Mrs. Riley touched his arm. "She opened her eyes when she heard the commotion. She asked to see the puppy."

Simon turned toward Kalinda's room. The child shouldn't be that lucid. He would examine her, then look over her medications.

"Did she say if she was in pain?" he asked.

Later they would teach her ways to manage her discomfort. That's what they called it. *Discomfort.* Not agony or torture or suffering. All the things a serious burn could be. Later she would learn about breathing and meditation and visualization. For now drugs would get her through.

"She said she wanted to hold the puppy."

He drew in a breath. "It was an eighty-pound mutt that doesn't belong in a hospital."

"Oh." Mrs. Riley's eyes filled with tears. "We had a dog. A small Yorkie. She died a few months ago. I know Kalinda misses her terribly. I remember reading something about hospitals using therapy dogs. Do you think that would help?"

She was a mother who loved her child and would do anything to help her. To keep her from suffering. Simon had seen it hundreds of times. The greatness of a parent's love never ceased to amaze him. Perhaps because he hadn't experienced it himself.

Simon would rather eat glass than have a filthy animal in his burn unit, but he also understood that the healing powers of the human body could be triggered by unexpected sources. If Kalinda was to survive, she would need something close to a miracle.

"I'll see what I can find out," he said, and turned toward his patient's room.

"Thank you," Mrs. Riley said, smiling

bravely through her tears. "You've been amazing."

He'd done very little. Surgery was a learned skill. The gift he brought to those skills came at a price, but one he was willing to pay. He lived for his patients, to heal them as much as humanly possible and then move on. To the next tragedy. The next child whose life had changed in a single flash and the lick of a flame.

"You're not going to prison," Max Thurman said firmly.

"I should. He was right. What happened was criminal."

Montana had had nearly an hour to beat herself up and she'd made use of every second. Her bravado when facing the angry doctor had faded and now she was left with little more than a sense of having messed up in the worst way possible.

"Dramatic much?" Max asked, his dark eyes bright with amusement. "You're taking this way too seriously."

"Fluffy was loose in a hospital. She ran around, knocked over a couple of carts, then got into the burn ward."

"I'm not saying we want wild animals running through a sterile facility, but it was an accident and, according to the hospital

19

administrator, no damage was done. You need a little perspective."

They were in Max's office, a bright room at the back of his house. The kennels were on his property, as was the training facility. Montana wasn't a very good judge of how much land made up an acre, but she would guess Max owned more than a few of them. She knew she had to drive a good three minutes from the road to even get to the house. Which could be challenging in winter.

"If you'd seen that doctor . . ." she murmured, remembering his coldness most of all. "He was beyond furious."

"So, apologize."

"To him?" She never wanted to see him again. That would really work best for her. "Or you could call back the administrator and tell her I'm really sorry."

Max's blue eyes crinkled with amusement. "Very mature."

"You know her."

"So do you."

"She likes you." Every time they'd had a meeting, the administrator had been unable to keep from staring at Max.

Montana thought he was pretty nice looking, although a little, well, old. He had steel-gray hair, rugged features and piercing blue eyes. He was tall and rangy. He looked like the kind of man who could take care of himself in any situation. Although nearly sixty, Max looked and acted much younger.

"If you're that concerned, you should call her yourself," he told Montana. "She understands it was an accident."

"Dr. Stick-Up-the-Butt didn't," she muttered, but without a lot of energy. Max was right. Montana should be the one to call. "I'm going to work with the dogs while I gather my courage," she told him and left the office.

Once she was outside, she crossed the large expanse of thick, green lawn. To the east, she could see the mountains rising high against the blue sky.

Max's property was nestled in the foothills of the Sierra Nevada at the edge of the town of Fool's Gold. South of Reno, east of Sacramento, the area was beautiful, with wineries, a large lake in the center of town and winter skiing only a few miles up the road.

Montana loved her town and she loved her job. She didn't want to lose either. Not that anyone could take the town away from her, but still . . . She was feeling a little vulnerable. Despite Max's support, she worried about what Fluffy had done. What

21

she'd allowed to happen.

She walked around to the large play area where, during the day, the therapy dogs ran free, playing or sleeping in the sun. Several of them hurried up to greet her as she let herself inside the gate. She gave pats and hugs, then looked into Fluffy's happy brown eyes.

"Max was right," she told the dog. "You're not therapy material."

Fluffy wagged her tail.

"We'll find you a nice home with kids. You'll like kids. They have as much energy as you."

She had more to say. She wanted to explain that none of this was the dog's fault. That sometimes you had to try something before you could figure out you weren't very good at it. But before she could get started, she heard a car pull up. She walked around to the other side of the play area and was surprised to see the town's mayor climbing out of her car.

Marsha Tilson had been mayor of Fool's Gold longer than Montana had been alive. She was a warm, caring person who had given up much of her life to serve the town.

"I was hoping to find you here," the mayor called when she spotted Montana. "Do you have a minute?"

"Sure."

Montana let herself out of the play yard and walked toward the mayor. The older woman was elegantly dressed in a suit and pearls. Her white hair remained perfectly in place, despite the light breeze. By contrast, Montana felt a little scruffy. Her sundress had been old last year and she'd slipped off her sandals as soon as she'd gotten in her car. Red marks from her new sandals dotted her feet, and a few puffy areas promised to turn into blisters later.

"There's a conference room in the kennel," she said. "Is that all right? Or do you want to go up to Max's house?"

"The conference room is fine."

Mayor Marsha followed her along the path, then into the large building. There was an office, a small bathroom, the conference room, a kitchenette, then wide doors led to the kennel area.

"Something to drink?" Montana asked when they'd entered the conference area. The oval table could seat twelve, although they rarely had that many people out for a meeting. "We have soda, or I could make coffee."

"I'm fine."

Marsha waited until Montana had pulled out a chair before taking the one across

23

from her.

"You're probably wondering why I'm here," the older woman began.

"To sell me raffle tickets?"

Marsha smiled. "I need your help on a special project."

Montana's first instinct was to bolt. A few months earlier, Mayor Marsha had asked Montana's sister Dakota to help on a special project. Dakota had ended up working on a reality show as the liaison between the town and the producer. The good news was Dakota had met the love of her life, gotten pregnant, engaged and had adopted a beautiful baby girl. It had been a busy time.

But even if the idea of another special project made Montana nervous, running wasn't an option. She was a Hendrix and a member of one of the founding families of the town. Not exactly as thrilling as being a member of the Daughters of the Revolution, but history was important.

"How can I help?" Montana asked, knowing she was making her mother proud.

Marsha leaned toward her. "There's a doctor visiting town. A gifted surgeon. He's brilliant, a little difficult, but what he can do for people. . . . Simon Bradley specializes in patients who have been burned. He also performs regular plastic surgery. We have him here for nearly three months. That's what he does — goes from place to place performing miracles, then moving on. I want him to stay. He would be a wonderful asset for the town."

Montana frowned. "He sounds really great, but what can I do to help?" She was assuming Marsha didn't want her to set herself on fire to get close to the good doctor. No doubt he was the type who would —

She instinctively started to stand, then forced herself to remain sitting. The room suddenly seemed a little stuffy. She wanted to say it wasn't possible, that no one's luck was that bad. But she knew differently.

"You, ah, said he's new in town?" she asked.

"Yes. He's been here about a week."

Montana swallowed. "Have you met him?"

"Yes. As I said, he's not the most talkative of men, but he has a gift."

"Does he also have a scar on his face? Just on one side?"

"Oh. You know him."

"Not exactly. I had a run-in with him earlier. Literally."

Montana explained what had happened. Instead of looking shocked, Mayor Marsha started laughing.

"I wish I'd been there," she admitted with a chuckle.

"Only if you'd taken my place." Montana sighed. "As much as I'd love to help, you can see why I'm the wrong person."

Marsha's humor faded. "Not really." She leaned forward. "You are absolutely the best person I can think of."

Montana nearly fell off her chair. "Why?"

"I have a feeling in my gut. I can't explain it better than that. I've met Dr. Bradley and there's something about him."

"A stick up his butt," Montana muttered under her breath. "He's already mad at me. Don't you want someone without such an unfortunate history?"

"I want you. Just be your normal, charming self. Befriend him. Show him around, maybe take him to meet your family. That sort of thing. Help him to see that Fool's Gold is a wonderful place to live." The mayor straightened. "I need you, Montana, and so does the town."

Montana wanted to offer more reasons why this was a mistake but the mayor had already said the magic words. Giving back was part of Fool's Gold's culture. When asked, the good citizens said yes. Even if they really, really didn't want to.

"I'll talk to him," Montana promised.

26

"But if he still hates my guts, you'll have to find someone else."

She couldn't imagine any circumstances under which Dr. Simon Bradley would want to spend time with her, which made her acceptance slightly less meaningful.

"Agreed," the mayor said, coming to her feet. "If the good doctor refuses to have anything to do with you, I'll find someone else."

Montana stood as well. They walked toward the door.

"I'm glad you're growing your hair out," Mayor Marsha told her. "It makes it so much easier to know which triplet is which. I don't have any trouble telling you three apart, but I've had complaints."

Montana laughed as she fingered the hair that had grown down to the middle of her back. "Seriously? People have complained?"

"You have no idea what I deal with on a daily basis."

Montana led her outside. "Last year my hair was dark. That should have helped."

"It did, although I prefer your natural blond color." As the mayor spoke, she eyed Montana speculatively. "I wonder if Simon likes blondes."

Montana held up both hands. "How far exactly am I supposed to go to convince

27

him to stay in town?"

The mayor laughed again. "You don't have to sacrifice your virtue, if that's what you're asking."

Virtue as in . . . virtue? That ship had sailed several years ago but she wasn't going to discuss that with someone old enough to be her grandmother.

"I'll do my best," she said instead.

"That's all anyone can ask for."

After the mayor left, Montana returned to the play area and worked with the dogs. Max was a big believer in constant reinforcement. Therapy dogs were expected to be well behaved and well trained. She worked with those dogs still in training twice a day and ran the more experienced members of the team through different sequences a few times a week.

Working with the dogs meant not having to think about the mayor's extraordinary request. Montana knew she would have to do her best but had exactly *no* idea of where to start. Apologizing to the man in question was probably a good place.

At noon, she went into the house to tell Max she was heading into town for lunch and would be back in an hour. Her boss grinned when he saw her.

"Guess who called," he said.

"Publishers Clearing House? I've won twenty million dollars?"

Max laughed. "Not exactly. Dr. Simon Bradley phoned. He would like to come by this afternoon."

Montana's appetite vanished and she had to resist the urge to whimper. "Why?"

"He wants to talk to you."

"Talk or throw rocks at me?"

"He said talk. Maybe he wasn't as pissed as you thought."

Oh, he'd been plenty pissed, Montana thought as she walked to her car. The question was what he was going to do to her as punishment.

CHAPTER TWO

Montana spent the next couple of hours trying not to go crazy. Although Dr. Bradley had threatened to visit, he hadn't said when that would happen, leaving her to constantly check the long driveway leading to the house and kennels. Knowing she wasn't at her mental best while she waited, she decided to clean out the outdoor runs.

The interior of the building had large individual kennels with raised platforms and size-appropriate beds. The space was kept heated in winter and air-conditioned in summer. Skylights and windows filled the cavernous room with light. Although several of the dogs had learned how to unfasten the simple latch on their kennels, they stayed where they were supposed to. Each dog had his or her own toys, water and a door leading to an outside area.

Pads of cement were enclosed by chain-link fencing. During the day, the dogs were either working or together in a common area. The pads were rarely used, but still got dusty. A brief rain shower the previous night had left them muddy.

Montana kicked off her sandals, stepped into a pair of rubber boots and grabbed the hose. She started spraying down the cement, reminding herself as she worked that her conversation with Dr. Bradley was going to be a great learning opportunity. With her personality, her default position was to feel guilty and act like a doormat, something she didn't want to do anymore. So this time she would be strong.

Yes, it was unfortunate that Fluffy had escaped into the hospital. It was a mistake. Neither Montana nor the dog was mean or evil. As far as Montana knew, there hadn't been any lasting damage, so Dr. Stick-Up-the-Butt was just going to have to get over it. If he thought he could come over and intimidate her, he was wrong. Well, mostly wrong.

By three she'd finished with the outdoor runs and had managed to work herself up into a frenzy of righteous indignation. Just because someone was a doctor didn't give him the right to make people feel bad about themselves. She wouldn't stand for it, and as soon as he got here she was going to tell him that.

She stomped over to the main faucet and turned off the water. Her feet were hot inside the rubber boots, but she still had to coil the hose before she could slip them off. She would take a few minutes, tidy herself and then —

"Max said I would find you out here."

The low, masculine voice came from nowhere. Montana spun toward the sound, nearly tripping over the boots and dropping the hose. Good thing the water was already off, she thought as she managed to stay upright and face the intruder. Or maybe not.

He was more amazing than she remembered. Not just the height or the broad shoulders. No, the thing that made him different, the thing that would make him *impossible* to forget was his face. The sheer perfection of his bone structure, the fullness of his mouth, the unusual color of his eyes. Even the sunlight seemed to shimmer around him as if it, too, were impressed.

He'd traded in his white doctor's coat for a long-sleeved, white, button-down shirt with gray pinstripes. His tie was loose and, on anyone else, that would have been sexy. Except he was too stiff in the way he stood, too controlled. As if he weren't comfortable being as mortal as everyone else.

"You know Max?" she asked, unable to think of another question and equally unable to stop staring at him. "You seem more the 'Mr. Thurman' type."

He frowned. "Is that his last name? He introduced himself as Max."

Which was like her boss. She shouldn't be surprised.

Her visitor shifted then, turning his head slightly, and she caught sight of the scars. Once again she noticed the starlike pattern of the way they shot across his face. The scars should have made her sympathetic and him appear more human.

"It was an accident," she told him, clumping toward him in her too-large rubber boots.

When she was only a few feet away, she came to a stop and put her hands on her hips. "You know there are accidents. What you do for a living proves that. No one hurts a child on purpose. Okay, a few do, but I would guess the kids you usually see have been hurt because of something unexpected. That's what today was about."

She didn't know why he'd wanted to see her but guessed it had something to do with threatening her, or worse.

"Obviously Fluffy isn't therapy-dog material," she continued, speaking quickly so he couldn't talk. "Max warned me, but I didn't listen. I wanted her to make it because she has such a good heart. She loves everyone. Maybe not gracefully or obediently, but there's still love and that's not wrong. I wanted to give her the chance to prove herself. I know you don't understand, but I swear if you say she's just a dog, I'll attack you with this hose and make you scream like a girl."

She took a breath, waiting for him to laugh, or smile or start yelling. Instead he stood as still as stone, watching her.

She let her breath out. He was a medical professional. Was he going to tell her there was something seriously wrong with her? And if he did, would she have to listen?

Montana stepped out of her rubber boots. If she was about to be drummed out of her perfect career, she wasn't going to endure it with her feet sweating.

"Say something," she commanded. "Or did you come all this way to attack me with your ray gun vision?"

"What do you do here?"

She frowned. "Excuse me?"

He motioned to the kennel behind her. "Tell me about the work you do."

Maybe it was just her, but wasn't he the one with the advanced medical training?

"I work with therapy dogs."

His eyes narrowed slightly and his mouth tightened.

Figures, she thought. She'd finally gotten him to show a little emotion and it turned out to be annoyance. Be careful for what you wish for and all that.

"Therapy dogs are used for a variety of purposes. They're different from service dogs, who are trained to help people with specific problems. Like Guide Dogs for the Blind and so on."

He nodded. "All right."

"Okay." She paused, not sure what he wanted to know. "Our dogs are used to provide comfort and companionship. We visit nursing homes and the hospital. Seniors' centers. There are a couple of dogs who spend afternoons at a group home for mentally challenged adults. I recently started a reading program. Kids who have trouble reading are often more comfortable reading to a dog than a person."

She explained a little about the program and how, now that school was out, they'd gotten permission to try the reading program at a local library.

"You mentioned hospitals, which means you bring dogs to hospitals." He was making a statement, not asking a question.

"Yes. Usually the visits go better than they did today."

"I should think so."

She bristled. "You know, you could have been nicer. It was, as I've explained several times, an accident."

"It's not my job to be nice. It's my job to help my patients heal."

She opened her mouth to snap back at him, only to remember that Mayor Marsha wanted her to be charming and convince him to stay in town.

She was so the wrong person for the job, Montana thought, dropping her arms to her side.

"If Fluffy were aware of what she'd done, she would be very sorry."

The man continued to stare at her without speaking.

It was probably good that he had such a sucky personality, she thought, wishing he would get to the point and leave. If he was charming *and* gorgeous, women across America wouldn't stand a chance.

"I want a therapy dog for one of my patients."

The words were so unexpected, she could have sworn she hadn't heard him correctly. Montana blinked several times. "You want a therapy dog?"

"Yes."

"In the hospital?"

"Yes."

What about the germs? What about infection and whatever else he'd yelled about that morning?

She decided it was better not to ask.

"A live dog, right?"

He sighed heavily. "A live dog would be best. My patient is a nine-year-old girl named Kalinda. She was badly burned when the family barbecue exploded a few days ago. She's had one surgery and is facing dozens more. Her parents are trying to cope. Kalinda is in pain and shock." A muscle twitched in his jaw. "I do have her mother's permission to be telling you this."

"Okay."

She wasn't sure why that mattered, then remembered something about medical confidentiality. No doubt he wanted to make sure she understood he wasn't breaking any rules.

"She's in bed, right? The girl? Kalinda? She's not walking around?"

"No."

Montana thought about the dogs they had. A small one would be best. If Kalinda suffered any lung issues, then avoiding dander would be good, too.

"I have just the dog for you," she said, smiling at him. "Come on. I'll introduce you."

The woman turned, as if she expected him to follow her. Simon didn't want to go anywhere with the dog-trainer person, but he was here on a mission. Anything for his patients. He'd always believed that. He would do whatever he had to do so they could heal. Dealing with the likes of the woman before him was simply one more challenge he had to overcome.

As she glanced back at him, her long, blond hair caught the sun. He was aware of the colors, the various shades of light and dark gold, the slight wave. Her eyes were deep brown and sparkling with amusement. He had no doubt she was laughing at him.

He was uncomfortable, but that wasn't news. He was uncomfortable anywhere that wasn't a hospital. In the familiar space that was his kingdom, he felt at home.

The woman — Montana, he recalled her boss saying — led the way to a fenced in, grassy area. He heard several dogs barking and yipping. They sounded happy. The afternoon was warm, the sun bright.

Montana moved with an easy grace. Her feet were bare, her pink-painted toes contrasting with the dark green of the grass. They were hidden when she slipped into a pair of clogs, then stepped inside what he would guess was the kennel area.

The space was cleaner than he had expected. He didn't notice any smell and the cages for the dogs were large. He saw big beds in plaid and plenty of toys. The lighting was good. It was obvious someone had put a lot of time and money into the facility.

"The dogs live here," Montana said, facing him. "Dogs are pack animals, so they're more comfortable in a group than in isolation. They're nearly always with someone. We have college kids who spend the night. Just to make sure everything is all right. Sometimes they bring their significant others along and that gets interesting."

She smiled as she spoke and it took him a minute to realize she meant the college students and not the dogs. Of course not the dogs. Dogs didn't have significant others.

"Max has plenty of stories, but that's not why you came," she continued.

"No."

He knew he should make some kind of small talk. It made people more comfortable. He'd never seen the point, but then he didn't see the point of most common rituals. Telling someone to have a nice day was beyond ridiculous. As if anyone had the power to make that happen.

She walked to a door that led outside. When she pushed it open and stepped onto the grass, at least a half dozen dogs came running. He followed, curious about them. He'd never had much contact with dogs. From the time he was eleven until he'd gone to college at sixteen, he'd been in a hospital. No dogs allowed.

Large dogs and small hurried forward with equal enthusiasm. He recognized the disastrous mutt from that morning and did his best to avoid her enthusiastic jumping. Montana petted them all, called out to a few and restored order more quickly than he had thought possible.

"Cece, come here, honey," she said, then looked at him. "I think she's going to be the right dog for you. Quiet, well behaved and, best of all, clean."

A small apricot-colored poodle made her way to Montana. The dog was maybe a foot tall to the top of her head, with long legs and a slender body. When Montana said, "Up," the dog turned so she could easily be scooped into the woman's arms.

"She would be very happy to curl up next

40

to Kalinda for as long as she would like," Montana told him. "She's great with kids, sweet tempered, and because she has hair rather than fur, no dander. We can keep her really clean, which I know is important."

As she spoke, Cece stared at him. Her eyes were darker than Montana's, and never left his. Her nose quivered, then her whole body began to tremble.

"Is she sick?" he asked, wondering if he should worry about transporting germs back to his patients.

Montana laughed. "Not in the way you mean." She whispered something to the dog, who swiped her tongue across her chin. Montana turned her attention back to him. "She has a crush on you."

"What?"

The dog was thrust toward him. He reacted instinctively, reaching for it.

She was lighter than he'd expected, with bones that felt delicate. Her fur was soft, her body warm. Even though he didn't know how to hold her, she snuggled close, perfectly content to be next to him.

"Support her butt," Montana told him.

He shifted slightly. Cece cuddled against his chest and stared at him with eyes that seemed able to see into his soul. He wondered if she was aware of all the flaws lurking there.

"She likes you."

Montana spoke in a tone that told him that she was really thinking, "There's no accounting for taste."

"She seems nice enough," he said, tentatively rubbing his fingers against the animal's back. "As long as Kalinda will be safe."

"You don't have to worry. Cece has a great temperament. And I'll be there the whole time."

He had his doubts about how much help she would be, but if Kalinda wanted a dog then, by God, he would get her one.

He passed Cece back and made arrangements for her to be brought to the hospital the following day.

"For a test run," he said. "If it helps, we continue the visits."

"Of course."

He turned to leave.

Montana, still holding the dog, walked with him. At the doorway they both paused, as if expecting the other to go first, then they moved at the same time.

They bumped into each other. People did it every day. Simon was used to all kinds of casual contact. He touched his patients, was passed things during surgery. Every now and then he even enjoyed the company of a woman for a few hours. So he had no reason to expect the brief brush of her arm against his to register.

But it did. The second Montana touched him, the second he felt the heat from her body, something large and uncontrolled stirred to life. He was so surprised he came to a stop, and she did, too. They bumped again, which caused her to grin at him.

"Okay. You first."

Easy words. A casual, happy smile. As if she couldn't feel the rage of desire that burst to life like an explosion.

He'd never felt anything like it before, had no way of knowing what he was supposed to do next. He wasn't sure he could keep from reaching for her, kissing her. Because that's what he needed — not just the possession of her, but her hunger as well.

"Are you all right?"

Simon forced himself back to the moment. He hung on to the ragged remains of his civility and nodded.

"Yes. Thank you for your time."

Her eyebrows rose slightly. He suspected she was remembering her comment from earlier in the day — when she'd accused him of having a stick up his ass. Better that than the truth, he told himself. Better for both of them.

He quickly made his escape. When he was back in his car, he was disgusted to find that his hands trembled and his sexual thoughts had produced a predictable manifestation. Pray God she hadn't noticed, he thought grimly, starting the car engine.

As he drove back to the hospital, he tried to figure out what had happened. He'd never considered himself overly sexual. Every few months, when the need became a distraction, he found someone who wanted what he did — physical release and little else. The events were pleasant enough, but more about biology than anything else. He'd never felt compelled. Driven.

It was chemistry, he told himself as he entered the main highway and headed back to Fool's Gold. One of those quirks of DNA that was intriguing but ultimately meaningless. So, he'd briefly wanted Montana. Later he would see her and everything would be fine. He had his work. Nothing else was as important. He had his work and his patients and that would always be enough.

CHAPTER THREE

Jo's Bar was one of Montana's favorite places in town. Unlike most bars, this one catered to women. The colors were girl friendly, with the large TVs turned to shows like *American's Next Top Model* and the shopping networks. Drinks were fun and the list of food came with a selection of offerings for the calorie conscious. As for the men, they had a room in back, with a pool table and plenty of sports. But at Jo's, women ruled.

Montana walked in and spotted her sisters already at a booth.

Technically Nevada was the oldest, with Dakota born in the middle and Montana last. They were separated by all of fourteen minutes. When they were young, they had truly been identical, nearly impossible for even family members to tell apart. As they'd grown, their personality differences had influenced their appearance.

Nevada was the most sensible of the sisters. A civil engineer, she favored short hair, jeans, shirts and boots that were practical on work sites. Dakota was as smart as Nevada, but slightly more nurturing. She was a child psychologist by trade, with a Ph.D. in her field. In the past three months, she'd adopted a little girl from Kazakhstan, fallen in love, gotten pregnant and then engaged.

Montana loved her sisters but there were times she felt like the family screwup. It was only the past year that she'd discovered what she really wanted to do with her life. Working with the therapy dogs was everything to her. She would deal with the fact that her love life was nonexistent another time.

"How's it going?" she asked as she approached the table.

"Great." Dakota slid in to make room for her. "Can I persuade you to order a lemondrop tonight?"

Montana greeted Nevada, then turned to Dakota. "Why?"

"I want to smell it."

Because being pregnant meant not drinking, Montana thought. She looked across the table. "And you wouldn't indulge her?"

Nevada motioned to her vodka and tonic.

"I offered to let her smell this."

Dakota shuddered. "No, thanks. Tonic water? I don't think so."

"Then I'll take care of your need to sniff," Montana said as Jo, the bartender, came over. "A lemondrop."

Dakota grinned. "Because she loves me."

"I could make you a virgin lemondrop," Jo offered.

"Isn't that just fresh squeezed lemons and simple sugar?"

"Uh-huh."

"I was hoping for more."

"We all need a goal," Jo muttered and walked away.

Montana watched her go. Jo had arrived in Fool's Gold a few years before and bought the failing bar. She'd had the money to completely refurbish it, but had never talked about where she'd gotten the funds. In fact, Jo rarely talked about her past. Rumors flew about everything, from her escaping an abusive husband to being a Mafia princess hiding out from her family. No one knew the truth and Jo wasn't the kind of woman who took well to questions.

"Finn home with Hannah tonight?" Nevada asked.

Dakota nodded. "They're watching *Sleeping Beauty*. He won't admit it, but I swear

47

he loves the movie as much as she does."

"Probably not news you want to spread around," Nevada told her.

Dakota laughed. "I'm not worried about what people might say. Let them get their own guy."

"I wish," Montana said wistfully, refusing to figure out exactly how long it had been since she'd been on a date. Too long, for sure. Soon, she promised herself. And this time it would go better. This time she wouldn't feel as if she wasn't good enough.

"We're a town with a man shortage, remember," Nevada said.

"Men are moving here. Last year we had busloads."

"Oh, yeah." Nevada picked up her drink. "I'm dying for a guy who can walk away from his life and take a bus to a place he's never been simply because he's heard there are desperate women there. That's my idea of a dream come true."

Dakota wrinkled her nose. "Have you considered your sarcasm is one of the reasons you're still single?"

"No. Sarcasm is my version of charm."

"How's that working for you?"

"Just fine." Nevada scowled. "I don't want to talk about it." She turned to Montana. "Distract her, please."

Montana knew just what to say. "Mayor Marsha came to see me today."

Dakota groaned. "That's never good. What did she want?"

"There's a new doctor in town. A plastic surgeon who specializes in children who have been burned. He goes from place to place, only staying a few months. She wants me to convince him to settle permanently in Fool's Gold."

As she finished talking, she instinctively tensed, waiting for her sisters to start laughing at her. After all, why would anyone think she could convince Dr. Simon Bradley of anything? But they didn't laugh.

Dakota shrugged. "Makes sense to me."

"Why? She said I should charm him. I'm not charming. I wouldn't know what to say or do."

Her sisters exchanged a glance. "Just be yourself," Nevada told her. "That's enough charm for any man. Trust me, he won't know what hit him."

"He seems amazingly unimpressed by me."

"Are you sure? Have you looked in the mirror?" Dakota asked with a laugh. "I know that in theory we're identical, but you're the pretty one. And funny. How can he resist you?"

Jo brought Montana's lemondrop. She appreciated the timing. Thanking the other woman meant it was more difficult for her mouth to drop open. The pretty one? Since when?

"I'm not pretty. I mean, not any prettier." She'd always thought that her sisters were gorgeous but that she was not quite there. As for being funny, maybe, but it wasn't always on purpose. "He's not like anyone I've ever met. He's really serious. Stick-up-the-butt serious." She told them what had happened at the hospital.

"I've met Fluffy," Nevada grumbled. "She's a menace. Adorable, but not the best-trained dog on the planet."

"She has a big personality."

"And no sense of her size. She needs to be with a family. One with boys."

"Dr. Bradley would agree with you."

"He came to see you," Dakota reminded her. "He needs your help. You can bond over that. Then show him around the town. That will give you things to talk about."

"Maybe. I could —"

The phone on the bar rang. Instantly the large room went quiet as everyone watched Jo pick it up.

"Is it time?" she asked, sounding worried. After a pause, she shook her head. "Not

50

Pia," she told the crowd.

Conversation resumed.

"Poor Pia," Dakota said sympathetically. "I know she's ready for the babies to arrive."

Pia was pregnant with twins. Everyone had assumed they would come early, in the way that twins often did. But not Pia's. So far they were hanging on until the very last day.

"She's huge," Nevada said. "I saw her two days ago and I swear my back started to hurt just looking at her."

Dakota raised her eyebrows. "Talk to Pia about your doctor friend. She knows everything about the town and it will be a distraction for her."

"Great idea," Montana said, holding out her lemondrop for Dakota to sniff.

"If that doesn't work, you can seduce him into staying," Nevada teased. "Wrap yourself in cellophane."

"I've never understood the point of that," Dakota admitted.

"You're a present," Nevada said. "Gift wrapped."

"I don't think Dr. Bradley is into that kind of stuff," Montana said. He was so stern. She couldn't imagine him smiling, let alone getting naked and having sex. Not that he

51

wasn't sexy — in a scary, distant kind of way.

"Then skip the cellophane," Dakota told her with a grin. "All men are into naked."

"Right," Montana said, laughing. "I'll show up at his hotel room naked. That will make Mayor Marsha so proud."

"At least it will give us all something to talk about."

Montana stepped out of the hospital elevator with Cece in her arms. As they approached the doors leading to the burn ward, she drew in a deep breath.

"There are going to be rules," she told the dog. "You're going to have to stay clean and not jump and generally be well behaved. Kalinda is really sick and you're going to make her feel better. At least, that's the theory."

She smiled into Cece's warm, brown eyes. "This would go a lot better if you spoke English."

"If the dog spoke English, we would have other issues."

Montana spun toward the speaker and saw Simon standing by the doors leading to the burn unit.

He was as tall as she remembered, and just as incredibly good-looking. At least on

the one side. The white coat was still intimidating, she realized as she swallowed.

She blinked at him, replaying his words in
her mind. "Was that humor?" she asked,
before she could stop herself. "Were you
being funny?"

Nothing about his expression changed.
"Apparently not."

She winced. "I'm sorry. I should have
laughed. I'm just nervous. You're really
scary."

One eyebrow rose. "Do you always say
what you think?"

"I try not to," she admitted. "Sometimes I
can't help myself."

"If you say anything to hurt my patient . . ."

Emotion flashed in his smoky-green eyes.
Anger and determination. A need to protect.

She supposed she should have been insulted or more frightened, but oddly enough
his intensity reassured her. "You take care
of them. Your patients, I mean."

"That's my job."

"But that's not why you do it. You care."
She smiled. "That's nice."

"I'm glad you approve."

He didn't sound as if he were glad at all,
but that was okay.

He motioned to Cece. "The dog is clean?"

"Yes. I spoke with one of your nurses this morning and used the soap she recommended. She's been kept away from the other dogs and hasn't been outside since her bath."

"Thank you." Simon frowned. "Won't she have to go to the bathroom?"

"Cece is paper trained. She can go on a puppy pad." Montana did her best not to smile. "Don't worry. She's not going to pee on the bed."

"Good to know." He glanced toward the doors, then back at her. "Since you're not a medical professional, you probably don't know what to expect. Kalinda's burns are recent. While she's bandaged, there are exposed areas of her skin. It's raw and unattractive. There's a smell, from the burns and the various medicines we use. She's in pain and is exhausted."

Montana nodded, her smile fading. "I wish I could do something to help."

"Hopefully the dog will accomplish that. Recovering from burns takes years. It's uncomfortable, to say the least. Despite our best efforts, the worst cases can never be what everyone would call normal. It's a failing."

She studied him, suddenly aware that he considered it a personal failing. As if he should be able to do better than everyone else.

"You'll stay fifteen minutes, then leave. We'll assess how the visit went before deciding if they will continue."

Before she was ready, he'd pushed open one of the doors and motioned for her to follow.

The last time she'd been on the burn ward she'd been more concerned about getting Fluffy under control than noticing her surroundings. Now she was aware of closed doors with warnings about isolation and cleanliness. As she walked with Simon, she was aware of his scars. When he spoke of the effort of recovery, he spoke from personal experience. She wondered what had happened to him and when.

They stopped in front of a half-closed door. Simon pushed it open and a woman in her late twenties stepped out. She was petite and obviously exhausted. Her skin was gray and dark circles shadowed her blue eyes. When she saw Montana or, more precisely, Cece, she smiled.

"You brought a little dog!"

Montana moved toward her. "I'm Montana Hendrix. This is Cece. She's a trained therapy dog."

"Fay Riley." The woman let Cece sniff her

fingers. "This is exactly what Kalinda needs. Thank you so much for bringing her." Fay's gaze moved to Simon. "And you for arranging it."

"Let's see how they get along," Simon said.

Montana moved toward the room. Fay put her hand on her arm. "Did he tell you about . . ." She swallowed and tears filled her eyes. "She was burned pretty bad."

"I'm so sorry for what happened," Montana told her as she drew in a breath. "We're going to do everything we can to make her feel a little bit better. That's what Cece's been trained for."

Fay glanced at Simon, then nodded and pushed the door open more.

Montana drew a steadying breath. Whatever she saw would be nothing compared to what Kalinda was going through. Montana only had to deal with the burns from a distance. Kalinda was living them. Montana vowed she wouldn't react in any way, no matter what.

But the promise was harder to keep than she'd expected. The girl on the bed seemed so small and helpless. Her arms were wrapped in white bandages, only the tips of her fingers exposed. Her face was a mass of raw skin, as was her neck. Thick ointment covered the burns.

The scent of disinfectant mingled with that of burned flesh and a rotting smell. For a second, Montana thought she might gag, but then she got herself under control and reminded herself to smile.

"Kalinda?" Fay said quietly. "You have a visitor."

The girl opened her eyes. They were startlingly blue against the angry burns. Montana's first thought was that she must have been a very pretty child, before the accident. Her second thought was she'd never seen that much pain in anyone's expression before.

"Hi. I'm Montana and this is Cece. Your mom said you liked dogs, so I hope it's okay I brought her to see you."

Kalinda nodded rather than spoke. She moved her head slightly, then winced and tears filled her eyes.

Montana felt her own throat tighten at her obvious suffering. She wanted to turn to Simon and demand he do something. Make it better. Yet she already knew he was doing as much as he could. Some things simply couldn't be fixed.

She set Cece on the bed. Simon moved to the other side, hovering protectively. She expected him to start issuing orders, but instead he waited.

Cece, all six pounds of her, studied Kalinda for a few seconds. Then she carefully made her way to the girl's side. She curled up between Kalinda's hip and her hand, stretched her neck a little and licked the exposed fingertips.

The girl smiled.

"Thank you," she whispered, her voice scratchy. Her eyes sank closed, but her fingers moved against Cece's side.

Montana stood by the bed for what felt like hours, but was probably only fifteen minutes. When Simon nodded, she picked up Cece and whispered a goodbye.

Fay followed them outside.

"That was wonderful," she said, wiping away tears. "She smiled. Did you see that? She actually smiled. Please say you'll come back."

Montana glanced at Simon, who nodded.

"Whenever you want," Montana told her. "If Kalinda is strong enough."

"Let's see how it goes," Simon said. "We don't want to tire her out."

"Whatever you think is best," Fay said, already moving back toward her daughter's room. "She smiled."

Montana felt a little sick to her stomach. While she was thrilled Cece had helped, she hated how both Kalinda and her mother were suffering. It seemed so unfair — the random cruelty of an accident.

The dog shifted in her arms, an attempt to get closer to Simon.

"Someone has a fan," Montana said.

Gray-green eyes locked with hers. "Excuse me?"

She motioned to the dog, who stared at him intensely. "Cece has quite a thing for you."

He barely glanced at the animal. "I'm sure she's like that with everyone."

"Not really." Montana paused, thinking she should probably excuse herself, only to remember her assignment from Mayor Marsha. She was supposed to get close to Simon, to charm him into staying in Fool's Gold.

"I could show you around town," she said before she could stop herself. "You're new and the town is great and I could show you around. You know, so you could see it." She cleared her throat and waited for him to say something scathing or simply walk away.

Instead he continued to stare at her with as much intensity as Cece stared at him.

"Thank you," he said. "That would be nice."

Montana continued to stand there in the

middle of the corridor long after Simon had excused himself and walked away. He'd said yes. She couldn't decide if that was a good thing or a bad thing. Maybe, the problem was, it was both.

CHAPTER FOUR

Simon was waiting by the Starbucks, as instructed. Montana paused on the opposite corner, both admiring him from afar and not sure if she had the courage to approach. Telling herself she was doing this for the greater good wasn't as helpful as it could have been. There was something about Dr. Simon Bradley. Something she couldn't put her finger on.

It wasn't just his patronizing attitude. She'd never met anyone quite like him — obviously intelligent, but an emotional puzzle. Plus, he was good-looking. Sure, he had those scars, but did they really matter? When a man like him looked at a woman, the rest of the world just seemed to disappear.

Not in a romantic way, she told herself quickly. She wasn't attracted to him. After all, it wasn't as if he was a nice guy. And wasn't that what she was looking for? A nice guy. If he happened to have those smoky-green eyes, well that was a plus. Except, not Simon. She might not know many things, but she knew he wasn't the one for her.

All of which was very interesting, but wasn't getting the job done. She drew in a breath, squared her shoulders and purposefully started across the street. Unfortunately, she didn't look even one way, let alone both, and had to jump back to avoid being hit by a Prius driven by a distracted tourist.

As she got closer to Simon, she realized he had traded in his white coat and dark trousers for jeans and a long-sleeved shirt. She hadn't known him for long, but he didn't strike her as a casual dresser. She would never have guessed he even owned jeans. Not that he didn't look good in them.

"Hi," she said as she approached. She was nervous and didn't know what to do with her hands. Should she offer to shake, or give a little wave?

"Good afternoon."

Simon's voice was as steady as his gaze. He looked calm, cool and completely unimpressed with her. How fair was that? He was the new guy in town. Shouldn't he be at least a little uncomfortable?

But he wasn't, and there was no getting around it. And if she didn't get out of her head pretty soon she was going to make herself crazy.

Purpose, she told herself. She had a purpose. She had been assigned a task by the mayor and she would see it through to the best of her abilities. Starting right now.

"I thought I'd show you the town," she said, hoping she sounded cheerful and confident. She was a happy person, so the cheerful part was easy enough. As for the confidence, weren't they always saying, "Fake it until you make it"? God knew she'd been faking it for years.

"That's what you offered," Simon said, watching her in that steady way of his. "A tour of the town."

She blinked. "Right. That is what I said." She tried to smile, found herself fighting nerves again, then went to a safer place. She'd been learning about the history of Fool's Gold since the first grade. When in doubt, stick to the facts.

She cleared her throat.

"In the early thirteen hundreds a matriarchal tribe called the Máa-zib settled on the shores of our lake. Not much is known about them. Legend has it that they're a branch of Maya Indians who came looking for a place where women and their children could live in harmony. Without men."

63

Simon raised his eyebrows. "So they died out?"

She laughed. "Okay, men were allowed in the village for certain purposes. They say there is a curse that keeps the men out. Maybe that's the reason Fool's Gold has a man shortage. Or at least we used to. More men are moving here all the time."

She thought about saying that he could move here, but didn't think that was especially subtle. Although having him agree would get her job done very quickly.

She motioned toward the park and started walking. Simon fell into step beside her.

"In fifteen eighty-one an English crewman who served with Sir Francis Drake wrote about being injured in the mountains and cared for by a matriarchal tribe of natives. His account suggests he was here in Fool's Gold and that the women were from the Máa-zib tribe."

Simon glanced at her. "Let me guess. He had sex with several of the women but they didn't let him stay."

She grinned. "You have to respect their ability to get what they want."

"Would you still respect their actions if the tribe in question had been men?"

"An unfair question. The women chose to get pregnant by him. I assume they wanted to refresh the gene pool, although they wouldn't think of it that way. That's completely different than a man getting a woman pregnant and walking away."

"Except he lost his children. He wasn't allowed to see them or raise them."

"A good point," she admitted. "But it's kind of the town thing to respect the women."

"I'll keep that in mind."

They walked down to the lake. As usual, children were feeding ducks, young couples picnicked on blankets in the shade of trees, and a few joggers made their way along the bike path.

Montana paused to take in the familiar scene. This had always been her home. She'd tried living somewhere else, briefly, and hated it. She knew some people left for the big city and she was sure any large urban area had its charms. But this was where she belonged.

She was aware of Simon standing next to her. He didn't say much, which wasn't a surprise. What she hadn't expected was how much she didn't mind his quietness. It was oddly relaxing. She was also aware of his height and his broad shoulders, but told herself not to be silly. Becoming interested in Simon as anything but a project for

Mayor Marsha was just plain stupid.

If he kept glancing at her, it was probably because he was waiting for the next burst of factoids or wondering if there was going to be a town history quiz. There was no way he was . . . She frowned. If she hadn't known better, she would have sworn Simon was looking at her mouth. Not possible, she told herself. No way she could attract a man like Simon.

Not that she would mind, but if the other men in her life hadn't found her to be attractive enough, she figured she would be woefully lacking in Simon's eyes, too.

She motioned to the trucks parked along the side road by the lake. "They're setting up for the Fourth of July celebration. Fool's Gold is known for its festivals. I don't know how many we have every year. A lot. There's the Book Festival and the Waterskiing Festival. The Fall Festival, which is before the Halloween party." She glanced at him. "It's fun."

"An active community."

She couldn't tell if he meant that in a good way or a bad way, and decided not to ask.

She led him back to the main street and started pointing out various businesses before continuing her discussion of the town. "Mayor Marsha is the longest serving mayor in the state of California. The festivals are run by my friend Pia. It's a big job and, now that she's pregnant, it's even more difficult. Although she has a new assistant, which is helping." She searched her mind for some other factoids. "My family was one of the founding families, on my dad's side. Not counting the matriarchal tribe, of course. There's Morgan's Books."

She led him to the store and showed him the window display of Liz Sutton, their resident mystery writer.

"Have you read her?" she asked.

Simon shook his head and shifted so he was on her other side. "Is she any good?"

"Of course. She's fabulous. She's married to my brother, Ethan. They have one son together and are raising her two nieces. It's complicated."

"Most family relationships are."

"Tell me about it." She started walking again and Simon fell into step beside her. "My dad passed away eleven years ago, so it's not surprising my mom has started dating. It really would have been okay, only she seemed fine alone and now we have to get used to this and it's strange. I want her to be happy, but it's the whole parental thing. She talks about her dates and we want to be supportive, but then she talks about kissing with tongue and I just want to cover my ears and hum."

She came to a stop. "You're a medical professional. Why is hearing about parents having sex so creepy? Okay, not creepy exactly, but strange."

"I don't have an answer to that."

"Didn't you go to medical school? Don't they have a class on this?"

And then it happened. Simon smiled at her. His lips curved, there was a flash of white teeth and a surprising dimple on his unscarred cheek.

Montana felt a sudden rush of sensation in her midsection. Not attraction exactly, but not disinterest either. The smile was unexpected and very appealing. It made her want to hear his laugh and maybe even make him smile again.

"I must've missed that day," he told her. "Sorry."

"You work at a hospital. You could ask around."

"Is it really that important to you?"

"I don't like feeling uncomfortable. Especially around my mother. I love her and we're really close. And I feel like a really good daughter would be able to talk about her mother's dating life."

"Not even a good daughter is expected to

68

discuss tongue."

She laughed and saw he was smiling again. Suddenly the morning seemed a little brighter, the sky a little bluer.

They came to a stop at the corner. Montana walked over to push the Walk button, then returned to Simon's side. "Where were you before you came to Fool's Gold? I heard you travel around a lot."

The pedestrian signal changed and she and Simon started across the street. As they reached the other side, he stepped around her.

"I was in India."

"That counts as travel," she admitted. "You go all around the world?"

"I go where I'm needed. I operate on whomever needs my help the most. Mostly children. But adults as well. After I leave here, I'm set to go to Peru."

That sounded very altruistic. "So you're a giver?"

"No."

She waited, but he didn't say anything else. There was no sign of the smile and she wondered if she'd annoyed him, or crossed some invisible line.

"Burns are my specialty," he said.

"You must get lonely, always being in a different place. What about family?"

"I have my work. That's enough."

It couldn't possibly be enough, she thought. He was a difficult man to understand. Obviously he was very gifted. His work was demanding and, from what she had seen, he was relentless when it came to taking care of his patients. But who took care of him?

No, no. Don't go there, she told herself. No rescuing. Simon was perfectly capable of taking care of himself. He'd been all over the world, doing amazing things. He didn't need her and she didn't need to make this assignment more than it was.

She'd had three serious boyfriends in her life. A guy back in high school, one in college and one shortly after. All three of them had ended things after making it clear she wasn't good enough. She hadn't been pretty enough or smart enough or ambitious enough. Was she really looking for an instant replay on emotional pain?

"Do you have a home base anywhere?" she asked.

"Los Angeles."

She wrinkled her nose. "I lived there for a while." With guy number three.

Simon glanced at her. "You don't sound as if you liked it very much."

"I didn't. I couldn't fit in — my boyfriend

was a disaster." She stopped in front of the Fox and Hound restaurant and faced Simon. "He was a doctor, too. Or he was going to be. He was still in medical school."

"What happened?"

A reasonable question. She'd set it up herself, so she had no one to blame. Thinking before speaking was an excellent characteristic, she reminded herself. One she was going to have to take up.

"We didn't want the same things."

Which was sort of true. The more important issue, which she wouldn't talk about, was that he'd destroyed what little self-confidence she'd had left. She believed no one could take that away without her permission, so she knew she was also at fault.

"His loss."

The words surprised her.

"Thank you." She tilted her head. "You're different from how you were before."

"Less stick-up-the-ass?"

She winced. "I'm sorry I said that. It was mean. You weren't out of line. Fluffy really could have done some damage."

"But she didn't. Sometimes I get a little intense."

Montana bit the inside of her mouth to keep from smiling. "I hadn't noticed. Thank you for understanding about Fluffy. It

71

wasn't her fault, it was mine. Max warned me. He said she wouldn't make it as a therapy dog, but I was determined."

"To fulfill her therapy-dog destiny?"

Humor sparkled in Simon's eyes. She felt herself getting a little breathless. The man could be devastating when he tried.

"I can't save the world, so my passion is a little smaller than yours."

"Not smaller. Different."

There was something about the way he stared at her. As if he was hungry. She shook her head. Talk about delusions of grandeur. Simon hungry for her? On what planet? He wasn't looking at her mouth. She must have a smudge or something.

As casually as she could, she rubbed her chin.

"Max is kind of an intriguing guy," she said. Because her boss seemed a safer topic. "A little mysterious. No one knows where he's from. He obviously has money. You've seen the facility — that doesn't come cheap. And it's not like the therapy-dog business pays very much. And there's a weird co-incidence with my mother. She has a tattoo on her hip. *Max.* My sisters and I don't think it's the same Max, though. That would be too strange."

She sighed. "Too much information, right?"

"Perhaps."

She started walking. He fell into step beside her.

"It was the tattoo. I shouldn't have mentioned my mother has a tattoo." She wasn't asking a question.

But instead of answering, Simon shifted to her other side. And then it clicked.

He always made sure he kept his good side to her. However they turned or moved, she was on his right.

Her throat got tight. She willed herself not to show any emotion at all. He wouldn't want that. She would guess he didn't even know he was doing it. That keeping his good side to people had started when he was much younger and was now unconscious.

Once again she wondered what had happened to him. How had he been hurt and why hadn't he taken steps to repair the damage? She didn't know that much about reconstructive surgery, but she couldn't help wondering if the scars could be made less noticeable.

Not that she was going to ask. Their time together today had gone well enough. She had done her duty and could now return to her regularly scheduled life. Only she didn't want to. She'd enjoyed her afternoon with Simon much more than she'd expected. Of course, she'd done most of the talking. The only new thing she'd learned was that he had a home base in Los Angeles.

Well, crap. She'd gone on and on about an assortment of topics that had probably bored him. She wasn't interesting enough for someone like him. No doubt he was used to women who —

They'd reached the park again. She came to a stop on the grass, close to a grove of trees, and mentally stomped her foot. No! She wasn't going to put herself down. She wasn't going to assume she was boring. There was nothing wrong with her, not physically or mentally or emotionally.

"Are you all right?"

She sighed. "Sorry. I was having a little discussion with myself. I'm done now."

"Did you win the argument?"

"I wasn't arguing."

"You looked serious about something."

Only her lack of self-confidence. Why were her sisters so much more secure than her? They were supposed to be identical. She should have the same genes, the same attitudes. But she didn't.

None of which was Simon's problem.

"I've kept you long enough," she said.

"You probably have a ton of things you would rather be doing this afternoon."

He faced her, his gaze locked with hers. "Is that what you think?"

Before she could answer, before she could form words or draw breath, she found herself moving toward him. But she wasn't making it happen. Strong hands had settled on her waist, pulling her forward.

She was caught completely off guard, barely able to process what was happening. Which was why she didn't stop it. There wasn't time. One second she was at a safe, socially correct distance and the next she was touching him everywhere.

Her breasts nestled against his surprisingly well-muscled chest. Her thighs brushed his. Heat surrounded her, which was also unexpected, but nothing when compared to his mouth lowering to hers.

Shock immobilized her. Kissing? Simon was kissing her?

But it had to be happening, because she had proof. The feel of his lips on hers. The hard pressure of his mouth as he claimed her in a kiss that was forceful and demanding, yet not in the least bit scary.

He moved his mouth against hers as if discovering her. As if . . . desperate. Starving for whatever she offered. One of his hands tangled in her hair, his fingers warm against her scalp. The other moved up and down her back, stroking her as if she were a cat.

Shock faded and she told herself to push him away. She barely knew him. Only she didn't want any more distance between them. Not when liquid warmth poured through her, making her feel alive and sexy and feminine.

She lightly rested her fingers on his broad shoulders, then gave herself over to the kiss. He must have sensed her surrender, as he shifted even closer and brushed his tongue against her bottom lip.

She parted her lips, wanting to know what his intimate kiss would be like. He plunged inside immediately, tasting and teasing. Shivers raced up and down her spine, following the path of his fingers. Her breasts began to ache and she felt that telltale swelling between her legs.

She kissed him back, liking the way he responded. His body tensed and his arms tightened around her. His kiss grew more hungry, more intense. His reaction fed her own. The heat intensified until she wondered if it was possible for them to get so lost in the moment they would never be found. She'd never been the type to have sex with a stranger, but for the first time in her life she was thinking it might not be the worst idea in the world.

But before she could decide if she wanted to make the offer, Simon abruptly stepped back.

They stood a couple of feet from each other, both breathing hard. She had a feeling her eyes were just as bright with passion as his were. Her lips felt well kissed and slightly swollen. She touched her fingertips to her sensitive skin.

"Did I hurt you?" he demanded, his expression hardening.

"What? No."

He half turned away, then faced her again. He didn't look happy.

"I'm sorry." The words were abrupt. "I shouldn't have done that."

She thought about asking why not, but thought that might send them down a road she didn't want to travel.

"I don't usually . . ." He cleared his throat. "I'm generally in control. You'll have to take my word on that."

"Not to worry. I believe you." She was pleased she could speak without her voice shaking.

"There's something about you. An attraction I can't shake. I —" He sounded frustrated and embarrassed. "I'm sorry."

Sure she must have heard him wrong, she held her hands up in the shape of a T. "At the risk of having you break out in hysterical laughter, are you saying you were overcome by passion and *had* to kiss me?"

She braced herself for mockery. Instead Simon nodded.

"I can't explain it," he admitted. "It's one of those chemical things." He looked away. "I don't usually have this kind of reaction to a woman."

She wanted to bask in the moment. No one had ever admitted unbridled passion for her before. Part of the reason could be that no one used the word *unbridled* anymore, but still.

"Why don't you usually feel this way about a woman? Please tell me you're not gay?"

A muscle twitched in his jaw. "No, I'm not. However, I can generally control myself sexually."

The tone was practically ice, but the words were hot enough to make her thighs tremble.

"Not around me?"

He sighed. "No."

Montana had no idea what to say to that. Part of her wanted to invite him back to her place. If a guy felt that strongly, she thought she should at least say thank you. Although her mother would probably tell her that a card was plenty. Part of her wondered if this was just a game. Except Simon was proud, and she doubted he would be willing to humiliate himself just to score points.

He took the decision out of her hands. "I've taken up enough of your time," he said. "Thank you for showing me the town. As for the kiss, it won't happen again. You have my word."

With that disappointing last statement, he turned and walked away.

Simon found refuge in his work at the hospital. As always, dealing with his patients, planning surgery, examining healing burns kept him occupied, both physically and mentally. But every now and then, and more often than he wanted, he remembered how he'd acted with Montana.

Now, sitting in the small office he'd been given for his three-month stay, he found himself thinking about the scent of her and the feel of her in his arms. He was distracted by the remembrance of her silky hair in his hands, the sound of her laughter and the way she looked when she smiled.

Heat and need threatened to overwhelm

him. Dammit all to hell, he thought grimly. Why now? Why her?

There wouldn't be an answer. Fate was nothing if not mysterious. He simply had to accept that when he was around Montana he was going to act like an idiot. If he didn't watch himself, he would slide past idiot status and into something more dangerous.

Now, as he stared at the chart but saw her face instead, he knew he had to find a solution. Bad enough to be stupid, but worse to be pathetic. He'd made the mistake of telling her why he'd kissed her. No doubt she felt sorry for him and was eager to stay away from him.

Normally he didn't care what people thought of him, but for some reason, Montana's opinion mattered. He wanted to impress her. Between his reaction to Fluffy exploding onto the ward and the kiss, he couldn't be further off the mark.

His cell phone rang.

Simon glanced at the screen before answering, then pushed the button. "What trouble are you in now?" he asked, smiling.

"The usual," the caller said. "Be impressed. I have cell service in Nepal."

"I am. How's it going, Alistair?"

"Good, and you?"

"The same."

"Where are you?" Alistair asked. "America somewhere?"

"Fool's Gold." Simon explained the location and a little about his cases.

"Sounds like work," his friend commented. "The same here. Burns. More primitive conditions in the outlying areas."

Simon had known Alistair since the year he'd spent studying in London. A Brit to his bones, Alistair had been his roommate and shown him much of his country. They'd become friends and, given that they did the same kind of work, stayed close.

"You're keeping busy," Simon said.

"Always." There was a pause and the sound of voices. "I'm sorry, Simon. I phoned to catch up but they're calling me down to emergency surgery. We'll talk soon."

With that, Alistair hung up. Simon sighed and tucked his phone back into his coat. He, of all people, knew how hard it was to maintain friendships in their field.

"Dr. Bradley?"

He glanced up and saw one of the nurses standing in the doorway. She was young and cheerful — something he was sure the patients appreciated but he personally found annoying. His gaze drifted to her name tag.

"Yes, Nora?"

She smiled. "Kalinda's resting. She keeps talking about that poodle who came to see her. What a great idea — bringing in a therapy dog. Especially one that small. I guess that's why you're the expert."

"I've never used a therapy dog before. It was an experiment. Sometimes I get lucky."

Her hair was blond. Her mouth widened slightly at his words. Humor and interest sparkled in her blue eyes. She was pretty and appealing.

"Which makes it a good day," she told him. "How are you enjoying Fool's Gold?"

"The town seems nice enough."

"We like to think we're a friendly sort. Can I prove that by asking if you'd like to come over for dinner? I'm sure you're getting tired of restaurant food. I have my grandmother's recipe for fried chicken, and I make a mean berry pie."

Long-term relationships were out of the question. Not only was he always moving from place to place, but he didn't see the point. He wasn't the sort of man who did forever. Still, when a woman indicated she was intrigued, he paid attention.

A companion for dinner and someone in his bed every now and then was all he wanted. All he required. Under other circumstances, he would accept Nora's invitation to dinner. But he couldn't.

Despite her easy smile and the hint there was more on the menu than dinner, he couldn't say yes. When he looked at her all he saw was a woman who wasn't Montana. Short hair instead of long. Blue eyes instead of brown. Until today he had considered women interchangeable. He might like one more than the other, but the difference wasn't measurable or important.

"Thank you," he said. "But I'm going to have to decline."

She raised her eyebrows. "Really?" She hesitated for a second. "Are you sure?"

Simon stood. "Very."

Perhaps he should have said more. Offered some kind of explanation. But what was there to say? That he was obsessed with another woman? One he barely knew?

He stepped into the hallway and was relieved to see Kalinda's mother walking toward him.

"She's sleeping," Fay said. "She's resting more comfortably. That's good, right?"

"She's healing." Simon hoped Fay wouldn't notice he hadn't answered the question. At this point in Kalinda's recovery, staying alive was good. Everything else was negotiable. Kalinda could turn with no notice, no warning. That was the hell of what he did — there was never a sure thing. Alistair always said they did their best and that was enough. Simon didn't agree.

"That little dog helped," Fay continued. "Cece. Montana said she would bring her back whenever we wanted. Is it all right if I call her?"

Simon rarely had to choose between what he wanted and what a patient needed. Not that there was a choice. Kalinda would come first. "Of course," he said with an ease he didn't feel. "As long as your daughter is holding her own, the dog can visit. Whatever we can do to help her."

Fay squeezed his arm. "Thank you," she breathed. "I'll call Montana right now."

He watched her hurry away, already pulling her cell phone from her jeans pocket. In a few seconds she would hear Montana's voice. Simon knew things were bad when he felt jealous of that.

He had to get a grip. He barely knew the woman. Maybe he needed vitamins.

Before he got any further in his self-diagnosis, one of the nurses came running toward him.

"We just got a call about an accident," she said urgently. "A boy. He's twelve. Fireworks. That's all I know."

Simon ran to the stairs and started down. The other woman was still talking but he wasn't listening and soon he was out of earshot. His mind cleared.

He'd seen the damage fireworks could do to the human body. A familiar, cold rage returned. Other people might enjoy the Fourth of July, but he loathed the holiday. Parents who let children play with fireworks should all be shot. Or set on fire themselves.

He let himself experience the anger until he stepped out of the stairwell and onto the ground floor. As he ran toward the emergency room, he let all the feelings go. He allowed himself only concern and the knowledge he would do everything in his power to fix what had been broken.

"I know we're supposed to eat outside," Montana's mother said. "It's tradition and all. But I feel like I've paid my dues. We ate in the backyard all the time when you were little. I dealt with the bugs and ants enough to last a lifetime. Besides, we're all grown-ups."

Montana did her best to keep her mother from seeing her amusement. They went through this every summer. For a woman who loved to garden, Denise was oddly reluctant to eat outdoors. Snacks were fine, but something about a meal eaten on the grass made her mother crazy.

"We're not all adults," she said just to tease. "Reese is only ten and Tyler just turned eleven. I won't even mention Melissa, Abby and Hannah."

Her mother sighed. "So you're saying that if I was a good grandmother, I'd serve dinner outside?"

Montana laughed, then walked over to her mother and hugged her. "You're an excellent grandmother. Nobody cares if we eat inside or outside. We'll go out later."

"If you're sure." Denise shook her head. "I don't know why I'm so frantic. I guess it's because nearly everyone will be here and that hasn't happened in a long time."

It was true, Montana thought. Only Ford would be missing. Her youngest brother was currently on a Navy ship in the Indian Ocean. Kent, the middle Hendrix brother, and his son Reese would be joining them. They hadn't made it for Christmas, something Denise had been unable to let go. Montana didn't know all the details. Kent and his ex-wife had been finalizing their divorce.

Unlike many women, Kent's ex didn't want custody of their son, although she expected to see Reese whenever it suited her. Montana's understanding of family law was that a parent had to pay child support or take custody so that the responsibility of having a child wasn't reduced to mere convenience.

Not her problem, she reminded herself as she set the table. It would be good to see her brother and her nephew. Reese was always fun, even if he did kick her butt at computer games.

She finished putting out the glasses. Most of the food had been prepared. The ribs were ready to go on the barbecue. Four kinds of salad were in bowls in the fridge, and frosted brownies tempted her from the counter.

"Your sister should be here soon," her mother said, glancing at the clock on the wall.

She meant Nevada. The single sisters arrived early to help. Until a couple of months ago, Dakota would have been with them. She had Finn now, not to mention her daughter, Hannah. And she was pregnant.

Montana wondered what that must feel like. To know you had a baby inside you. As far as she knew, her sister hadn't felt any movement in her growing tummy. Still, the realization that a life was inside her must be powerful stuff.

Fierce longing swept through her, startling her with its intensity. She wanted to fall in love and get married and have kids. She'd never been that passionate about the subject before. Maybe because she hadn't figured out what she wanted to do with her life. But now she was settled in her job and ready for the next step. Unfortunately, no guy lurked on the horizon.

Without wanting to, she remembered Simon's kiss. But he'd made it clear that he didn't plan to kiss her again. While technically kissing wasn't required for pregnancy, she had a feeling it helped. Besides, she didn't want just a baby, she wanted a husband. Simon didn't strike her as the sort of man who'd settle down.

"Are you all right?" her mother asked.

"Fine. Just thinking about Dakota's baby."

"Hannah is going to enjoy having a baby brother or sister."

Montana thought of her sister's adopted daughter. She'd only been a part of the family for a couple of months, but already no one could remember what it had been like without her. She had spent the first few months of her life in an orphanage in Kazakhstan yet she'd adjusted to the family as if she was blood.

"Maybe she'll have twins," Montana said

with a grin.

"Don't let your sister hear you say that," her mother warned.

Montana laughed. "More grandchildren for you."

"I wouldn't say no. But she might want to go more slowly. So . . . are you seeing anyone?"

The question was asked casually enough, but Montana wasn't fooled. Her mother would want details. Not that she had any to share. She hadn't been on a date in months. And her tour of town with Simon didn't count, even with the kiss.

"No, are you?"

Her mother leaned against the counter and sighed. "I've been on a few dates, but nothing special." She wrinkled her nose. "I don't understand it. There are so many younger men asking me out. Why? Where are all the good men in their fifties and sixties?"

Montana looked at her mother. Denise was as pretty as she had been twenty years ago. She could also fit in the same clothes. Her blond hair was short and stylish. She understood why younger men were interested in her mother, even though she didn't want to hear about it.

For a second, she thought about mentioning Max. Her boss was about the right age and in the year Montana had known him, he'd never been out with anyone. At least she didn't think he'd been on a date. They didn't exactly talk about their personal lives. So, he was a possibility. Except for the issue of the name Max tattooed on her mother's hip. Whoever *that* Max was, their relationship had been very intense. There might be name associations her mother wouldn't appreciate.

"Your sister told me about your conversation with Mayor Marsha," her mother said.

"We really don't have to talk about that." She glanced at the clock, wishing someone would show up. Anyone would be a distraction.

"It's nice of you to help the town. What's he like?"

"Quiet." A great kisser. But that was a factoid she was not going to share with her mother.

"Do you think you'll be seeing him again?"

Before Montana could figure out how to answer, the phone rang.

Saved by the bell, she thought humorously.

Her mother reached for the receiver. "Hello?"

Montana turned toward the refrigerator

to get herself something to drink. But a sixth sense made her turn around.

"Are you sure?" Denise asked, her face going white. "I'm sorry. Of course you're sure. Yes. We'll be right there."

She hung up the phone, then pressed her hand against her midsection. Tears filled Denise's eyes.

Montana was at her side in an instant. "What is it? What happened?" She could feel her mother shaking.

"There's been a car accident. Kent and Reese. They're on their way to the hospital."

Montana was already grabbing her purse. "We'll meet them there."

CHAPTER FIVE

Montana told herself to keep her attention on the road. What she wanted to do was panic. Instead, she was going to be strong. If anyone had the right to freak out, it was her mother.

"I wish they'd told us more," her mother said, clutching her hands together and straining in the seat as if willing them to go faster.

Montana resisted the urge to speed. They were driving through the center of town and there were pedestrians everywhere. She wasn't willing to hurt someone just to get to the hospital a few seconds more quickly.

"Two more minutes," she said, signaling to turn into the hospital parking lot. "I'm going to pull up in front of the emergency room. You go in and I'll park."

Denise nodded and jumped out of the car.

Montana found a parking space, but before getting out, she paused and sent off a brief prayer that everyone was going to be all right.

She hurried across the parking lot and through the automatic doors. Relief washed through her when she saw her brother Kent holding her mother. He looked shaken and pale, and had a bandage across his forehead, but otherwise he was all right.

Kent looked up and saw her. He freed one arm and held it open to her. She ran into his embrace.

"I'm okay," he was saying. "Reese is going to need surgery." His voice shook as he said the words. "He got cut pretty bad. Mostly his face, some on his arm. They're telling me the injuries aren't life threatening, but they scared the hell out of me." He swallowed.

Montana sensed he wanted to say more, to share the experience. But he was holding back because of their mother. No doubt he was concerned that too many details would upset her. Montana had a feeling that the details involved a lot of bleeding and knew her brother was making the right decision. They could catch up on the specifics later.

She drew back slightly and studied him. Like his brothers, Kent was tall and broad shouldered, with dark hair and dark eyes. He looked a lot like their dad. Handsome, with an inner strength.

"Where is Reese now?" Denise asked.

"Being prepped for surgery."

Before he could say more, a doctor approached him. The badge on her coat said Dr. Lawrence. Montana had seen her around the hospital and knew she had a good reputation.

"Reese is just fine," the doctor told Kent. "He's calm — we've given him something for the pain. He should be in surgery in the next half hour or so." She gave them a warm smile. "The best news I have to give you is that the doctor who will be working on your son is extraordinary. I would go so far as to say gifted. If there is one surgeon I would pick to work on my child it would be Dr. Bradley."

Montana blinked at her. "Simon is going to do the surgery?"

"You know Dr. Bradley?" Dr. Lawrence asked.

She felt everyone looking at her. "Yes. I take one of my therapy dogs to see one of his patients." She turned to her mother and brother. "Simon, ah, Dr. Bradley, is a renowned plastic surgeon. He mostly works on burn patients."

Dr. Lawrence nodded. "That's true. He's just finishing up surgery on a boy right now.

As soon as he's ready, we'll take Reese in to him. The surgery itself shouldn't take very long."

They were given a few more details, told where to wait. When Dr. Lawrence left, Montana took her mother's arm and leaned against her brother.

"It's going to be okay," she told him. "Dr. Bradley is the best."

"I'm relieved," Kent admitted, leading the way to the waiting room.

They settled onto surprisingly comfortable chairs, clustered close together. Their conversation was more idle chitchat than anything meaningful. Just something to pass the time while they each privately worried.

Nevada showed up next. Dakota was there a few minutes later, baby Hannah in her arms. Hugs were exchanged while everyone was brought up to date. Then Ethan and Liz arrived and they went through it all again.

As everyone talked, Montana realized this was what families did. They comforted each other, they waited in hospitals, they prayed. No matter what happened, she would always have this. People who loved her and would worry, and wait. She was one of six children and didn't know any other way to live.

Out of nowhere, a thought occurred to

her. What about Simon? Who waited and worried for him?

Simon made the last, impossibly small, even stitch. The procedure had been straight-forward. The cuts looked worse than they were. Not too deep, not too wide. There might be some minor scarring but he doubted it.

He stood in the operating room while the boy was wheeled to recovery. Most surgeons would have left already. He didn't linger out of concern. Instead he waited because he knew what was next. He would go tell the family that everything was going to be fine. That the worst the boy would have was the faintest hint of a scar. Nothing frightening. Barely noticeable.

They would be grateful. The families always were. They would surround him and thank him and want to offer him something. The women would try to hug him and the men would shake his hand. He went through it hundreds of times and he never found it easy. He didn't want their thanks. All he wanted was to slip away. To take on the next case, to lose himself in the work.

This time would be especially awkward. According to the nurse, his patient was Montana's nephew. He would be forced to see her again, to stare into her dark eyes and know that he couldn't have the one thing he most wanted. Worse, he would have to do it in front of her family.

He doubted she would say anything. She was too kind for that. But she would be thinking it. That he had kissed her, practically forced himself upon her. It had been so unlike him.

Knowing he was putting off the inevitable, he walked to the waiting room. He saw them at once, the large family clustered together, talking, comforting one another. He'd been told that waiting was the worst and he believed it. At least he was always busy doing something.

In the second before they noticed him, he saw Montana had sisters. No, more than that. He saw the identical bone structure, the shape of the eyes that was exactly the same. Minor differences caused more by time than DNA.

A triplet. She hadn't mentioned that. And brothers. She came from a large family, something he couldn't relate to. How did people find quiet with that many family members around?

Montana glanced up and saw him. "Dr. Bradley."

Everyone shifted, allowing one of the

brothers and the petite, pretty woman in her fifties to move toward him. Montana's mother, he realized, taking in more similarities.

The brother, a tall man, held out his hand. "Kent Hendrix," he said. "Montana tells us you're the best. How is he? How is Reese?"

They were all staring at him. All waiting to hear that their loved one was fine. He never knew what to say, even when the news was good, so he stumbled on as best he could. The boy was doing well, the scarring minimal. No surprises in surgery.

Montana moved to his side and smiled. "I was so happy when I heard it was you." She turned her attention to her brother. "I've seen his work. It's very impressive."

Simon's first thought was that she wasn't angry. He felt as if he'd been given a reprieve, for whatever reason. His second thought was to realize the only work of his she'd seen was with Kalinda. No layperson could look beyond the bandages and raw skin to see the work he'd done.

Concerns for another time, he told himself.

Kent Hendrix continued to shake his hand. "I can't thank you enough. When I saw him lying there, and all that blood . . ." He paused and glanced at his mother. "I didn't know what to think."

"It's difficult when a family member is injured," Simon said stiffly.

He managed to free his hand from Kent's, only to be hugged by Denise.

She straightened and stared into his eyes. "Please tell me he's going to be all right. I know you said it, but I need you to say it again."

Love shone in her eyes. Love and concern and worry. She was everything a mother and grandmother should be. He had seen it time and time again in his practice. The mothers who didn't love, the mothers who deliberately hurt their children, were rare. He'd always known that, but it still surprised him that so many parents were good.

"He's going to be fine."

"Very light scars," Montana said, touching her arm. "It'll make him a chick magnet."

Denise managed a strangled laugh. "Just what every grandmother wants to hear." She drew in a slow breath, then let it out. "Dr. Bradley, we were supposed to have a family dinner today. I suspect that's going to be postponed until tomorrow. Please join us."

Anything but that, he thought grimly. He didn't want to have dinner with them. He didn't want to socialize or spend time with them. He never knew what to do with himself, how to act with strangers. He knew the invitation was more about their need to thank him than anything else.

Which was why he always refused. He kept things separate. He wasn't the kind of doctor who got personally involved.

The rest of the family echoed the invitation. Their words washed over him, easily ignored. Until Montana turned to him.

"Please say you'll join us," she said. Her gaze was steady.

Despite his reluctance, he found himself nodding. He couldn't resist spending time in her company.

Denise said something about the time and rattled off an address. He wasn't listening. Instead he focused on the two sisters, the ones that were identical to Montana. If it was chemistry, if it was simply some quirk of genetics, shouldn't he be equally attracted to them?

He studied them, trying to imagine talking to them, touching them, kissing them. Instead of being interested, he felt uncomfortable and more than a little foolish. No, it was only Montana.

"Let's not make him find his way," Montana said, still looking at him. "Simon, I'll pick you up at your hotel around four. Does that work?"

No, it didn't work. He couldn't spend time with her in front of other people. What if he did something ridiculous again? What if he kissed her?

He reminded himself he had always been able to force his body to do more than anyone anticipated. He'd healed faster, gotten better range of motion, kept up his grades in school. He determined his own fate, within the confines of the rules. Of course he could have dinner with Montana and her family without embarrassing himself.

"It's Tuesday," she added.

He allowed himself a smile. "I do manage to keep track of the days of the week."

"As busy as you are, I thought they might blur." Humor brightened her eyes. "I've always heard you genius types have trouble with ordinary details."

"I struggle through. Tomorrow at four. I'll be waiting."

"I'm looking forward to it," she admitted.

For a second, it was as if the rest of the world disappeared. Only the two of them existed. Then one of the other sisters laughed and he was brought back to reality.

After accepting another round of thanks, he excused himself. He still had patients to see and work to do. But as he stepped into the elevator he thought only of Montana and how being with her seemed to make everything better. Reality be damned.

Montana stood in the hospital parking lot, the one reserved for doctors. She'd found Simon's car easily enough. It was sleek and expensive, some kind of Mercedes convertible. Her brothers would probably know the make and model and be impressed. All she knew was she wasn't comfortable leaning against it. She didn't want to risk scratching it.

The bag in her hand got heavier by the second. But what concerned her more than the temperature of the takeout was how stupid she was going to feel if she had to wait much longer.

She'd been told Simon would be done close to eight. She'd gotten him dinner and had shown up to wait. It was now eight-fifteen, the sun had nearly set and she was wondering if she'd been an idiot.

Buying him dinner had seemed like the least she could do. After all, he'd saved her nephew. For him, it was probably no more than part of his regular day's work. But for her and her family, it had been a miracle. She wanted to say thank-you, and providing dinner had been a start. It was also possible she was curious . . . maybe even intrigued by the thought of seeing Simon again in private. There was something about him, something about the way he kissed her. Something about the way he'd looked at her in the hospital waiting room. She couldn't define it, but she found she liked it.

She checked her watch again. She would wait until eight-twenty, then leave. She dropped her arm to her side, only to see Simon walking toward his car. He saw her and came to a stop.

She tried to read his expression and couldn't. She had no idea what he was thinking, which meant she began to question herself and her decision. Maybe bringing him dinner had been a bad idea.

He began walking again, only to stop when he was a few feet in front of her.

"What are you doing here?" he asked.

His tone was neutral. There wasn't any emotion in his eyes. She shook her head. That wasn't true. Plenty of emotions swirled in his eyes, she just couldn't read them.

"I heard that you'd been in surgery most of the day. You haven't gotten a break at all or a chance to eat." She held up the bag. "You must be exhausted. I brought you dinner. It's from the Fox and Hound. They make a great stew. And there's bread and a salad."

"Aren't you feeding me tomorrow?"

"That's my mom. This is from me."

Okay, so this hadn't been her best idea. The poor man probably thought she was stalking him. She wished she could think of something clever to say. Something smart and funny. Anything that would stop him from staring at her.

"I didn't know you were a triplet," he said.

"For as long as I can remember." She smiled. "I have three brothers, so there were six of us. My mother stayed amazingly sane despite the chaos."

"You must've been impossible to tell apart when you were younger."

"We were. It was fun. Now we try to be different."

"You outgrew the need to try to fool everyone?"

The tension in her body faded away. Well, that wasn't completely true. The nervous tension was gone, but a different kind took its place.

She was aware of Simon standing close to her. Of the lines of weariness around his mouth and eyes. But even with the exhaustion, he had an energy that drew her. She wanted to step into his embrace and hold him against her. She wanted his mouth on hers, taking her the way he had before, as if he couldn't help himself. No one had ever wanted her like that. Being desired was more seductive than she had ever known.

"By the time we were teenagers, we were ready to be more distinct." She tilted her head. "What about you? Any brothers or sisters?"

"No."

He said the single word with great finality. As if there would be no more discussion about family. At least not his.

While she was trying to figure out what to say next, he opened his car and took the food from her. After setting it on the passenger seat, he straightened and faced her.

"I don't think coming to dinner tomorrow is a good idea," he said. "I'm not the family type."

She didn't know very much about him. Finding out he was an only child practically doubled her knowledge pool. But sometimes she was good at guessing about people. Her gut told her Simon spent most of his life alone, even when he was around others.

"There's no entrance exam. It's dinner. You've done dinner before."

One corner of his mouth twitched slightly,

as if he were going to smile. A flicker of anticipation danced through her.

"Besides," she continued, "you need a family dinner. It will do you good. Make you less stuffy."

"Is that how you see me?"

"Sometimes. But not in a bad way."

He raised his eyebrows. "Because there's a good stuffy?"

"Maybe. It can work if you're British."

Now he did smile. His whole face changed as the amusement turned him from merely handsome to completely irresistible. She supposed some women would be put off by his scars, but she barely noticed them.

"I don't do a very good accent," he admitted. "Although I have a friend who's British."

"You should practice the accent. Because women really love that. Not that the doctor thing isn't working for you."

"The doctor thing?"

"Don't pretend you don't know what I'm talking about. There you are, a good-looking doctor. Better yet, a surgeon. You're like catnip."

The smile faded. He stared at her with an intensity that made her want to take a step back. She knew she'd said something wrong, but couldn't figure out what it was. She didn't think he was mad, exactly. But he was —

He reached for her. His large, strong hands cupped her face, his thumbs lightly caressing her cheekbones. Then he was kissing her, his mouth on hers, claiming her with the passion she remembered from their last kiss.

She was less startled this time, more ready to step closer and lose herself in the feel of his lips against hers.

The heat was familiar, as was the need that rushed from him to her. She surrendered more quickly, putting her hands on his shoulders, then tilting her head so he could deepen the kiss.

She inhaled the scent of skin and night and the faint smell of the dinner she'd brought him. He tasted of coffee and mint. Stubble lightly scraped against her skin.

She was aware of the smooth wool of his suit jacket, the breadth of his shoulders, the tension in his muscles. Then he parted his lips and his tongue swept in to claim her.

It was exactly as she remembered, she thought happily as desire flooded her. The erotic dance, the way he kissed her, as if desperate and starving. She answered stroke for stroke, letting his kiss sweep her away because getting lost had never felt so right.

He dropped his hands to her waist and pulled her hard against him. She felt the strength of his body and had a vision of them naked together. Skin on skin. She shivered, her breasts becoming more sensitive, her nipples getting tight. Heat pooled in her belly before slipping lower.

He dropped his hands to her hips. His fingertips lightly grazed the curve of her butt. Her belly came into contact with his groin and she felt his erection.

She instantly wanted to touch him. No, that wasn't it. She wanted to be on her back, naked, ready. She wanted his mouth everywhere.

The images were so real, for a second she thought she had begged to be taken, standing there in the parking lot. Instead of being embarrassed, she wanted to grab his hands and place them on her breasts or between her legs.

She'd been kissed before, had made love before, but she'd never been so . . . hungry.

Without warning, Simon stepped back. His breathing was ragged and his expression stark with passion. If he asked her back to his hotel, she wasn't sure she could say no. Having sex with someone she barely knew wasn't exactly the wisest thing to do, regardless of how good it would feel.

But he didn't ask. He *apologized.* If one could call it that.

"Sorry," he said gruffly. Then he turned from her and got in his car. As she watched, he started the engine, then drove away.

"A hit-and-run kisser," she whispered when she was alone. A dangerous man. She would have to be more careful when it came to Simon Bradley. He was the kind of man who could easily break her heart.

CHAPTER SIX

Tuesday afternoon, Simon stood in the center of his hotel room, not sure what to do. He didn't usually allow himself to be indecisive. In his line of work, decisions had to be made quickly. He'd learned to trust his instincts, to believe that his training and his ability would guide him. But this wasn't surgery. This was regular life and he'd never done very well there.

He fully expected Montana to have given her mother some reason why he couldn't show up. After what had happened yesterday, there was no way she would be waiting for him in the hotel lobby. He hadn't just kissed her, he'd claimed her. Once again he'd been unable to resist, and this time she'd felt the proof of what she did to him. His inability to restrain himself humiliated him, yet he knew if given the chance he would do it again.

He glanced at his watch. It was nearly

four. He'd gone to all the trouble of arranging to leave the hospital early. Either he went through with the damn meal or he went back to work. Compelled by a force he couldn't explain, he made his way downstairs. Even if she didn't show up, he owed it to her to be waiting. It would be his penance.

But when he stepped into the lobby, she was all he saw. Her long golden-blond hair, tumbling across her shoulders. The pale blue sundress that left her arms and legs bare. She was beautiful and sexy and he wanted her with a desperation that robbed him of speech.

He saw other men glancing at her and wanted to step between them and her. He wanted to announce to all the world that she was his and no one else could have her. The primitive need shocked him. He wasn't that man. He was always in control.

Except with her.

She saw him and smiled, then walked toward him. Her hips swayed, enticing him. Every movement was sensual, a siren's call to pleasure.

"Look at you, wearing jeans again. You're doing it to mess with my head, aren't you? We both know you're much more the suit type."

Because that was how she saw him. What was it she had said? That he had a stick up his ass?

"About yesterday," he began.

She shook her head. "Don't you dare apologize. You can't kiss like that and then say you're sorry. Because if you really are sorry, I'll have to punch you hard in the stomach. I've accepted that you're a hit-and-run kisser. Luckily for you, you're the best one around."

"There are others?"

She laughed. "No. Just you."

He could see she wasn't angry. If anything, she was teasing him. He'd hoped she enjoyed kissing him. She'd kissed him back — he'd felt her response. But he didn't know if he'd taken it too far. While that wasn't an excuse for his behavior, her acceptance made him feel a little better.

She placed her hand on his chest. He supposed it was casual, or at least intended to be. But he felt the heat of her touch burning down to his soul.

"You should do that more often," she said, staring up at him.

"Kiss you?"

She laughed. "That's not what I meant, but maybe. I was talking about you smiling. You don't smile very much. I suppose that comes from being a very serious man."

In her world, was being serious good or bad? He had a feeling it would fall on the bad side and wanted to tell her he could be as much fun as the next guy. But he knew he was wrong. All the fun had been burned out of him a long time ago.

She dropped her hand to her side. For a moment he wanted to protest, telling her that he needed the physical contact between them. Instead he said nothing.

"Come on," she said. "Everyone in my family is waiting to treat you like the hero you are."

"I'm not a hero," he said, following her out of the hotel lobby. Far from it.

Sometimes, not often, but sometimes, he wanted things to be different. He saw the world around him and wanted what other people had. Connection. What was that old saying? No point in howling for the moon.

"You're a hero to us," she told him.

They stepped out into the warm afternoon. The sidewalk was surprisingly crowded with families and couples talking as they walked. From the little he'd seen of the town, it was an open, friendly place. Like something out of a movie or a sitcom. Not that it tempted him. When his time here was finished, he would be moving on.

Montana made her way to a beat-up Subaru wagon. A few dings scarred the doors and the paint wasn't very shiny, but what caught his attention was the large dog in the back. He recognized the big eyes, the slobbery grin and the sweeping tail with nearly magical powers of wreaking havoc.

He stopped beside the car. "It's that dog."

"You don't have to say it like she has a disease. Yes, this is Fluffy. You probably remember her from that little incident at the hospital."

He raised his eyebrows. "Little incident?"

"What would you call it?"

"You don't want to know."

Montana sighed. "I have already admitted I overestimated Fluffy's ability to change. She's a happy, exuberant dog and most of the time that's a good thing. Just not so much for therapy. I'm taking her with us because I want her to meet Kent and Reese. Kent has been thinking about getting them a dog. Fluffy would make a great pet."

She narrowed her gaze. "Don't you dare say anything."

"I'm sure Fluffy would make a great pet." As long as the dog never got onto his ward again, he would be happy.

"Oh." She unlocked the doors.

He slid into the passenger seat. Fluffy

lunged toward him, but Montana told her to stay in the back.

"Kent and Reese have been going through a bad time. Reese's mom took off about a year ago." Montana started the engine, then glanced at him. "She just left. What kind of mother does that? She rarely sees Reese. Kent said she barely calls, but when she suddenly gets an itch to play mom, she expects Kent to drop everything and bring Reese to her. I don't think that dog can take the place of his mother, but sometimes unconditional love can really help."

Simon thought of his own mother. Compared to her actions, leaving would have almost been kind. But Montana wouldn't know much about the monsters in life. She'd been spared, and he found he was pleased by that. He didn't want her to know what life could really be like.

"I didn't tell Cece that Fluffy was coming with us," she said with a grin. "I didn't want them fighting." She glanced at him out of the corner of her eye. "She really has a thing for you. It's so cute."

He thought about the small poodle. She wasn't a bad dog and seemed to do well with Kalinda, which he appreciated. "I think you're giving her too much credit."

"You only say that because you don't

know her. Just wait. Cece is going to win you over."

Before he could respond, she began pointing out the various sites in Fool's Gold. They drove by the park and through the small downtown before turning into a residential neighborhood.

From what he could tell, the houses were older but well maintained. Large trees and green lawns gave the neighborhood an idyllic air. A few bicycles leaned against porches. He supposed this was normal for a lot of people. Middle America. The kind of place where most kids grew up, or at least imagined growing up. He'd never experienced anything like it. His life with his mother had been spent in a series of small apartments in grim neighborhoods. He'd spent his teen years in hospitals.

No doubt many of his patients lived in houses like this, but he never visited them there. He made it a point to keep his work separate. He didn't want to know them more personally than necessary. In fact, he had never accepted an invitation to someone's home. This was a first. And it wasn't because he wanted to get to know the Hendrix family. It was all about Montana.

She parked in front of one of the houses. It looked freshly painted and the roof was new. The yard well cared for. There were already several cars in the driveway. As he got out of the car, he braced himself to once again deal with people he didn't know. Not his strong suit, he thought grimly.

Montana let Fluffy out of the back and quickly clicked the leash onto her collar. Even so, the large dog practically dragged her toward the porch. Before they got there, the front door burst open and people spilled out.

"Welcome," Denise said, hurrying toward them. She held her arms open.

He wanted to take a step back, to turn away, to make his excuses. But everything happened too fast. Denise embraced him, holding on as if she would never let go.

"He came home this morning," she said as she hugged him tight. "Just like you said. He's going to be fine and it's because of you." Still holding on to both his upper arms, she stepped back and looked at him. "I want to spend the next several hours thanking you, but that might make you uncomfortable. So I'm going to say it now and try to let it go. Thank you."

"You're welcome," he said, hoping he didn't sound as awkward as he felt.

She linked arms with him and led him toward the waiting family.

He remembered Kent from the previous day. After they shook hands, he was introduced to Ethan, the oldest of the six children, and Ethan's wife, Liz. Next up were the remaining triplets, Dakota and Nevada.

Dakota was holding a toddler. Hovering close by was Finn, Dakota's fiancé.

"The kids are in the backyard," Denise told him. "You know Reese, of course. Then there are Ethan and Liz's three. My youngest son, Ford, is overseas in the military."

As she spoke, she led Simon through the house. The large, bright rooms and comfortable furniture were welcoming. He found himself relaxing almost against his will.

Once they went outside, everyone drifted to the tables set up in the shade under the trees. He heard the other two sisters teasing their mother about eating outside. Montana moved next to him.

"You doing okay?" she asked.

He glanced at her. "Fine."

"I'm only asking because I know this isn't your thing." She smiled. "Families. Groups."

He wondered if it was that obvious. "I appreciate the invitation," he began.

She cut him off with a laugh and a shake of her head. "Oh, please. You can say that to them, but we both know the truth. You would rather have a root canal than be here today. Which makes me really appreciate you agreeing to come."

He had never considered himself the kind of man who had a preference for a physical type. The women in his life were temporary, a convenience. But now, staring into Montana's brown eyes, he wondered if he would ever be able to look at another woman without thinking of her.

They settled in chairs next to each other. Nevada joined them, sitting across the table and leaning toward him.

"I won't get into the whole 'we really appreciate what you did' thing," she said. "Mom will thank you for all of us. I would guess at some point the thanks get tedious."

"Not tedious," he corrected. "Uncomfortable."

She smiled. "Not into the gushing thing?"

"No."

The curve of her mouth, the flash of teeth, was nearly identical to Montana's. Yet his reaction could not have been more different. He wasn't the least bit interested in Nevada. She was nice enough and pretty enough, but nothing like her sister. Quite the trick, considering they were identical triplets.

"Montana tells me you're in town for a temporary assignment. You go from place to

119

place doing surgery and then leave?"

He nodded. "I don't usually go to large cities unless there is a special case. Every couple of years I spend a few months in other countries. I'm going to Peru as soon as I'm done here."

"Doctors Without Borders?" Montana asked.

"I've worked with them and with other organizations. There is a massive need for surgeons in the Third World."

"But you mostly work with burn patients, right?" Nevada asked. "Don't they require long-term care?"

"Yes. I do the preliminary surgeries and their local doctors follow up with long-term care. Sometimes I go back a few years later." If the case was difficult enough.

"Aren't you kind of young to be doing what you do?" Nevada asked. "You're what? In your early thirties?"

"I started college early and got through quickly. I knew what I wanted to do and was motivated."

Montana enjoyed listening to the exchange. She didn't know very much about Simon and having her sister grill him would make it easier for her to make some headway with Mayor Marsha's request.

Although from what she could tell all he

did was move around. While that sounded exciting, didn't he eventually want a home?

As he and Nevada discussed the rigors of his education, Montana studied his face. She wasn't surprised that he had seated her on his "good" side. But when he turned to her sister, she could see some of the scars. They were thick and angry, tugging at his skin. They went down the side of his neck. She wasn't sure where they ended. At his shoulder? Did they go all the way down his back, his chest?

What had happened to him, all those years ago? How had he been hurt and how had he recovered? "Who was Simon Bradley?" she asked herself somewhat dramatically.

Before she could figure out how to ask, Kent and Reese walked up, Fluffy bounding beside the boy. There were bandages on the side of her nephew's face and he had a couple of bruises. He was still kind of foggy from the accident and the surgery. At both his father's and grandmother's insistence, he was spending the afternoon in a lounge chair, while his cousins played around him. She had a feeling that come tomorrow he would be running around with the rest of them.

"How are you feeling?" Simon asked the boy.

"Okay. My face hurts a little. I'm kind of tired. Dad says you're the doctor who operated on me."

Simon nodded. "You were my easiest case of the day."

Reese leaned against the table. He had the same dark hair that all the Hendrix men possessed. Montana could see a lot of her brother in his son.

"Doesn't all that blood bother you?" Reese asked.

"I'm used to it."

"It's pretty sweet, the way you help people and all. But I'd worry about throwing up with all that blood."

Kent looked surprised. "Are you thinking you want to be a doctor?"

Reese grinned. "Dad, I'm ten. I kind of want to be everything. But I think what Dr. Bradley can do is special. You know, fixing people."

Montana watched her brother struggle. She knew him well enough to guess that he wanted to point out his profession was interesting, too, although she wasn't sure how many ten-year-olds dreamed of being a math teacher.

"A doctor would be good," Kent said. "You have to go to school a lot."

"He has plenty of time to decide," Simon

said easily, then smiled at Reese. "You won't be so tired tomorrow. And your face will stop hurting."

"Sweet."

Kent excused them both and went back to the house. Fluffy trailed along with them.

"I should go help Mom," Nevada said, rising.

Montana started to stand but her sister waved her into place.

"Entertain our company," Nevada said with a knowing smile. "I'll take care of setting out the food."

Montana sighed, then glanced at Simon to see if he'd noticed the not very subtle "pay attention to the cute guy" reference. Fortunately, he seemed intent on watching Fluffy.

Through the open sliding door, they could see Reese had plopped down on the sectional sofa. Instead of staying outside with the other kids, Fluffy settled at his feet.

"She's protecting him," Montana pointed out. "She didn't have the personality to be a therapy dog, but she had the heart."

"Disappointed it wasn't enough?"

She studied her nephew. "I think a dog will be good for him, so no. Still, it would have been nice to add Fluffy to the team. Big dogs work well in a lot of situations."

"Such as?"

"If we're visiting a large group, like a nursing home. The bigger dogs can easily go around and be patted. They're also easier for residents with walkers and wheelchairs. No little paws getting underfoot. The bigger dogs seem better suited for the reading program, too. You'd think a large dog would scare a little kid, but they don't. Plus they can lean on them or cuddle, which takes away some of the stress. Not to dismiss the work of the small dogs. You saw what Cece did for Kalinda. It's hard to get an eighty-pound Lab onto a bed with a sick kid."

She shook her head. "Sorry. I can get carried away."

"I like hearing about your work."

"It's nothing when compared with what you do."

His gray-green gaze was steady. "I disagree. The ability to read is just as important for a child as fitting into our societal norms, physically speaking."

He had a point, but still. "You save lives."

"When you bring a dog to visit someone who is lonely, aren't you saving their life, too?"

"In the moment."

"Isn't life about moments?"

This was a side of him she hadn't expected

to see. "I thought all surgeons had huge egos."

"I have my moments, too." One corner of his mouth twitched. "Plus, that stick up my butt takes a lot of room."

She winced. "I shouldn't have said that. I'm sorry."

"Don't apologize. I can be too focused. I need that skill for my work, but after a while I forget to turn it off."

He flashed her a smile and she felt her stomach clench. There was something about this man, she thought. She wanted to ask about his scars — how he'd gotten them and why he hadn't entirely fixed them. Maybe they couldn't be fixed. And while she was wondering things, what about his personal life? From what he'd said, he went from place to place, with no real roots. Didn't that get lonely?

Usually conversation was easy for her, but with Simon she felt she had to tread more carefully. Strange, considering the man had had his tongue in her mouth. After that intimacy, he shouldn't be so intimidating. But it wasn't that she was nervous around him. Rather, she didn't want to scare him off. Talk about confusing.

"I'm guessing that means you didn't have a dog when you were growing up," she said, wondering if she could get him to talk about his past.

"No." The humor left his eyes as he spoke and his mouth straightened. "No dog. It was just me and my mother. Until I went into the hospital."

With the burns, she thought, eager to find out what had happened. But before she could figure out what to ask, he spoke.

"You and your sisters are the youngest?"

"Yes. Mom wanted one girl and instead got three. That can't have been easy. The multiple birth thing. My friend Pia is pregnant with twins. She's due any minute. I can't imagine what that's like — especially since they're not hers. Not biologically."

"Someone donated the eggs?"

"Our mutual friend Crystal had frozen embryos. Crystal died and left them to Pia, who freaked out." Montana smiled at the memory. "She wasn't exactly prepared to be a mother. But she couldn't say no and then she met Raoul and now they're a family." She sighed. "It's wonderful. Don't you love a happy ending?"

"You believe in that?"

"Of course. Fool's Gold is the Land of Happy Endings. Don't you believe in them?"

"Sometimes."

The air was warm and the scent of her mother's flowers drifted by. She could hear the sound of the kids playing, talking and laughter coming from the house. Still, all that faded until there was only Simon.

"Only sometimes? Because other times they don't make it," she whispered, understanding that for him, not saving someone, even if he knew there wasn't a way to make that happen, must be terrible.

"I've accepted it."

"You don't mean that."

He stared at her. "I don't mean it," he admitted. "I'm supposed to be able to save them all." He put his hands on the table. "It's here. In these, and in my head. I'm good at what I do — one of the best. I always knew that I had a special talent, and that if I dedicated everything to becoming the best, I could save lives."

That wasn't ego, she thought, although she wasn't sure how she knew. It was something else. Something more profound and integral to who he was.

"You're complicated," she told him.

"No. I'm fairly simple. You're the complicated one."

She laughed. "I don't think so. My life is very normal. Boring, even."

"Not boring."

She wished he was telling the truth. "I always wanted to be exotic. Different. Instead I'm one of six kids with parents who loved each other. I guess being a triplet was unusual, but in a way it only added to the sameness. It's hard to be an individual when you're one of three." She shook her head. "I'm not making sense, am I? The thing is, I love my family and my sisters so much. But they always knew what they wanted and, until recently, I didn't."

"Hence your concern about Fluffy's destiny?"

She laughed. "There's that word again. *Hence.* You and your fancy education."

"That's me. Fancy."

"I'm glad you came today," she said impulsively, touching her hand to his.

His skin was warm and made her remember being in his arms. Talk about a place that felt good.

Simon studied her intensely. "I am, too. I don't spend a lot of time with families."

By choice, she thought suddenly, thinking of his travels. He could have chosen to settle in one place, to raise money and have the patients come to him. But he hadn't. He'd done this deliberately, which left the question of why.

Ethan strolled over. "All right, Simon, I've

come to give you a break. Kent and I are going to grab a beer and watch the game. Want to join us?"

Montana would have preferred to keep him to herself, but wasn't sure what he wanted to do.

"Go ahead," she told him. "I'll help Mom in the kitchen."

They went into the house. Ethan grabbed them each a beer, then the guys settled in front of the big TV in the family room. The space was large, with comfortable sofas. Although it opened onto the kitchen, the guys were so far away that the sound from the TV barely made it to the kitchen.

The kids were out back, playing. Nevada and Dakota were with Denise, finishing up the last prep work for dinner. Baby Hannah sat in her playpen, happily digging into a quilted bag filled with fabric animals.

"Let me guess," her mother said as Montana entered. "They're going to watch the game."

"Of course."

"Men and sports. I'll never understand it." Denise leaned against the counter. "How your father loved baseball."

"And football," Nevada added. "Remember that Thanksgiving when the game went into overtime and the turkey was done?"

Dad had been desperate to see the end of the game, but had taken one look at his wife's face and turned off the TV. Denise had been so impressed, she'd had Ethan and Ford drag the TV into the dining room while Ralph was carving the turkey in the kitchen.

"He would have missed the end of that game for you," Montana reminded her mother. "He loved you so much."

"He did. He was a good man." Denise looked at her, then at Nevada. "I want you two to find a man like him."

"I'm not opposed to it," Montana said, doing her best not to look toward the family room or even think about Simon. First of all, she barely knew the man. Fabulous kissing did not a relationship make. Second, he wasn't the kind who stayed, and she wasn't the kind who left.

"I'm not convinced what you and Dad had still exists," Nevada grumbled. "There aren't that many good guys around."

"Sure there are," Dakota told her.

"Thanks. Rub in the fact you found the last one."

"Maybe not," Denise said, eyeing Simon. "Any sparks?"

"Mom!" Montana waved her hands. "Shh. What if he hears you?"

"They're at the other end of the room with the TV on. He can't hear me." Still she lowered her voice. "I saw you two talking outside. Anything?"

Montana didn't know what to say. Simon was smart and good-looking and kissed in a way that left her breathless. But . . .

"I don't know," she admitted. "We don't have that much in common."

"How much do you need?" Nevada asked.

"I'm not sure. He's very solitary. I can't figure out how much of that is by circumstance and how much is by design."

"You mean, is he mysterious, or is there something wrong with him?" Dakota asked.

Montana grinned. "Exactly."

"You could find out," her mother reminded her.

"I could."

CHAPTER SEVEN

Denise tightened the belt on her cotton robe as she waited for the coffee to brew. Although she'd grown used to having the big house to herself, it felt good to have some of her family back home with her, even if it was only temporary. She'd been a widow for more than ten years — she'd long since gotten used to the silence. But having people in the house was better — especially when those people included any of her grandchildren.

Kent walked into the kitchen. He'd already showered and shaved. She studied his dark slacks, light blue shirt and patterned tie.

"Nervous?" she asked as she poured them each a mug of coffee.

"A little. I really want to get the job."

Kent was back for a final interview at Fool's Gold High School. He would be coming in with the possibility of running the department when the current head retired in a couple of years.

"Not that I'm not thrilled to have you moving back to town," she began, staring at her son. "But I want you to be sure."

Kent gave her a smile that was so much like his father's it made her chest hurt. "Mom, we've talked about this already."

"As if that matters. I want you running toward something, not running away."

He held up his hand. "Don't hold back, Mom. Tell me what you really think."

"You know what I mean. You and Reese have gone through so much in the past couple of years. I want you to be sure."

"I am." He set down his coffee and leaned against the counter. "Lorraine isn't coming back. I know that. Staying in that same house is hard on both Reese and me. Too many ghosts. I want to start over — it'll be good for both of us. Where better than here? The town is great. Reese already has friends here from all our visits. We have family. I want to be here, Mom."

"Okay. If you're sure."

"I am."

She took another sip. "I'm sorry about Lorraine."

"No, you're not."

She sighed. "I'm sorry you're hurt."

"That I'll believe."

Denise had hated being one of those mothers-in-law who never approved of the woman their son married, but she'd been unable to help disliking Lorraine from the second she'd met her. Clichéd or not, the woman wasn't good enough for her son. She was beautiful but cold. Denise remembered wondering why someone so ambitious and determined had married a guy who wanted to be a math teacher.

Their marriage had been tumultuous from the first day, with Lorraine walking out several times. Eighteen months ago she'd announced she wanted a divorce. She'd left again, but that time she hadn't come back.

While Denise felt terrible for Kent, the person she most ached for was Reese. Lorraine rarely saw her son and had missed his birthday a few months before. Talk about a selfish . . .

"You sure you don't mind me staying here?" Kent interrupted her line of thinking.

"It's a big house. I'll enjoy having the company. I'm more worried about you."

He grinned. "A guy in his thirties, living with his mother? I'll be a chick magnet."

"I think you will be. When you're ready."

The smile faded. "I'm not. I thought I'd

found what you and Dad had. I thought she was the one. Maybe for me she was, but it doesn't really matter. She's gone."

Denise wanted to tell him not to give up. That he was too young and there was too much life to be lived. But she learned a long time ago that it was better to hint and nudge than outright direct her children's lives.

"All that can wait," she said, while thinking that once he was here and settled, she would find a way to introduce him to a few women around his age. There were plenty in town. "First you have your final interview."

"Speaking of which, I'd better get going." He crossed the kitchen and kissed her cheek. "Thanks, Mom. You're the best."

"I'll believe that when you get me a plaque."

Kent left. Denise walked to the window and looked out at her backyard, remembering how life had been different when Ralph was alive. Better. Before him, there had been Max, whom she'd also loved. She'd been very lucky, she reminded herself. Even now, as she kept her secrets, she couldn't ask for much more than she'd been given.

About a half hour later, a very sleepy Reese wandered into the kitchen. He wore a T-shirt over loose pj bottoms and his hair was sticking up all over.

"Hey, you," Denise said fondly, walking over and hugging him. "How are you feeling?"

"Better. My face doesn't hurt at all, just like Dr. Bradley said."

"That's good news."

Reese hugged her back, then slumped at the table. Denise crossed to the refrigerator and pulled out a pitcher of orange juice.

"I can make waffles for breakfast," she told him as she poured. "What do you think?"

He grinned. "That would be great." He took the glass she offered and thanked her. "Grandma, do you know there are lots of kids at the hospital?"

"Yes." She collected ingredients. "There's a whole floor for children. It's called pediatrics."

"I guess I knew that." Reese frowned. "Kids get sick, too, but it was weird to see them there. A lot of them are really, really sick and have to stay there a long time. If they have cancer or something." He reached for his glass. "One of the nurses told me."

Denise felt an instant protective need to shield him from life's unpleasantness, then reminded herself that learning about other people's hardships often helped a child to understand compassion.

"It must be very hard for them and their families," she said.

He nodded. "Plus it's summer and they can't be outside playing." He put the glass back on the table. "Do you think I could visit a couple of the kids? Ones who don't have any friends close by? Maybe we could play a computer game or something."

Pride filled her. Not only in Reese, but in Kent for getting it right with his son. "I'll talk to your aunt Montana. She takes therapy dogs to the hospital regularly. She'll know who to ask."

"Sweet."

He grinned at her and at that moment, he reminded her so much of her boys when they were his age. Kent might have hideous taste in women, but he was a wonderful father. At least his ex-wife hadn't been able to take that away from him.

The Fool's Gold library had been built around 1940. It had been a WPA project, complete with carved columns and twenty-foot murals. Montana loved the library. She loved the sweeping stairs leading to huge carved double doors, the stained glass windows, and the ever-present scent of old dusty books.

Before going to work for Max, she'd had a job at the library. She'd enjoyed her work and had been offered a full-time position. Even though she'd known she probably should have accepted, a voice inside had told her that her true passion might lie elsewhere.

Fortunately, Mrs. Elder, the head librarian, was the forgiving sort. When Montana had approached her about starting a summer reading program using therapy dogs, Mrs. Elder had been enthused.

They were starting small, with a single dog and three students. The premise was simple. Kids who had trouble reading worked with a tutor for half an hour. The tutor went over the vocabulary list, and made sure the students understood what the words meant. Then the students read a book aloud to a dog.

Montana had chosen Buddy. Not only was he gentle and supportive, he tended to worry. Montana had noticed children responded to doggie concern with reassurance. But any kind of reassurance required a little bit of confidence, something the students who couldn't read tended not to have.

Mrs. Elder introduced Montana to a skinny boy about Reese's age. "This is Daniel." The librarian smiled at the boy. "Daniel, I'd like you to meet Montana and her dog Buddy."

The boy glanced at her, his eyes barely visible through his long bangs. "Hi."

The word came out more like a sigh than a greeting and Montana figured he wasn't excited about spending a warm summer afternoon in the library.

Mrs. Elder nodded at them and left.

They were working in one of the small rooms off the main library. As Montana had requested, there were several beanbag chairs and large pillows on the carpeted floor. When a child was reading to a dog, it helped for everyone to be at eye level.

Montana sat on a beanbag chair and patted the one next to her for Daniel. "Buddy is very excited to hear the story. I was telling him about it earlier, and he can't wait."

Daniel slumped onto the floor, then rolled his eyes. "Dogs don't get excited about books."

"How do you know?" Montana asked. "Buddy isn't having a very good day and stories make him feel better."

"You can't expect me to believe that."

"Of course I do. Look at him. Does he look like a happy dog?"

Daniel dutifully turned toward Buddy. As

always, the dog's expression was one of concern, as if he had the weight of the world on his shoulders.

"He does look kind of sad," Daniel admitted. "But reading isn't going to help. Dogs don't care about stuff like that."

"Really?" Montana picked up the two books Daniel had carried in. She held them both out to Buddy. "Which one?"

The dog lifted his left paw and tapped the book on the left.

Montana handed that one to Daniel. "See, he has an opinion."

Daniel's eyes widened. "Whoa. I've never seen anything like that." He turned to the dog. "Buddy, you really want me to read you this story?"

Maybe it was Montana's imagination, but she would swear the dog nodded.

"Okay." Daniel looked at Montana. "You're not going to stay are you?"

Montana rose to her feet. "Nope. You're on your own."

She left the room, but hovered just outside the open door. Daniel began to read, his progress painfully slow. He sounded out each word, stumbling every now and then, but pressing forward.

She'd come up with the idea of having the dog pick the book a few weeks ago. Teaching the trick was easy and if it helped the kid believe, then it was time well spent.

She glanced at her watch, then headed outside. She would check on Daniel in ten minutes.

She'd barely settled in the shade of a large oak tree when her cell phone vibrated in her pocket. She pulled it out.

"Hello?"

"Montana? This is Fay Riley, Kalinda's mother. Have I caught you at a bad time?" Fay sounded beyond tired, as if she hadn't slept in days.

She probably hadn't, Montana thought, remembering how small Kalinda had looked in the hospital bed.

"This is a good time. How can I help?"

Fay sighed. "She's having a bad day. The pain is horrible and she can't sleep. Would it be too much trouble to bring Cece by? I think it would really help her. I'm not trying to make you feel guilty," she said in a rush. "Oh, hell. Maybe I am. I'm desperate."

Montana could hear the strain in her voice, along with tears. "Of course I can bring her by. I'm at the library and I'll be here another hour. Then I'll go get Cece. So about three-thirty?"

"That would be great." Fay swallowed a sob.

"It's okay," Montana said softly. "I'm happy to help any way I can."

"I appreciate it. I'm sorry to be so weak, it's just the burns. They're so horrible and I don't know what to do."

"You're with her and you love her."

"If only that were enough." She cleared her throat. "I'm sorry. You're being wonderful and I'm . . ."

"I understand. At least as much as I can."

"Thank you, Montana. This will mean so much to both of us."

After they hung up, she put the phone back in her pocket. There was no way she could get what that family was going through. There was no way anyone could, unless they'd been through the same thing. All she had to offer was the company of a small poodle. Today that would have to be enough.

Montana rode the hospital elevator, a clean and excited Cece in her arms. The poodle seemed to recognize the setting. Montana wondered if her quivering was at the thought of seeing Kalinda or Simon. The little dog had liked them both, although Simon was by far her favorite.

142

If she were being completely honest with herself, Montana wouldn't mind a little Simon time, as well. Not just for kissing, although that was pretty fabulous, but also to talk to him. She wanted to know more about his life. She wanted to find out about his scars — how he'd gotten them and why he didn't get them fixed.

She stepped out onto the floor and headed to the burn ward. After checking in with the nurses' station, she walked toward Kalinda's room. Fay moved into the hallway and spotted her.

Although it had only been a few days since Montana had brought Cece by, Fay looked more exhausted and frail than she had before. The dark circles under her eyes looked permanently etched into her skin and her mouth trembled with what Montana would guess was overwhelming emotion.

"Thank you for coming," Fay said quietly. "Kalinda's in so much pain. The nurses keep telling me they're doing what they can, but then she cries for me to help her and there's nothing . . ." Fay swallowed. "I'm sorry."

Montana felt helpless. "Don't apologize, please. This is so hard for you and your family. You need to vent, so feel free to use me."

"You're very kind."

Montana wasn't sure of that, but she would do whatever she could.

"I didn't tell her the dog was coming," Fay admitted. "She'll be so happy."

"Cece is pretty excited, too."

They went into the room. To Montana's untrained eye, the girl's burns looked worse than they had before. The raw skin was more angry, the smell worse. Cece quivered and squirmed to get out of her arms, as if she remembered Kalinda from her last visit.

The girl opened her eyes. "Oh, you brought Cece."

"I thought she might make you feel better," her mother said.

Kalinda managed a shaky smile. "Thanks, Mom. She does."

Montana set Cece on the bed. The tiny poodle walked carefully across the blankets to Kalinda's side. She stared at her for a few seconds, then licked the girl's fingers. Kalinda managed a weak laugh. "She likes me."

"Of course she does," Montana told her, feeling a bit of emotion herself.

Cece curled up beside Kalinda. The girl petted her gently, her eyes closing.

"This is nice," she whispered.

Fay motioned for Montana to follow her

144

into the hall. "Can you stay for a bit? I was thinking she might relax enough to sleep."

"Of course. I'll sit right here." Montana looked at her. "Why don't you take a break? Get something to eat."

"I'm not hungry, but I would love to take a shower." She glanced back toward the room. "I hate to be away from her."

"I'm not going anywhere." Montana pulled a book out of her purse and held it up. "I promise."

"The nurse has my cell number if anything happens." Fay still hesitated. "I wish it had been me instead of her. Everything about this is so hard. The pain, the healing, all the surgeries. She misses her friends but they're too far away to visit. Plus, I'm not sure her friends would want to see her while she looks like this."

Montana remembered her mother telling her about Reese's desire to visit children in the hospital.

"Do you think she'd like a visitor closer to her age?" she asked. "My nephew is ten. I could bring him by for a few minutes."

Fay looked more worried than pleased. "Could he handle it? I wouldn't want him saying anything that might hurt her feelings, or acting shocked."

"I'd talk to him first. We could go online

145

and do some reading about what she's going through, so he knows what's going on.
Reese is a pretty good kid. Plus, Kalinda's
hands aren't burned very much, so maybe
they could play a game or something."

Some of the worry faded. "I would like
her to see someone other than me and the
staff," Fay admitted. "We'd have to make
sure it was a good day. So far there haven't
been very many of those."

"You think about it," Montana told her.
"In the meantime, I'll talk to Reese and his
dad. If Reese is game, we'll do the research
so he's prepared."

Fay nodded. Tears filled her eyes. "We're
not from around here. We only came to
Fool's Gold because Dr. Bradley's here.
He's the best. And everyone in town has
been so welcoming. It's very unexpected."

Montana impulsively hugged her. Fay
hung on for several seconds, as if she
needed the support.

"If you need anything, just let me know,"
Montana told her. "Whatever it is, I can
probably figure out how to get it."

"Right now a shower is plenty."

Fay collected a change of clothes from the
small suitcase she had stored in her daughter's room and went down the hall. Montana
slipped back into Kalinda's room. The girl

was asleep, her hand tucked protectively around the little dog. Cece's head rested on the child's palm.

"You do good work," Montana whispered.

Cece's tail wagged, but otherwise she didn't stir. Montana settled in the chair and opened her book, but instead of reading, she found herself offering a prayer for the child who hurt so much and the others in the world who were just like her.

Montana sat across from her friend. Pia looked beyond pregnant — she was swollen. While her face, arms and legs were still their usual size, her belly was more extended than Montana had thought was possible, and her poor ankles were the size of balloons.

"Are you really okay?" Montana asked, trying not to wince as she stared at her friend.

"However bad it looks, it feels worse," Pia said with a sigh, as she shifted to get comfortable in the oversize chair. "Don't elephants stay pregnant for a couple of years? How do they do it without going crazy? I'm *so* ready for these babies to come. Twins are supposed to be early, but are mine? Of course not."

She rested her hand on her belly. "I'm

bloated and gross and whiny. Raoul is going to leave me."

Montana smiled. "He adores you."

"He adores me, not the freak I've become. I swear, if I had any medical training, I'd take the babies out myself."

"I don't think I could watch that," Montana admitted. "What does the doctor say?"

"To be patient. That every day the twins stay in me is better for them. I used to like Dr. Galloway, but I'm starting to think she's part of a conspiracy. By the time these babies are ready to be born, they'll be eligible for college."

Montana was torn between sympathy and amusement. "Anything I can do to help?"

"Listening is nice. So thank you for that." She shifted slightly in the chair, then groaned. "The thing is, I don't know if it's going to get any better when the babies are born. What if they hate me?"

Pia had been worrying about that for a while now, Montana thought. Pia had never considered herself overly maternal. Despite that, when her friend Crystal had died and left frozen embryos in Pia's care, she'd taken the extraordinary step of having them implanted.

"Your babies are going to love you," Montana said firmly. "You know they are."

"Only because they won't know any better. I'll be the only mother in their life. What choice will they have? Can you bring by one of the mean service dogs?"

Montana frowned at the non sequitur. "We don't have any mean service dogs. By definition of their job, they pretty much get along with everyone."

Pia whimpered. "I thought if I could make a difficult dog like me, I would have a better chance with my babies."

Montana rose and crossed to her friend. She bent over and hugged her. "You're making yourself insane."

"It's the hormones. Okay, a little of it is me, but it's mostly not my fault."

Montana straightened and returned to her seat. "Try to relax. You're going to be a great mom. You agreed to have someone else's babies. That's how much love you have to give."

Pia sniffed. "I'll try to remember that." She drew in a breath. "Let's talk about something else. How's the world? I haven't been out in it for a couple of weeks. I'm either here or at the doctor. Is there still a sky and trees?"

Montana laughed. "Yes to both. The planet orbits the sun and the days progress."

"Good to know. You're doing well?"

"Yes. I've started the summer reading program at the library. The dogs and I make the usual rounds at the nursing home and assisted living places." She hesitated, wondering if Pia could help with one of her more pressing problems. "There's a new doctor in town. Simon Bradley. He's a gifted plastic surgeon who mostly works on children. His specialty is burn victims. He goes to a place for two or three months to help, then moves on. Mayor Marsha came to see me and wants me to convince Simon to stay in Fool's Gold."

"You've got to love our mayor." Pia leaned her head back against the chair. "Do you know if he likes sports? Baseball, golf, that sort of thing?"

"No, but aren't all doctors into golfing?"

"I think so. Let me talk to Raoul. Maybe he and Josh and Ethan could take Simon golfing. Or at least out for a drink. Guy bonding and all that. What does he like to do?"

Montana remembered Simon's intense, toe-curling kisses but didn't think that was what Pia meant. "He doesn't talk about much other than work. Kent and Reese were in a car accident about a week ago and —"

Pia nearly came out of her chair, a trick

considering how pregnant she was. "What? I didn't know about this. Are they okay? What happened?"

Montana was on her feet again, hurrying to her friend's side. "Sorry. I thought you knew. They're both fine. You have to relax." Raoul would kill her if Pia went into labor because she'd gotten upset.

"I'm fine. When did this happen?"

"Right before the Fourth. Kent wasn't hurt, but Reese got a few cuts on his face. Simon worked on him and he's not going to have much in the way of scarring. Mom invited him over for a belated Fourth of July dinner. Even she couldn't get much information out of him."

"What do you think of him?"

Montana considered the question. "He's very solitary. Fierce when it comes to his work and his patients, but otherwise, he's quiet. He doesn't talk about himself. If my mother couldn't get him to talk, then even a professional CIA operative would have trouble extracting information."

Pia laughed. "That's true. Denise isn't obvious about it, but she usually ends up with whatever information she wants."

"He's not a traditional loner," Montana said. "I think of those people as choosing to be by themselves. They prefer their own company. With Simon, I wonder if it's coming from the outside. I know that doesn't make sense, but it's like it's imposed on him." She paused. "He has scars on his face and neck. From a burn. From one side, he's beyond gorgeous, but from the other . . ."

"He's a monster?"

Montana half smiled. "It's not that bad, but I keep thinking something could be done about the scars. Does he keep them like that to have physical proof for his patients that he knows what they're going through? Or am I being naive and assuming something that isn't true? But what happened to him? He's never said and I don't know how to ask."

She paused, only to find Pia staring at her. "What?"

"Wow." Pia grinned. "You've fallen for him."

Heat exploded on her cheek and she ducked her head. "Don't say that. I think he's interesting. It's nothing more than that."

"It's a whole lot more than that."

It was the kisses, she thought. How was she supposed to ignore them?

"Even if he was my type, I'm sure not his." So far she'd managed to avoid being anyone's type.

"Why? From what you've described, you might be exactly what someone like him needs. But I won't embarrass you by talking about it anymore. Let me think about different ways to convince the good doctor to stay in town. Does he have any family?"

Montana stared at her blankly. "Family?"

"You know. Kids. I'm assuming there isn't a wife."

"Not that I know of," Montana told her, even as the *W* word bounced in her head. A wife? He'd never said and she'd never thought to ask. "He's never mentioned anything." He'd more than hinted he was alone. But still.

A wife?

It was a question that needed an answer very, very soon.

CHAPTER EIGHT

Simon was in his office when he heard the page. He called down to the nurses' station.

"Montana Hendrix would like to see you, if you have a second."

The anticipation was instant. A tightening in his body, a rush of heat. He quietly cleared his throat before speaking. "Please send her here," he said, then hung up the phone and stood.

His office was on the small side, with a desk, a couple of chairs and a mostly empty bookcase. He wasn't on staff, so he didn't deal with a lot of paperwork beyond his patient charts. The hospital had provided a computer and printer. He didn't need much more.

Now, as he looked around at the stark room, he wished it were some color other than plain white, with a picture on the wall or a plant in the corner. Something to make it seem less institutional.

He told himself he was being an idiot. Whatever Montana wanted to talk about, it had nothing to do with his office. No doubt she wanted to discuss bringing a pony into the hospital, or perhaps juggling monkeys. Whatever it was, he would listen. Hearing her discuss a tax audit would be appealing. He liked the sound of her voice, the way she moved her hands when she talked. He liked the flashes of emotion in her brown eyes and the way she always seemed on the verge of smiling.

She was alive in every sense of the word. Alive and vibrant, and she saw a world filled with possibilities. No one had hurt her, not in a way that had left her broken. He found himself wanting to stand between her and reality, to make sure that didn't change.

He crossed to the door and held it open. A few seconds later Montana turned the corner. She'd replaced her customary summer dresses with jeans and a short-sleeved shirt. Both hugged the shape of her body, showing off curves and making it more difficult than usual for him to maintain any semblance of control.

Her long blond hair hung down her back in a cascade of waves, making him want to tangle his fingers in the silky smoothness. Her smile both pleased and taunted him.

He wanted to know the feel of every inch of her. He wanted to *know* her because in the knowing he believed he would find solace.

"Hi," she said as she approached. "I hope I'm not interrupting."

"If you were, I wouldn't have had the nurse send you to my office." He motioned for her to step into his office, then followed her. He was careful to leave the door partially open. Perhaps knowing that people could see in would allow him to maintain his distance.

She stopped in the center of the room and turned to face him. Her brown eyes danced with amusement. "You're not a big believer in social niceties are you?"

"What do you mean?"

"I know that if you were busy, you wouldn't have seen me. You don't have to say it."

"What's wrong with saying it? It's the truth."

She laughed. "I know, but my comment about hoping I wasn't interrupting was —"

He waited patiently.

"You're not supposed to say it," she said.

"Why not?"

"You're just not."

"As long as the rules are clear."

She laughed again and he found himself

smiling, even though he couldn't say why.

"I heard you were in to see Kalinda the other day," he said. "I appreciate you taking the time."

The humor faded from her eyes. "Fay called me and sounded pretty desperate. I guess it's been difficult. I'm glad Cece and I could help. Well, mostly Cece."

"Having that little dog around makes a difference."

"I'm glad."

Somehow they were standing closer together than they had been before. He consciously took a step back, wanting more space between them. No, he thought. Not wanting it, but apparently needing it.

They stared at each other. He could feel the tension crackling in the room. His gaze was riveted on her mouth, and the need to kiss her nearly overwhelmed him. He took another step back.

"Is that why you stopped by?" he asked, his voice sounding more stressed than pleasant.

She blinked. "No. I was thinking about the town. You haven't seen very much of it. There's so much more than what you saw on our mini-tour. You're only here for a short time. It would be a shame for you to miss seeing the real Fool's Gold."

"Of course," he said. "How would my life be complete?"

The humor returned to her eyes. "Mock me all you want, but you just wait. Fool's Gold is a special place. We have a varied history that includes Spanish pirates and Mayans. Specifically, female Mayans."

"You mentioned them before. It sounded intriguing."

"I want to put together some kind of plan for you to see as much as possible. So maybe you should tell me about your hobbies or likes and dislikes."

He noticed she wasn't looking at him. She seemed to have become fascinated by the back of his computer monitor. And instead of standing comfortably, she shifted her weight and twisted her fingers together. Almost as if she were nervous.

"I don't have a lot of hobbies."

She cleared her throat. "Yes, well, it might not just be for you. It might be about other people."

"What other people?"

"Your other people."

She'd lost him. "What are you talking about?"

"Your family. Children." She paused. "Mrs. Dr. Simon Bradley." She glanced up at him. "You never said if you were married."

Now it all made sense. She was worried. He probably shouldn't like that, but he did. He liked her hesitation and the flush on her cheeks. He liked the implication that the answer to the question was important to her.

"I'm not married."

Her eyes brightened. "Really?"

"It doesn't seem to be something I would have forgotten."

"You'd be amazed how many men do."

"Are you speaking from personal experience?"

"No. The men in my life haven't been married. Just not that interested in me."

"I find that hard to believe."

"You do?"

He took a step toward her. "Very much."

"Thank you."

"You're welcome." He took another step. "I wouldn't have kissed you if I were married."

"That's what I thought, but I wanted to be sure."

"Very sensible of you."

"No one has ever called me sensible before," she whispered, staring into his eyes. "No one sees me that way."

He wanted to ask how other people did see her and how she saw herself. He wanted to know everything about her, but those questions were for another time. Right now what was important was being close to her.

He pulled her into his arms. She went willingly, stepping into his embrace with an eagerness that excited him.

They'd done this enough times that the feel of her was familiar. But instead of that making him less interested, he found himself wanting to experience every part of kissing her again and again. He wanted to inhale the scent of her body, to feel her soft mouth against his. He wanted her taste, her curves, all of her.

Their kiss began slowly, almost tentatively, as if they were both taking their time. Lips clung, creating heat that ripped through him before settling in his groin.

He moved his hands up and down her back, then set them on her waist. She tilted her head and parted her lips. The invitation was clear and he began to circle her tongue with his, beginning the erotic dance of desire.

She tasted sweet, like ice cream or candy. Without thinking, without planning, he continued to kiss her deeply while moving his hands higher and higher. Before he knew what he'd done, he'd cupped her breasts, feeling the weight of her full curves.

In the back of his mind, he was aware of the partially open door, of the fact that anyone could see them, but he couldn't bring himself to stop. Not now that he'd touched her so intimately. He had to know more. He had to know everything.

He explored her curves with his fingers, then brushed his thumbs against her nipples. Relief battled with need when he found they were already tight and hard, visible and tactile proof of her reaction to his touch. He lingered there, rubbing, massaging, then felt the uncomfortable heaviness of his erection when she moaned quietly.

He stretched out one arm and pushed the door shut. The second he heard the latch engage, he drew back from their kiss and pulled up her T-shirt. He unfastened her bra with an easy flick of his surgeon's trained hands and pushed up her bra as well.

Her breasts were perfect. Full and pale, with pink areolae. He leaned in and took her left nipple in his mouth, sucking deeply.

The taste of her was beyond exquisite. The warmth of her soft skin enticed him. He moved his tongue over and around, savoring everything. He used his hand on her other breast. She rested her fingers on his shoulders.

He was aware of her head falling back, of the quickness of her breathing. He flicked his tongue against her nipple and she moaned. The sound — the most erotic he'd ever heard — was followed by a shudder that swept through her body.

He moved to her other breast. Now her breathing came in pants as she squirmed to get closer. He knew she was wet and swollen, as aroused as he was. It would only take a second to rip off her jeans and panties, to bury himself inside her.

Even at the thought of filling her so deeply he got lost, he was distracted by the thought of how her wetness would feel against his fingers. He wanted to explore her there, to find her most sensitive spot, to tease and rub and circle until she had no choice but to come. He wanted to kiss her intimately, to taste her and do with his tongue what he'd done with his fingers. He wanted her trembling from exhaustion, weak from the pleasure.

From the other side of the door he heard low voices and then laughter. The images of making love with Montana faded as reality returned.

Reluctantly, he straightened. He held her around the waist with both hands and stared into her eyes.

Her gaze was unfocused, her face flushed. She had the look of a woman who wanted a man. He smiled.

"Thank you," he murmured.

She blinked slowly, as if coming awake. "You're, ah, welcome. Anytime. Seriously."

There were more voices. She glanced toward the closed door.

"I forgot where we were," she admitted.

"I wish I could have."

He reached for her bra and smoothed it into place. After turning her, he fastened the hooks. She pulled down her T-shirt and faced him.

Her gaze met his. With a mischievous look in her eye, she placed her hand on his belly, then slipped it lower until she cupped his erection. He saw the surprise in her face.

"Wow," she whispered.

"Did you doubt?"

"Maybe. A little. You're just so . . . I'm not really your type."

"How can you not be my type?" he asked, doing his best to pretend not to care when she moved her hand away. "You're beautiful and fun." He shook his head. "You're right. You're not my type."

She tilted her head and the corners of her mouth curved up. "You prefer unattractive

163

women who have no personality?"

"I want to say no, but my past speaks for itself."

He'd always gone with women who were safe — predictable. Women who would understand the rules. Montana wasn't like that, but he still couldn't seem to resist her.

"Mine, too," she murmured.

He lightly touched her cheek and knew he couldn't rest until he had her. "I want you. In my bed. Naked. Please say yes."

It was the most direct invitation Montana had ever heard. Simon's need was raw. She could see it etched on his face, feel it in the tension in his body. Being desired this much made her weak.

In the past, she'd found herself not feeling as if she was enough. The men she'd fallen for had either left her or tried to change her until she'd been forced to escape, rather than becoming someone else. To be wanted for who and what she was left her practically floating.

She stared into his eyes. "Yes. But not in your bed, if that's okay. You're staying at a hotel and I know everyone in town."

"Then your bed."

"My bed."

He leaned in and kissed her again. The

contact was short and hot and full of promise.

"Tonight," he said when he straightened.

She nodded, then gave him her address. They settled on a time.

As she turned to leave, he touched her arm. She looked back at him.

"You know I'm not here for very long."

He wasn't talking about the night, she thought sadly. He was warning her about who and what he was. A man who couldn't or wouldn't settle down. A man who left.

"I know."

"I'm going to Peru as soon as I leave here. Nothing about that will change."

She nodded.

She sensed he wanted more of a reaction from her. He wanted her to explain that she was sophisticated and did this sort of thing all the time. That she wouldn't mind him walking away after their affair was over. But none of that was true, so she simply opened the door and stepped into the hallway.

She might not be that girl, but she also wasn't going to protect herself at the expense of not knowing what it was like to be in Simon's arms. She had a feeling that experience would be worth the risk.

Montana's previous sexual experiences had

been limited to two of her three long-term boyfriends. She'd given her virginity to her college boyfriend, and her battered heart, ironically, to a doctor she'd met during her brief time in Los Angeles. Neither had appreciated the gift.

The former had taught her that a man saying he loved her didn't mean he would keep his promises. The latter had convinced her she would never be good enough. So it made sense to be wary around Simon. Only she wasn't.

Standing in front of her closet, trying to figure out what to wear for a date that was pretty much about sex, she knew she probably *should* be concerned. Simon was well traveled, sophisticated, emotionally distant. Not exactly a great bet. She wasn't sure what he was looking for in a woman, but she doubted the female in question would be a small town dog trainer.

But Simon was also kind and when she stared into his green-gray eyes, she found herself wanting to get lost in him. Nothing else mattered. She liked his smile, his attention to detail, the way he kissed, how he'd apologized for having a stick up his ass. She wanted to know about his past, his scars and what he most regretted.

She knew she was taking a chance —

she'd never given her body lightly. What made her think she could hand it over to a man who'd made it clear he was leaving? Shouldn't she try to protect herself more? But she couldn't seem to muster the least bit of self-preservation.

If she was into fooling herself, she would say that making love with him was a way to get to know him better. Maybe that was true, but in reality she wanted Simon in her bed because she had a feeling he was going to take her places she'd never been, and didn't a girl deserve a little of that in her life?

Which led to her current dilemma. What to wear? Even though they were going to end up in bed, and probably fairly quickly, showing up naked was too aggressive for her. Silky lingerie was an obvious choice, but she didn't have anything remotely sexy or silky. Her nicest nightgown had been a Christmas present from her mom, and she didn't think Simon would be blown away by white cotton covered with cartoon dogs. She did, however, own one black lace matching bra and panty set. The panties were actually more G-string than brief, but she could survive that for a couple of hours.

Some kind of dress would be good, she thought, looking through her options. She had a simple blue one that was sleeveless and slightly fitted. The long zipper down the back would make the undressing part of the evening simple. Although, based on how Simon had managed her bra with a quick touch of his fingers, she probably shouldn't worry about clothing complications.

Still smiling at the thought, she dressed, then checked her makeup. She was wearing enough to make her eyes look bigger, but not so much that she would smear it all over him. Shoes weren't going to be a problem. She would be barefoot.

A quick glance at the clock confirmed she still had an hour to wait. Anticipation danced in her stomach. Maybe she could call him and suggest he arrive earlier. Or she could —

Her cell phone rang. As she grabbed it, she saw Simon's name on the screen.

"I was just thinking about you," she said by way of greeting.

"Montana, I can't come over. There's been an accident."

She sank onto her sofa. "Not with you."

"No. A guy on a motorcycle. He's going into surgery now. He has internal injuries. When they're done, I need to work on his face." He drew in a breath. "I'm sorry."

"Me too."

"I wouldn't have canceled except —"

"Simon, you don't have to explain. This is what you do. Saying you have to help someone isn't unreasonable."

"You're not angry."

"No. Wildly disappointed, but not angry."

"Good. I didn't want you to think I was trying to get out of our evening."

"Sex," she teased. "You mean sex."

"I do mean sex."

She thought about how he'd touched her. "I'm pretty sure you were looking forward to that. I'm okay with waiting."

"As long as it's not too long."

"Sooner would be better than later," she told him.

There was a pause. "I have to go. I'll call you when I can."

"I hope he'll be okay."

"Me too."

Then he was gone. Montana sat there for a few seconds and then stood. It looked like this wasn't going to be a G-string night after all.

She walked into her bedroom and changed her clothes. She'd barely slipped on sandals when the phone rang again. She saw a different man's name on the screen.

"Is it time?" she asked breathlessly.

"It's time," Raoul shouted. "It's time.

She's in labor." His voice was thick with panic. "She's too damn calm. We're going to the hospital. You've got the list, right? There's a list. You know what to do?"

"Breathe," she instructed. "We all know what to do. I'm calling my mom first. She'll be there in less than ten minutes. If I don't get her, I'll come over and stay with Peter until she's available."

Pia and Raoul weren't just expecting twins — they'd also adopted a ten-year-old boy. Denise had promised to stay with him when Pia went into labor.

"Okay. Good. One of the neighbors will be here until then." He swore again. "I gotta go. Pia's in labor."

Montana grinned. "I got that part. Go on. I'll make the calls and we'll all meet you at the hospital. Oh, and tell her I love her."

"I will. I'm hanging up now."

"You do that."

The phone clicked.

For a guy who had guided an NFL team to a Super Bowl championship, Raoul sure was flustered. She guessed childbirth had a way of doing that to a person.

She quickly called her mother. Denise answered on the first ring.

"Hello?"

"Pia's finally in labor."

"Thank goodness. She's been desperate for weeks. I'm all packed. I'll head over to their house right now."

"Great. I'm going to make calls and then go to the hospital."

"Keep me informed."

"I promise."

Denise laughed. "I can't wait to hear if they're boys or girls. It's going to be a good day."

"It is, Mom. I love you."

"I love you, too, honey."

Montana hurried to the living room. The call list was sitting on the coffee table. She started dialing.

"If it's twins, does it take twice as long?" Nevada asked.

Montana laughed. "I don't know and I'm not sure I want to. Labor would be the same, wouldn't it? I guess the delivery would be different."

They were sitting in a waiting area on the maternity floor. Other families gathered together, talking, anticipating their own miracle, but Pia's group was the largest. Mayor Marsha was already there, as were Charity and Josh Golden and their baby. Montana's brother Ethan was there with his wife, Liz. The girls and Tyler had been left at home.

Food had been spread out on the various tables, and a cooler filled with water bottles and soda stood in the corner. The other people waiting had been invited to eat and drink. The atmosphere was more like a party than a hospital setting. Something Pia would have appreciated.

"Did I tell you Dakota called?" Montana asked.

Her sister shook her head. "Is she coming?"

"As soon as she gets Hannah to sleep. Finn is going to stay home with Hannah."

Denise came in with a redheaded boy at her side. Montana stood and walked over to them.

"Peter," she said, giving him a hug. "You doing okay?"

The boy looked more curious than worried, which was probably a good thing. He'd been through a lot, losing his birth parents in a horrible car accident. He was the only one who'd survived. After a couple of years of foster care, he'd found a home with Pia and Raoul. Now he was about to get a couple of baby brothers or sisters. Or possibly one of each.

He hugged her back. "I wanted to see," he told her, looking both defiant and a little embarrassed.

"He was concerned that we were all worried," Denise said, resting her hand on Peter's shoulder. "And hiding it from him."

"I love Pia," he said simply. "I want her to be okay."

"We all want that," Montana told him, taking him by the hand and leading him over to the table.

He picked a peanut butter cookie and took a bite. "So she's okay?"

"We haven't heard any differently."

There was no point in discussing the possible complications of childbirth. Statistically Pia was going to be fine. Montana didn't see the point in worrying a ten-year-old needlessly.

"Do you think Raoul is scared?"

Montana laughed. "I'm sure he's terrified. You're an easy kid to have around, but babies are small and helpless and they can't tell you what's wrong."

Peter nodded. "I guess I'll have to help. You know, be a big brother."

She wrapped her arm around him. "My parents appreciated my big brothers helping with me and my sisters."

Dakota arrived a few minutes later. Mayor Marsha claimed Peter and sat chatting with him. Denise shared a sofa with her daughters.

"You'll be next," she said, smiling at Dakota.

Dakota touched her still flat stomach. "I'm not due until early March, Mom. We've got a ways to go."

"Still. I'm very excited."

Nevada sighed. "I'm feeling pressure."

"I didn't say anything," Denise said.

"You didn't have to."

Denise looked at Montana. "Do you feel pressure, too? I don't want you to. While it would be nice to have more grandchildren, if you're not interested in starting a family or in carrying on the Hendrix tradition, I'm fine with that." She paused and drew in a deep breath. "My heart will mend eventually."

Montana looked at Nevada. "Pressure? I have no idea what you're talking about."

A doctor came into the waiting room. Everyone turned toward her, but she walked to another family.

Dakota heard Mayor Marsha telling Peter, "Pia thought she would get the cat instead."

The boy laughed. "I'm glad she didn't. We have a dog now. Dogs are better than cats." He glanced around the room, then added,

"You can play with a dog. Cats like to sleep a lot."

"So I've heard," Marsha told him.

Montana listened in on other conversations. Moments like these reminded her why she loved living in Fool's Gold. This was more than a small town — it was a real community. People took care of each other. She knew that when Pia went home, women would bring her all kinds of casseroles. That she wouldn't have to cook for at least a month.

She knew that mothers and grandmothers would stop by regularly to offer advice and free babysitting so Pia could nap or take a walk. Raoul would find himself drawn into the lives of those around him in ways he didn't expect. She liked being a part of this — having a place she could depend on. Fool's Gold wasn't like other places. Living here meant belonging.

Raoul stumbled into the waiting room. Everyone stopped talking and looked at him.

The normally handsome former football player still wore scrubs. His hair was mussed, his gaze unfocused. He glanced around, as if not sure where he was.

He saw Peter and grinned at the boy.

"Girls," he said at last. "We have two girls.

They're so beautiful. Perfect. I don't know how I got so lucky. First you and now these girls — Adelina Crystal and Rosabel Dana, in honor of Keith and Crystal Danes. Our friends will live on in our daughters."

As one, everyone stood and rushed toward him. There were cheers and hugs and calls of congratulation. Montana made sure her mom was with Peter, then slipped out of the room. It would be a while before anyone could see Pia or the babies. She wanted to check on Simon.

She made her way to surgery and stopped at the nurses' station. The older woman there glanced up from her computer screen.

"How can I help you?" she asked pleasantly.

"I'm checking on Dr. Bradley. He's in surgery. Do you know how long he's going to be?"

The nurse's smile faded. "He's not in surgery this evening. Would you like me to page him?"

Montana opened her mouth, then closed it. Not in surgery? But he'd said . . .

She swallowed. "No, thank you."

She turned away. Heaviness settled on her chest.

Simon had lied. She couldn't believe it, except there was no other explanation.

Obviously he'd had second thoughts. He'd changed his mind about sleeping with her, but rather than tell her, he'd made up some stupid story.

Her eyes burned, but she refused to cry. It was bad enough that she'd been willing to give herself to him without even the hint of a relationship. She wasn't going to make it worse by wasting tears on him.

She turned to leave, then shook her head. No. She wasn't simply going to walk away. Dr. Stick-Up-the-Butt might think his behavior was okay, but she was going to let him know it wasn't. She might not be sophisticated or elegant or whatever it was he usually went for, but she wasn't going to let him treat her like this. Not without telling him exactly what she thought of him.

CHAPTER NINE

Montana found Simon on the burn ward. He stood outside of Kalinda's room, the door slightly open. He didn't look up as Montana approached.

"Fay went home to shower and get some clean clothes," he said quietly, studying the sleeping girl. "There will be another surgery in a couple of days. She's healing well."

Montana stared at him. "That's it?" she asked, keeping her voice low so as not to wake the girl.

Kalinda and the other patients were the only reason she wasn't screaming. And possibly hitting. Ethan and Kent had made sure she and her sisters knew exactly how to punch so that it hurt.

Simon glanced at her, frowning slightly. "What else did you want me to say?" he asked. "She's —"

He swore under his breath. "You came to check on me."

"No," she said, firmly. "I came because a friend is having a baby. Then I decided to check on you."

"It's not what you think. I didn't change my mind. There was a patient —"

She put her hands on her hips and put as much energy into the glare as possible. In a perfect world he would turn to mush and melt right there on the hospital floor.

"I wasn't in surgery because I didn't get the chance to operate. He died before I started."

Montana opened her mouth, then closed it. Her mind went blank, which was probably better than the guilt she was going to feel any second.

Simon took her hand and pulled her down the corridor. He drew her into an empty room.

"I'm sorry," she said, facing him. "I shouldn't have assumed the worst."

"Why not? You don't know me well enough to think otherwise."

The room was dark, the hospital bed stripped of sheets, the blinds on the window open to the night. His forgiveness unnerved her. She'd thought he would get angry, rather than understand.

"I'm sorry," she repeated. "Losing him like that must be hard."

He shrugged. "I never saw him. He died before I got started. Sometimes it happens like that. It's not always my job to save them from death. I'm there to make them look as normal as possible. There are limits to what it means to fit in."

Although he was looking at her, she had a feeling he didn't *see* her. He was staring at something else — something from his past.

Was he talking about himself when he mentioned fitting in? Yet he wore his scars like a badge of honor. Or were they a reminder?

She raised her hand and rested her fingers on his cheek. The spiraling marks were raised and hard. He pressed his hand on top of hers, as if holding her in place.

"They're not just here," he said, his gaze more intense. "They go down my neck and across my chest. There are a few on my back and my arm."

She didn't know what to say, what he needed from her. Telling him she wouldn't have minded didn't seem to be enough.

"You don't have to worry," he continued. "You wouldn't have seen them. If we'd made love tonight, I would have kept on a T-shirt. It's easier."

"Easier for who?"

"Both of us."

She wasn't sure she wanted it to be easier. Seeing him was a part of being intimate. Or maybe that's what he didn't want. He didn't want to be seen. Not fully.

If that was true, who had hurt him? Who had taught him it was better to conceal the truth? Or had he decided that by himself?

She found herself wanting to see the scars, to touch them. Ridiculous, she told herself. It wasn't as if she could heal him.

He lowered his hand and she did the same. Still staring into his eyes she said, "My friend Pia just had twins. Girls. That's why I'm here. It's kind of a town thing. We're filling up the maternity waiting room. There's some food. Are you hungry? My mom's here. I know she'd want to say hi."

"I'm not the party type."

"It's not a party. Just people getting together. Birth is a time to celebrate."

He turned away from her. For a second she thought he was going to leave, but then he faced her again.

"This is who I am," he said, his voice a low growl.

"I don't understand."

"I'm a brilliant surgeon. I can work magic in the operating room. I can take someone who has to creep in the shadows and turn him or her into someone who can pass for normal. Do you know what that means to them? To be just like everyone else?"

She shook her head, not sure what he wanted.

His mouth twisted. "You can imagine, but you'll never know." Now he touched her face. "You have the gift of beauty. Do you know what we find beautiful and what we find ugly is a difference of millimeters? Eyes too small, an uneven mouth. Not even inches. Fractions." He traced her lips with his thumb. "You're physically perfect."

"I'm not."

"Close enough. But there are others like me — the monsters. I take them from the shadows." He raised both his hands in front of her. "Like magic. Training, hard work and a gift. But it comes at a price. I don't belong, Montana. I don't have your beauty and I don't have your world. I do my work, I stay apart. It's better that way."

"That's so much crap," she said before she could stop herself. "There's nothing that says you have to sacrifice yourself to be good at what you do. Yes, you have a great talent and you've worked hard to nurture it. You've decided to be the best and you are. But there's no giant accountant in the sky. No one who says if you have a life, if you belong, you lose everything."

"You don't know that. I do."

Was this the problem? Simon at his essence? A man who believed the price to save the world was to sacrifice himself?

She couldn't imagine such a thing, but knew he wasn't lying.

The room was dark enough that it was difficult to make out his features. She could see the scars, and knew the unmarked side of his face illustrated the beauty he had talked about. The perfection. When he stared in the mirror, he saw both halves of what he did as a surgeon. He was the before *and* the after. The creature of the shadows and the man of light.

Words bubbled to the surface, but none of them would make a difference. She didn't fully understand the problem, nor was she qualified to fix it. She only knew he was in pain and somehow she wanted to make him feel better.

"Come with me," she instructed and took his hand.

She expected him to protest, but he went along with her. They walked to the elevator, then got inside. She pushed the button that would take them down two floors.

The nursery windows were lined with people pointing and waving. Denise had left, probably to take Peter home, and

Dakota had returned to her family. But Nevada was still there, along with Mayor Marsha and everyone else who had waited to hear the news of the twins' birth.

Marsha saw them first.

"Montana, there you are. Oh, and you brought Dr. Bradley." She approached them. "We met when you first arrived."

"I remember."

Simon shook hands with her.

"I'm here to welcome our newest citizens," Marsha said with a smile.

Montana wasn't touching Simon, but she still felt the stiffness in his body. This was exactly what he'd wanted to avoid. There was no way to tell him that she hadn't brought him here to talk to other people. Instead, she'd wanted him to see the babies.

Fortunately, Mayor Marsha excused herself and most of the other visitors drifted away. Montana was able to walk to the glass and stare at the two sleeping newborn girls, with the last name of Moreno tagged on the bassinets.

"These are the embryos that Crystal left Pia. She had them implanted and now they're born." She glanced at him. "You can't do anything that compares with this."

"I know."

"Do you? Every day people get to create a

miracle. They have children, grandchildren. And there's no price put on that. No exacting from the gods. Why do you think what you do is so damn special that you have to pay for the rest of your life?"

His expression went carefully blank. She had no idea what he was thinking, but she had a feeling it wasn't good. She'd hoped to convince him that he didn't have to suffer to be brilliant.

But instead of saying he understood, or arguing, he simply stepped back, said, "Excuse me." And then was gone.

She was left alone by the nursery, aware that instead of making Simon understand, she'd insulted him and caused him to feel even more isolated. She'd had her chance and she'd blown it.

Denise stopped at the corner and waited until the car to her right cleared the intersection.

"Renting will give you a chance to figure out if you like the neighborhood," she said as she accelerated.

"It's Fool's Gold, Mom," Kent told her from the passenger seat. "There aren't any bad parts of town."

"True, but you want to be where there are people your age and Reese can have friends.

You and your brothers were always bringing home neighborhood kids."

Her house had been the one where everyone had hung out. While having a dozen or so boys playing in the yard or watching TV had created a lot of extra work — not to mention the expense of feeding them all — she'd liked having her boys at home and knowing all their friends.

"Are you worrying about me?" Kent asked as they pulled in front of a two-story Craftsman house.

"Yes, and don't say I shouldn't. I'm your mother. It's part of the job description." She glanced at the house. "This is nice."

"Josh owns the house," Kent grumbled. "I'm not sure I want him as my landlord."

Josh had moved into their house when he'd been ten or twelve, Denise thought fondly. His mother had abandoned him, literally. The town hadn't wanted to turn him over to the state, so she and Ralph had taken him in. He'd been one more kid in an already crowded house, but they wouldn't have had it any other way.

"On the other hand, you can threaten to humiliate him by telling stories about when he was younger."

Her son grinned. "Good point."

They got out of the car and walked toward

the house. Josh had said he would leave it unlocked, so she turned the knob and they stepped inside.

The foyer was small, opening onto a good-size living room. While the floors were freshly refinished and the paint was new, the Craftsman details — built-in cabinets and beams over the doors — had been left untouched.

"It's lovely," she breathed, heading for the dining room.

"Lorraine would really like it," Kent murmured. "Craftsman was always her thing."

Denise came to a stop and had to consciously unclench her teeth.

It had been over a year since Lorraine had walked out on Kent and Reese. Like Josh's mother, she'd abandoned her husband and her child. A case could be made for ditching a spouse, but what kind of woman left her kid? Lorraine rarely saw Reese, didn't call or even text. And she wasn't dead. Apparently Kent had made sure of that. From what he'd told her his ex-wife was living a different kind of life now and didn't want to be married or deal with her child. Not that she was willing to contribute to child support either. Denise had begged her son to take her to court over that, but he refused.

Kent walked into the kitchen. "This seems fine. Lorraine always liked big windows over the sink."

Even as Denise told herself this wasn't her rock to carry, she stalked into the kitchen. She stopped in the center, noted the blue granite went really well with the white cabinets and tile floors, then put her hands on her hips and faced her son.

"It's been over a year," she said, hoping she sounded more calm and reasonable than she felt. "A year. Lorraine isn't on vacation — she walked out on you and Reese. She left her son, Kent. Not a word, not a note, nothing. This isn't an example of a woman who has feelings. She's not a good person and she's not coming back."

Her son stood with his back to her. She saw the tension in his back and the way his shoulders hunched, and felt crappy.

"I'm sorry," she said quickly. "I shouldn't say anything. I just hate to see you like this."

He faced her, defeat in his gaze. "I can't help loving her, Mom."

"Have you tried letting go? Are you doing anything to get over her?"

"Are you over Dad?"

Ralph had been gone long enough that she could hear the question without having to deal with the pain. "I still miss him, if that's what you're asking, but, yes, I have moved on. I have a life."

"Good for you, but I'm a different person from you. Lorraine was the one."

No, Lorraine was a bitch, Denise thought, lowering her arms to her sides. "There can be more than one great love. Maybe if you got out there and started dating, it would help."

"I don't want to."

"So you're going to spend the rest of your life pining for a woman who doesn't care about you?"

His body flinched and he looked away. "You weren't there, Mom. You don't know what she was like. We have a past."

Not a very good one, Denise thought, grabbing on to her patience. As for knowing what Lorraine was like — everyone but Kent had figured that out years ago.

"I love you and I hate to see you like this. I want you to at least consider trying to put your marriage behind you. If not for yourself, then for Reese. Don't you think he knows how much you're hurting?"

"I don't talk about it."

"He's a smart kid. He's going to guess. Having you in pain hurts him. Don't bother trying to tell me I'm wrong. I remember how you kids were every time I cried."

He walked to the window and looked out. "Maybe."

It wasn't much of a concession, but she was going to take it all the same.

He turned toward her. "What about you? Are you really moving on with your life?"

"I'm dating," she said. "So far not very successfully or with much enthusiasm, but I'm trying. You need to do the same."

"Will you get off me if I say I'll think about it?"

She smiled. "Of course."

Which wasn't exactly the truth. What she really meant was "for now." But Kent didn't need to know that. At least not yet.

Cece dropped the small ball she held in her mouth and gazed at Kalinda expectantly. The girl giggled, picked up the ball and tossed it toward the end of the bed. Cece bounded toward it, captured it and returned to Kalinda's side.

They'd been playing the game for nearly ten minutes. Even as Montana watched Kalinda start to tire, Cece dropped the ball and cuddled up next to her. The girl rubbed her back. Cece rolled over to get a tummy rub, as well.

"She trusts you," Montana told her. "Cece doesn't let just anyone rub her belly."

Kalinda smiled. "I like her a lot."

"She's certainly helping," Fay said from the other side of the bed, where she'd pulled up her usual chair.

"Can she stay longer tomorrow?" Kalinda asked, her blue eyes pleading. "Dr. Simon said she could."

Fay's expression turned wry. "We probably should have discussed it with you first. I'm sorry about that. We were talking about how Kalinda loves having Cece around. Dr. Bradley said we could use his office as a sort of home base for her. He hardly uses it at all and said she wouldn't be any trouble."

Montana supposed she should be pleased that Simon had come so far on the dog front. No longer just germy annoyances, the service animals had become a tool he could use for healing. Yay, her.

But she couldn't get excited about the plan, mostly because he hadn't bothered discussing it with her. Not surprising, considering she hadn't seen him in nearly a week. To say he was avoiding her was to state the obvious.

It was her own fault, she thought sadly. First she'd assumed the worst about him and then she'd taken things too far. Why had she thought it was her place to fix anyone, let alone him? Why did she have to

191

push things? If Simon had some weird ideas that got him through the day, who was she to tell him he was wrong?

But had she considered any of that? Of course not. She'd plowed ahead, pushing in where she wasn't welcome, and now he was avoiding her and she really missed him.

Aware that Fay was waiting for a response, she forced a smile. "I think it's a great idea to have Cece spend the day with the two of you. I can bring her in the morning and take her back in the evening. She's crate trained." She turned to Kalinda. "That means her dog crate is her home. She sleeps in it whenever she's in the kennel. It makes her feel safe."

Kalinda smiled. "It's like she can take her bedroom with her."

"Exactly," Montana said. "I'll bring the crate, along with some food and a couple of dishes. As long as she gets a walk once or twice in the morning and afternoon, she'll be fine."

"Thank you," Fay breathed. "It sounds like a lot of work for you. You don't have to bring her every day. Just when it's convenient."

Montana could see Kalinda wanted to disagree with her mother. Montana knew having the dog around helped the little girl.

Much of her face was bandaged today, the skin Montana could see was red and angry. She was aware of the IV that delivered pain medication on a regular basis. The kid was going through enough. If having Cece around helped, Montana was going to bring her by.

"I'll make it work," she promised.

"Thank you," Kalinda whispered, her eyes drifting closed. Beside her, Cece curled into a ball as if she'd figured out it was time to rest.

Fay and Montana walked toward the door.

"Did you get a chance to talk to her about my nephew?" Montana asked.

"I don't want to see anyone," Kalinda said.

Montana turned toward her. "Are you sure? Reese is your age. I was thinking you could play a game or something."

"No! I don't want to see anyone."

Even as Montana asked herself when she was going to learn to butt out of other people's business, she found herself asking, "Aren't you lonely?"

Tears filled Kalinda's eyes. "I can't," she whispered. "I can't let anyone see me like this."

Fay moved to her daughter's side and took her uninjured hand. "Oh, honey. You can't hide forever."

"Why not? I'm a monster. I'm ugly."

Sympathy and pain jumbled together in her chest. Montana remembered what Simon had said about making people normal. Would Kalinda ever get there?

"He really wants to meet you," Montana said. "To be honest, Reese isn't all that. I don't think you'd have to worry."

Kalinda stared at her for a long time. "You promise he won't say anything?"

Hoping she was doing the right thing, she nodded. "Just ten minutes. If he gets on your nerves I'll take him away and you never have to see him again. Is that fair?"

"Okay."

"Don't worry. I'll give you plenty of warning." She glanced at Fay. "Are you all right with this?"

"We both need to get back into the world," Fay told her.

Having Reese stop by wasn't exactly the same as the world, but it was a start. Now all she had to do was make sure everything went perfectly.

Simon sat in his office, updating charts on his computer. Despite his laserlike focus, he was aware of a small dog carrier in the corner of the room, along with two dishes.

One was filled with water, the other with kibble.

He'd agreed to let Cece use his office as a temporary home. Having her around helped Kalinda heal, which was his primary concern. But the cage or crate or whatever it was called distracted him. Stupid but true.

Worse, he found himself anticipating seeing the dog. She was small enough not to be a bother, and friendly. He'd never considered himself a pet person, but she wasn't too bad.

He finished with the chart and leaned back in his chair. Who was he trying to kid? While he thought the dog was fine, the person he most wanted to see was Montana.

It had been eight days since that night. Eight days since he'd told her the truth about himself and she'd explained why he was wrong.

He'd always known no one would understand. Still, he'd found himself hoping she would get it, that she would see what he went through. She hadn't.

He supposed the fault wasn't hers. After all, she didn't have any life experiences to prepare her for someone like him. Her world had been safe, kind. The most important person in her life hadn't turned on her.

There was no resentment in the thought.

Knowing that Montana believed in goodness and the kindness of strangers made him sleep easier at night.

He missed her. There it was — the uncomfortable truth. He missed looking at her and talking to her. He wanted to have her tell him about her life and then he wanted to make love with her. Slowly the first time, savoring all that he could, then taking her hard and fast, both of them breathless.

He closed his charts and stood. Before he could leave his office, someone knocked on the partially closed door.

"Come in," he called.

Two men entered. They were about his height and age. One was blond. He recognized the other man. Ethan Hendrix. Simon had met him at the family picnic after the car accident.

"Are we interrupting?" Ethan asked.

"I was just finishing paperwork. Good to see you again." The two men shook hands.

Ethan introduced his friend. "This is Josh Golden, the second most famous athlete in Fool's Gold."

Josh grinned. "Give me a break. You really think Raoul could ride a hundred and eighty-plus kilometers in the high mountain stage of the Tour de France?"

"Sure."

Josh chuckled. "Right." He turned to Simon. "Admit it. You've heard of me."

Ethan laughed. "You don't have to do any upper body workouts, do you? Carrying that ego around is more than enough."

Josh laughed. "You're jealous because all the ladies love me."

"I'm only interested in one lady loving me. You can have the rest."

Instead of looking pleased, Josh seemed to deflate. "Good point. I only want Charity, too. Well, damn. What am I supposed to do with the rest of them? Simon? Interested?"

He found himself agreeing that there was only one woman who had recently captured his attention. "I would be a poor substitute."

They continued to banter with each other. Simon found himself enjoying the conversation, even though he wasn't saying much. They had obviously been friends for a long time — something he missed with his lifestyle. He was never in one place long enough to make connections that lasted.

Without wanting to, he remembered being eleven and standing in his mother's small kitchen. His ears were ringing from the backhanded slap that had just landed across his cheek.

"He's a freak," his mother's boyfriend had complained, pulling back his arm to hit

Simon again. "Make him stop looking at me."

Instead of defending him, his mother had yelled for him to leave the room. As Simon had run away to his bedroom, he'd heard the man say he was a creepy kid. That there was something not right about him.

That wasn't the first time Simon had heard the words. He didn't know how to fit in. He was smarter than all the other kids — already skipping two grades. School came easily to him. He remembered wondering what it would be like to be just like everyone else.

Something he would never know, he thought, returning to the present.

"You golf?" Josh asked.

"You don't have to ask," Ethan said. "They have to learn it in medical school."

Simon chuckled. "I missed that class, but I do play occasionally."

"We heard you have the afternoon off. Pia has a houseful of women and is throwing Raoul out for the afternoon. Come with us. It'll be fun."

Although Simon didn't know either of the men, he wanted to go with them. An afternoon away from the hospital would help clear his head.

"Let me tell them I'm leaving," he said,

picking up the phone. He paused and looked at them. "We play for money, right?"

Both men laughed.

"You're going to fit right in," Josh told him.

CHAPTER TEN

Steve was an attractive man. Tanned, fit, reasonably intelligent. He had blue eyes, which Denise liked. So far they'd talked about his job as a district manager for a computer parts distributor, the upcoming art festival in town and the weather.

She glanced surreptitiously at her watch and hoped the man sitting across from her didn't notice. She held in a groan. Had it really just been twenty minutes? Thank God they were only having drinks.

"Do you come here often?" Steve asked.

"To the winery? No, I don't get here much." She looked around at the patio. Tables and chairs had been set out. The summer evening was warm, but a light breeze kept the temperature bearable. The mountains were to the east, the vineyard to the west. It was a perfect romantic setting. So why did she feel like banging her head against the table?

"I was reading in the paper that they're having a good summer for grapes," she said. "If the favorable weather continues, this is going to be one of those excellent years for California wines."

She held in her second groan in the past three minutes. Talk about inane conversation.

Maybe it was the setting. Too forced. The truth was, she didn't have that many places she could go on a first date. Living in Fool's Gold meant she knew everyone and everyone knew her. Talk about a dating challenge, especially at her age.

"Do you get to Fool's Gold often?" she asked.

He smiled. "No, but I could change that."

Oops. She hadn't seen that coming.

"So business is good?"

He leaned toward her. "Good and getting better. Technology is always changing and people want to keep up. In a lot of industries you have to wait until the equipment breaks. Think about it. Would you replace your washing machine just because there was a new, fancy model?"

"Of course not."

"Right. No one would. But people think nothing of getting a new phone, just because it's new. It's a kind of built-in obsolescence."

"You sound like you really enjoy your work."

"I do. I like sales a lot and I really like having access to the newest toys."

He pulled a slim phone out of his pocket, tapped on the dark surface and showed her the screen. It was a maze of little boxes. *Apps* — was that the word?

"I'm so the wrong person to try to impress," she admitted. "I've had the same phone for two years. I'm terrified it's going to stop working and I'll have to figure out how to use a new one."

"I could help you," he said, meeting her gaze.

He was obviously interested, she thought with a sigh. She supposed she should be flattered and she was, a little. But while he was nice to look at and seemed charming enough, there was no . . . spark.

He was smiling. Denise frowned as she realized there weren't a lot of wrinkles around his eyes or gray in his dark blond hair.

They'd met last month, when Steve had been in town for some kind of conference. She'd bumped into him at Starbucks. Despite the spilled coffee, he'd been funny and friendly and when he'd asked for her number she'd impulsively given it to him, assuming he was close to her age.

"How old are you?" she asked.

"Forty-two."

Had she been drinking her glass of Merlot, she would have choked.

"I'm more than ten years older than you." She braced herself for the skid marks he would make as he raced away.

Steve shrugged. "Age is just a number."

"That's not what my mirror tells me every morning."

He leaned toward her again. "Don't sweat it. I don't. You're an attractive, vital woman. Sexually in your prime."

A second opportunity to choke, she thought, torn between hysterical laughter and the burning need to call one of her children to come rescue her. Sexually in her prime? She'd been dating for a while now and could barely bring herself to kiss a man. Sex was impossible to imagine.

She drew in a breath. "Steve, this has been great," she began.

"It has. I want to see you again."

"Why?"

His blue eyes crinkled as he smiled. "I like you, Denise."

"You're very nice, too," she murmured, "but let's be realistic. Have you been married?"

"Divorced."

"Any kids?"

"No."

"Want them?"

"Sure."

"Exactly. Not to be too blunt, but that ship has sailed. I have six children, the oldest of whom is . . ." She had to swallow hard. "The oldest is about eight years younger than you."

"So you were a baby when you got married. It doesn't matter."

"It does. I have grandchildren. I don't want to start over with someone. I want . . ."

She pressed her lips together when she realized she didn't know *what* she wanted. The impossible, she supposed. A man who made her heart beat faster, who understood her and her world and found both were exactly what he'd been looking for. A man she could picture clearly, but was taking great pains to avoid.

"It's been great," she said, rising to her feet. "Thanks for the drink."

He stood as well. "You're leaving?"

"I'm saying goodbye."

With that she walked through the tasting room and back to her car. But when she got there, she didn't get inside.

She'd barely had five sips of her wine, so she wasn't worried about driving. Still, she stood in the fading sunlight and fought back tears.

There were times when she missed her husband so much she thought she would rip apart from the inside out. Times when it had seemed impossible to go on. Today wasn't one of those, because as she stared out at the mountains, she wasn't thinking about her late husband.

Ralph hadn't been the one to bring her here. That had been Max. Dangerous, exciting Max, who rode a motorcycle and had kissed like he meant it. Max who had shown her what it meant to be swept away by passion and love.

He'd left, because that was what men like him did. By then, she'd already met Ralph and realized he was the kind of man she could love her whole life. Being with him had been different from being with Max. There hadn't been danger at all. Where Max had withheld, Ralph had offered.

He'd given her six beautiful children and the happiest years of her life. He'd been her other half. They'd loved each other faithfully long past his passing.

She got in her car and started the engine. While she didn't believe there was only one great love in each person's life, she did believe that a man like Ralph wasn't likely to come along again. That left her with the choice of accepting second best or simply giving up on the whole dating thing.

She drove out of the parking lot and headed for home. If she hurried, she could still join Kent and Reese for dinner, take Fluffy for a walk and lose herself in the familiar. Wasn't that better than anything a man had to offer?

"You know what to do, right?" Montana asked. "You're clear on the rules?"

Reese looked at her with a combination of patience and pity. "We've been over the rules three times."

Probably a good enough answer, she thought. "I'm nervous."

They were in the hospital elevator, going up to see Kalinda. Montana had left Cece at Max's place, thinking it would be easier to only deal with Reese for now.

When they exited the elevator, Reese stopped and looked at her. "I'm not going to say anything bad. I promise. I know she looks different and maybe seeing her will scare me a little. But I'll get over it. I don't know how she's feeling, but I'm not a little kid. I know she feels bad."

"Look at you," Montana said, feeling impressed. She hugged her nephew. "You're growing up."

"Six more years until I get my license." He grinned. "I know how many days, even."

She winced. "You probably don't want to mention it to your dad. I think knowing how close you are to driving would give him a heart attack."

Reese laughed.

They walked toward the burn unit. Once they were inside, she led the way to Kalinda's room. Fay met them at the door.

"She's a little tired," Fay said by way of greeting. She looked more cautious than excited and Montana suspected she was having second thoughts.

"Are you sure about this?" Fay asked.

Montana glanced at Reese, who nodded.

"Okay, then."

He drew in a breath and stepped into the room. Without hesitating, he walked up to the bed and smiled. "Hi. I'm Reese. You're Kalinda, right?"

She was half sitting in her bed, only a few strands of blond hair sticking out from white gauze. Her bandages were in place on her face and arms. The parts of her neck and cheeks they could see were raw. The smell of medicine and sickness seemed to linger in the air, fighting with the scent of antiseptic.

When she didn't answer, he continued, "Montana told me you can't get up and move around a lot. I guess that's why you want a small dog visiting you. My dad and I just got a dog a few weeks ago. Fluffy would sure make a mess of things in here." He smiled again. "She's real friendly, but she doesn't get how big she is. She practically knocks me over with her tail and you should see what she did to the glass dishes on my grandma's coffee table." He frowned. "Montana, didn't Fluffy come to the hospital?"

Now it was her turn to be uncomfortable. "Just the one time. Accidentally."

Kalinda surprised her by giggling. "I remember. I saw her. Dr. Bradley was mad."

"He sure was." She didn't like thinking about their first meeting. Not that he was any happier with her today.

"Do you like Dr. Bradley?" Reese asked. "I was in a car accident and he did the stitches." He pointed to the small bandage on his cheek. "He doesn't think I'm going to have a scar, which is okay, I guess. I wouldn't mind if I did. I think scars are interesting."

Kalinda turned away, then looked back. "I have scars. Or I'm going to."

Reese's expression turned sympathetic. "Does it hurt a lot?"

The girl nodded. "They give me stuff for the pain. It makes me sleepy. A barbecue exploded. I caught fire."

Reese pulled up a chair and sat down. "Like on TV? But not in a good way."

"Just like that."

Montana backed out of the room. Fay stood with her in the hallway.

"She's talking to him," Fay whispered. "I didn't think she would. I thought she'd tell him to go away. This is good, right?"

"I think so. It's a form of normal."

There was that word again — the one that always made her think of Simon. Not that she needed much help in that department. The man was always on her mind.

"Thank you for suggesting this," Fay told her. "I'm going crazy here, watching her suffer, knowing there's nothing I can do to help."

"You're with her. That means everything."

"I hope so."

Reese came to the door. "Do you have any games we can play? Kalinda's hands aren't burned too bad, so she could use a joystick or control."

"Or you could play a board game," Montana told him.

He sighed heavily. "Yeah, that would be great."

Fay laughed. "You're just like my daughter. I did bring in her Playstation 2. Does that sound better than a board game?"

"Lots." He grinned. "I know how to hook it up to the TV and everything."

Fay excused herself.

Montana was left standing alone in the hallway. She decided she would find a waiting area close by and read. An hour should give the kids enough time to enjoy the game without tiring Kalinda too much.

She started toward the nurses' station only to turn the corner and nearly run into Simon. They both came to a stop.

He was as tall as she remembered, and the right side of his face was just as perfect. She barely noticed the scars, except that she knew they were significant to him.

"Montana."

"Hi. I brought my nephew to visit with Kalinda. So far it's going well. They're playing video games."

One dark eyebrow rose. "That sounds like it will be fun for her. Good. We don't want her getting depressed. It interferes with healing." He cleared his throat. "I'm glad I ran into you. I wanted to speak to you about something. Several children will be by the hospital tomorrow to get out their stitches. If the first one starts crying, it upsets the rest and the morning goes badly. I was wondering if you could bring a service dog by to distract them."

She nodded, even as she thought about her schedule. "Of course. What time?"

"Nine-thirty. For about two hours."

"I don't have any appointments with the dogs until afternoon. I'll bring one of the bigger dogs. That'll make more of a diversion."

"Good."

He sounded so formal. Distant, even. That was her fault. She'd been the one to cross the line.

She reached out and touched his arm. The fabric of his white coat was smooth under her fingers.

"I'm sorry," she said quickly. "About what I said before. It's not my place to tell you what to believe or how to live your life. I barely know you. I was trying to show you something and I got it all wrong. I apologize for hurting you or offending you or whatever it is I did."

His expression gave nothing away. "And if I say it was nothing?"

"I won't believe you, but I won't argue."

"You like to argue."

"No, I don't." She stopped and sighed. "I don't mean to like it."

211

"Then that changes everything."

She studied him, trying to figure out what he was thinking. "Are you mad?"

"No."

"Do you hate me?"

"No."

Do you still want me?

She didn't speak those words. Her courage only took her so far.

"Do you forgive me?" she asked instead.

"Yes."

She smiled. "Thank you for saying that, instead of telling me there was nothing to forgive. I really am sorry."

He raised his hand as if he were going to touch her face, then lowered it back to his side. Disappointment swelled inside her. Terrified she'd blown it, she didn't know what to say. How was she supposed to ask a man to want her again?

Restless from her encounter with Simon, Montana decided what she needed was a good book to distract her. An evening curled up on the sofa reading would make her feel better. When she was done with work, she swung by Morgan's Books.

As usual, the place was busy, with a dozen or so people browsing and chatting. The scent of fresh coffee filled the air, along with the distinctive and delicious smell of brownies. Morgan's daughter Amber must have come by with a fresh batch from her bakery.

Montana waved to people she knew and headed for the romance section. Her love life was in the toilet, but there was no reason not to live vicariously through others, she told herself. She scanned the shelves, looking for a book that fit her mood, and stopped in front of a red book with a picture of a woman on the cover.

"Visions of Magic," she murmured, studying the flame tattoo on the woman's back. She'd never read Regan Hastings before, but was intrigued.

She reached for the book, only to bump hands with someone else.

"Sorry," she said, stepping back and turning. "Oh, hi." She recognized the curvy blonde as new to town. "Heidi, right?"

The woman, about her age, but much prettier, smiled. "Yes. And you're one of the triplets. I'm sorry, I can't tell you apart yet."

"Montana."

"Right." She tilted her head, as if studying Montana and hoping to find a difference.

Montana grinned. "If it helps, Dakota is pregnant, so for the next few months she'll be easy to find."

"Great. Thanks for the tip."

Heidi had golden blond hair she wore in two braids and large green eyes. Green eyes that made Montana think about Simon, which she didn't want to do.

"You and your grandfather bought the Castle Ranch outside of town, right?"

"That's us."

"How are you settling in?"

"We're figuring it out as we go. The house needs a complete renovation. I don't think anyone has lived in it for a while."

Montana tried to remember who had lived there last. "Old man Castle died ages ago. Maybe twenty years or so. I can't remember. He had a family living there. The mom was the housekeeper and her three boys worked the ranch. It wasn't much, even then. I don't know what happened after that. When he passed away, the family left. There was talk of someone from back East inheriting, but no one ever showed up."

"The place looks like it." Heidi wrinkled her nose. "I remind myself I've lived in worse. At least the plumbing and electricity work and the roof will last another couple of years, but seriously, when was the last time you saw an avocado-green stove?"

Montana laughed. "Once. In the movies."

"If you want to see the real thing, let me know. I have one."

Montana hadn't heard much about Heidi and her grandfather. "Are you running cattle on the ranch?"

Heidi shook her head. "No. I'm not big into cows. There are a few roaming around. They're wild or feral or whatever it is cows get when no one is around to take care of them." She paused. "I have a few goats I milk and I use the goat milk to make cheese."

Goats? "Your name is Heidi, you live with your grandfather and you have goats?"

Heidi laughed. "The irony is not lost, believe me. The difference is Glen, my grandfather, is very friendly, so I won't have to act as a liaison between him and the villagers." She glanced around the bookstore. "I'll bet Morgan has a copy here. When was the last time you read *Heidi?*"

"I think my mom read it to me and my sisters when we were pretty little. Wasn't there a girl in a wheelchair?"

"I sort of remember that." Her smile faded. "My mom read it to me, too. It's a good memory."

Sadness replaced humor and Montana had the feeling Heidi had lost her mother a long time ago. Having suffered through the death of her father, she knew what that was like.

"Do you get to town much?" she asked. "We have a girl's night out, or sometimes in, every few weeks. Just a bunch of us getting together to talk. If you want to give me your number, I can let you know when the next one is and you can join us."

"I'd like that."

Montana pulled out her cell phone and took Heidi's number.

"Are you and your grandfather okay out there by yourselves?"

The humor returned to Heidi's expression. "Despite the hideous appliances, we're doing great. This is the first real home we've ever had. We always traveled around a lot. I can't tell you how good it feels to finally be settled. We have a lot of plans for the ranch."

"I take it they don't include cows."

"Probably not. But I want to expand my herd. I plan to create a cheese empire." She laughed. "Plus, we're both really loving Fool's Gold. Everyone is so friendly and welcoming. And in an unexpected turn of events I can't decide if I'm okay with or not, my grandfather is quite the hit with the ladies of a certain age."

Montana wasn't surprised. The man shortage had been mitigated by several new businesses and lots of guys moving to town, but few of them had been past middle age.

"It'll keep him young," Montana told her.

"As long as I don't walk in on him having his way with one of them, I'm good with it."

Montana reached for the Regan Hastings book and grabbed two copies. "Let me buy you this. Sort of a welcome-to-town gift."

"Wow. This is why I love it here. Let me just announce to the universe, I'm never leaving. Wind, snow, a herd of locusts, I'll outwit them all."

"I like that — a plan. Did you know that Fool's Gold was originally settled by a group of Mayan women? They called themselves the Máa-zib. It means something like *few men.* I heard they kept men as love slaves."

Heidi grinned. "Don't you miss the good old days?"

"All the time."

Montana told herself not to be excited about the clinic with Simon. Kids were getting their stitches out — that was hardly a reason for her to want to break into song. The thing was, she was far more tingly about seeing him again than thinking about kids, which probably made her a bad person.

"Something else I have to work on," she

told Buddy as she opened the back door of her car, stepping to the side so he could jump out.

Buddy looked at her, a faintly worried frown pulling his doggie eyebrows together.

She'd debated which dog would be right for the event, and had settled on Buddy. Children sensed he was a worrier and spent their time reassuring him. Focusing on something else was probably a good thing. Plus, he was big enough for the little ones to lean on and he always loved a heartfelt hug.

As they made their way to the clinic, she reminded herself that she was here in a professional capacity. She should be grateful that Simon trusted her and her dogs to assist him.

"Not technically," she added to Buddy as they went in through the main doors. "I don't think removing stitches would be something you'd do well. No offense."

Buddy glanced at her as if to say none was taken.

They made their way to the clinic. Buddy's service dog vest allowed them to pass through the various departments with hardly a second glance.

As she approached the nurses' station, she was greeted by an efficient-looking nurse in her forties.

"Dr. Bradley said you would be here." She smiled cheerfully. "He's been telling me what a difference your service dogs can make. I'm looking forward to seeing this one in action."

She reached out and petted Buddy, who responded calmly, wagging his tail. But his frown deepened as if he was concerned about the added pressure.

Montana was more confused by Simon saying nice things about her. Obviously he understood the dogs could help — otherwise, why bother inviting her? But to talk to someone else about what she did was unexpected.

The nurse showed her to a small examining room. A tray sat on the counter. Although it was covered, she imagined all sorts of shiny, sharp medical tools and instantly understood why the waiting children would be apprehensive.

She glanced around, taking in the padded table where the patients would sit, the extra chairs on the side of the room, the bright overhead lights. Not exactly a friendly setting.

The door opened and Simon stepped in. She felt an instant surge of excitement, hope and, well, lust.

"Good morning," he said briskly. "Thank you for coming to the clinic."

His impersonal words, the way he barely glanced at her, deflated her anticipation.

"We're happy to help. This is Buddy."

Simon surprised her by crouching so he was eye level with the dog. "Nice to meet you, Buddy." He rubbed the dog's ears. Buddy perked up at the attention.

"He's very friendly," she said as Simon straightened. "But he always looks concerned. Kids respond to that by reassuring him. I thought that might distract them."

"A good idea."

She might as well have been anyone on the staff, she thought sadly. Apparently he'd recovered from his need to be with her. No more kissing for her.

The nurse stuck her head in. "They're ready, Doctor."

"Give me a couple of minutes and send the first one in."

"Sure."

She stepped out.

Simon crossed to the sink and washed his hands. When he was done, he dried them, then pulled on gloves. "It doesn't take long to remove stitches. Assuming no complications, we should be out of here in about an hour. Would you like to go get coffee with me?"

She was so busy being sad, she almost missed the invitation. "I have Buddy," she said, stumbling over the words.

"The Starbucks has outdoor seating."

"Right. Um, sure. That would be nice."

"Good."

The first patient was brought into the room.

Her name was Mindy and she was twelve years old. Simon explained that she'd been cut by flying glass when a neighborhood kid had thrown a baseball through a plate-glass window. She had stitches along her jawline and down the side of her neck.

"That must have been scary," Montana said as Mindy hugged Buddy.

"It was. There was blood everywhere." She sounded both horrified and proud.

"We're still getting it out of the carpet," her mother joked.

Mindy climbed on the table. Simon pulled a chair up next to it and motioned for Buddy to jump up on the chair. Mindy wrapped her arms around him, while keeping the stitches facing Simon.

"What are you going to do this weekend?" he asked, as he began to snip the stitches.

Montana had never seen him work before

and was impressed by how quickly he removed each stitch. There was a sureness in his movements. Utter confidence.

"We're going to the Summer Festival," Mindy said, her face turned away. "We go every year. It's one of my favorites, although I like all the stuff we do at Christmas, too."

"I've never been to Summer Festival."

Shocked, she looked at him. "You have to go. It's the best. There are rides and booths and elephant ears."

"What are elephant ears?"

Her eyes widened. "They're delicious. All warm, with powdered sugar."

"They go right to my thighs," her mother murmured.

"Ow."

Simon's fingers never slowed. "We're almost done."

Tears filled Mindy's eyes. "Can you stop now?"

Buddy gently whimpered and pressed the top of his head against her chest.

She turned her attention to the dog. "It's okay," she whispered. "I'm okay."

"We're done," Simon told her.

Mindy looked startled. "That was quick. It didn't really hurt that much. I was surprised is all."

Her mother moved close and studied the

work. "It barely shows and it's not even finished healing."

Simon nodded. "I'm not expecting her to have a scar. You have the instructions for what to do as soon as the scab falls off?"

"Yes."

Mindy stared at her mother. "So I'll still be pretty?"

Simon helped her down from the table. "You're already beautiful. I don't think there's anything I could do to make you more beautiful. I'm not that talented."

Mindy beamed at him, then hugged him. "Thank you. I was scared but this wasn't bad at all."

"I'm glad," he told her with a smile.

He was so different with his patients, Montana thought. More himself — open and giving. It seemed that was the only place he allowed himself to relax. The rest of the time there was a wall between him and the world.

Mindy and her mother left. The nurse let in a small boy accompanied by a woman Montana would swear she recognized from the social services office. The boy had cuts all over his face and dozens of stitches.

Simon immediately dropped to a crouch and put his hand on the boy's shoulder. "Hello, Freddie."

"Hi."

The boy's voice was soft and high-pitched. He was probably six or seven, skinny and small boned.

"I heard about your aunt coming to get you."

Freddie's mouth turned up but he didn't actually smile. It took Montana a second to realize that because of all the cuts and stitches, he couldn't.

"The judge said she could and she's taking me back to Hawaii." Freddie looked at the social worker. "My cousin Sean is my best friend, but Dad said I couldn't see him anymore. Now I can."

Simon motioned for Buddy to approach. "My friend Montana brought in a very special dog. His name is Buddy. He's kind of scared to be in the hospital but when I told him about you, he wanted to visit anyway."

Humor twinkled in Freddie's eyes. "You can't talk to dogs."

"I'm a doctor, young man. I can do anything." Simon turned to the dog. "Buddy, are you nervous?"

Buddy's eyebrows drew together even more and he whimpered.

"Whoa." Freddie looked impressed. "Okay, Buddy. Thanks for wanting to come see me."

Buddy held out a paw to shake.

Simon helped the boy onto the table. This time Buddy jumped in the chair without being asked. Freddie put an arm around him and the dog leaned close.

Simon went to work. Unlike the last time, there were no tears, no requests to stop. Freddie flinched a few times, but otherwise he was completely stoic.

Montana realized Freddie had been through this before and wondered what could have happened to him. Why was he having more surgeries? Except for the lines from the cuts, he didn't look deformed.

After Freddie there were three more children. When they were finished, Simon escorted Montana and Buddy out of the hospital.

"I have an idea," she said. "Would you get us our coffee and I'll meet you there in a second?"

Simon nodded. "Of course."

While he walked toward the center of town, she and Buddy headed for her car. Fifteen minutes later, coffee in cupholders, they were driving up the mountain.

"We're not going far," she told him. "I know this beautiful meadow where we can talk and Buddy can run around."

225

Simon reached back and patted the dog. "You've earned a romp."

She pulled off the road and into a makeshift dirt parking lot. After letting Buddy out, she grabbed a blanket from the back and led the way to a meadow.

The sun was warm, the grassy area dotted with small flowers. The hum of insects mingled with birdsongs and the soft breeze. It was a perfect kind of morning in a perfect kind of place. She spread out the blanket and motioned for Simon to sit.

"Tell me about Freddie," she said when he settled. "How did he get hurt?"

"His father. He cut him. This wasn't the first time."

Montana stared at him. "I don't understand."

"Not all parents are like yours. Some have mental or emotional problems. Some are just cruel. Freddie's father would tie him up and then cut him with a hunting knife. His back, his chest. This is the first time he went to work on his face."

Her chest was tight and she found it difficult to breathe. Her eyes burned. Rather than give in, she looked past Simon to where Buddy chased a butterfly — for once having fun rather than worrying.

"Why wasn't Freddie taken away from

him before now?"

Simon shrugged. "The kid didn't say how it happened and he slipped through the cracks."

"What kind of parent does that?"

"The bad kind. It happens more than you would think."

Her gaze shifted to his scars as an impossible thought formed. Had one of Simon's parents been responsible for his burns?

"I can't believe something like that would happen in Fool's Gold," she whispered, because she was too afraid to ask.

"It happens everywhere, but if it makes you feel better, Freddie and his father have only been in town a few months. The E.R. staff figured it out immediately and called social services. Freddie was taken away from his father that day."

"I'm glad. I hope he's locked up for a long time."

"Me, too."

"I guess you see a lot of awful things."

"How the wounds happened is sometimes worse than the injury itself."

"Can you ever forget it? Does the reality haunt you?"

"I'm used to it."

She was sure that someone in his position would have to find a way to disconnect. To compartmentalize. Still, when he was alone, there must be ghosts.

"I shouldn't be telling you this." He sipped his latte, then looked at her over the lid. "You don't need to know."

Simon should have looked out of place in his suit slacks and shirt and tie. Instead he was as relaxed as he'd ever appeared. The only place she'd seen him completely comfortable before was the hospital.

"I'm not as innocent as you think," she told him.

He smiled. "Sure you are. You're the kind of girl who wants to fall in love."

"Doesn't everyone?"

"No."

Meaning not him. "You've never been in love?"

"Not even once."

"That's too bad."

"Why? I'm content."

"Don't you want to be happy?"

"Happiness is elusive. My work is enough."

She knew he was wrong, but didn't think there was any point in telling him that.

"Why aren't *you* married?" he asked.

She took a moment to adjust from interviewer to interviewee. "No one has ever asked. I've had a couple of serious boyfriends, but they both left. They weren't in love with me. I wasn't . . ." She shrugged. "I wasn't enough for them. One cheated and one just broke it off. The last one kept saying I would be 'perfect' if I changed my clothing style, or hair cut, or makeup. It was starting to seem like a never ending list of how I could be better."

She did her best to speak the words as if the truth didn't hurt her.

"They were fools."

"Thank you."

"I'm not being polite, Montana. You are the kind of woman men dream about having."

His statement left her breathless.

"Even you?" she asked before she could stop herself.

"Especially me." His gray-green eyes darkened. "If I was looking for something permanent."

"Right."

"And you're the kind of woman who is looking for forever."

She didn't want to agree, but couldn't seem to keep herself from nodding.

"I go to Peru in a few weeks. Then on to somewhere else." He looked at his coffee, then at her. "I could come back, to visit."

"But not to stay."

"No," he said with finality. "Not to stay."

CHAPTER ELEVEN

Montana didn't usually attend city council meetings. Her job had never been political. Before working for Max, she'd been a part-time librarian. But Mayor Marsha had asked, so here she was.

The agenda was much as she had expected. Information about road construction — in this case a project funded by the state. A few permit issues. An update on the Summer Festival, only two days away.

Gladys, the city treasurer, turned to Mayor Marsha. "I assume Montana is here to talk about the Dr. Bradley issue."

"She is." The mayor smiled at Montana. "How is our project going?"

Montana realized she shouldn't have been surprised by the shift in topic. If she'd thought about it for even a second, she would have known why she'd been asked to attend. Unfortunately, she went completely blank.

"I, ah, I don't know what to tell you."

"Is he enjoying Fool's Gold?" Marsha asked.

"Yes. Everyone has been very welcoming and I think he appreciates that. He's not much of a joiner, though. I haven't found that he has any hobbies."

"He went golfing with Josh and Ethan," another council member said. "Raoul Moreno joined them for the last nine holes."

"Do you think he would be impressed by sports celebrities?" Marsha asked earnestly. "Should I suggest Josh and Raoul spend more time with him?"

Montana felt everyone staring at her. She did her best not to squirm. "Not really. He's not that kind of man. He's quiet and thoughtful. He only seems comfortable opening up to his patients."

"I don't suppose you've had sex yet?" Gladys asked.

Heat flared on Montana's cheeks.

"That is not our business," Marsha announced firmly. "I asked Montana to be his friend, to show him around town and talk about the benefits of living here. She's not expected to give her, ahem, all for the sake of the town."

"In my day we understood a good sacrifice," Gladys mumbled.

Marsha ignored her. "Montana, do you feel you're making progress?"

"I don't know. I'm never sure what he's thinking."

The mayor nodded, then the meeting moved on to other topics. When it was over, Mayor Marsha asked her to stay behind.

"Do you know how he got his scars?" the older woman asked when it was just the two of them.

She asked the question in such a way that Montana realized the mayor knew the answer.

Montana shifted in her seat. "He hasn't told me."

"Do you want to know?"

The tone was gentle, the expression caring. Mayor Marsha wouldn't tell her if she didn't want to know.

Montana nodded.

Marsha slipped on her reading glasses and opened a slim folder in front of her.

"From what I've been able to find out, his mother was largely a disinterested parent. There's no word on Simon's father. He seems to have disappeared fairly early on. Possibly while she was pregnant. According to the police reports, her boyfriend left because he found Simon . . . disconcerting."

Marsha glanced at Montana, looking over her half-glasses. "He was very intelligent, even when he was young. He'd skipped a couple of grades by the time he was eleven and was expected to skip even more."

Montana gripped the edge of the large conference table. She sensed she was going to need the support.

"When the boyfriend took off, Simon's mother blamed her son. She pushed him into the fireplace." Marsha looked up again and removed her glasses. "Obviously we've all seen his scars. When he tried to climb out, she pushed him back in. It's something of a miracle he didn't die."

Don't throw up, Montana told herself as her stomach turned over and over. *Don't think about it and don't throw up.*

Horror swept through her. Her brain flashed to Freddie, whose father had cut him on purpose.

"The neighbors called an ambulance, who in turn called the police. When Simon was taken away, the mother confessed all. She didn't care if she went to jail. She never wanted to see her son again. As far as she was concerned, Simon had ruined her life."

The mayor slipped on her glasses and continued to read. "He spent nearly four years in the hospital. There were countless surgeries. Amazingly, he was able to study on his own, without the benefit of much more than a part-time volunteer teacher. He achieved nearly perfect scores on the SAT and ACT tests and was given a full scholarship to Stanford at the age of sixteen. From there he went to UCLA medical school."

Montana couldn't listen anymore. "Excuse me," she said, pushing her chair away from the table. "I have to go."

She grabbed her purse and hurried out of the room. The door to the outside seemed miles away, but finally she made it and was able to breathe again.

This wasn't happening, she thought, bent over slightly, sucking in air. She didn't want to know.

But the knowledge couldn't be unlearned. The reality of Simon's past horrified her. She'd seen Kalinda's burns. Simon's would have been as bad. Maybe worse. She knew they were on his face and went down his neck. They were also on his body, she remembered. He'd told her that.

His mother hadn't just pushed him into a fire, she'd tried to keep him there. She'd tried to punish or even kill him in one of the worst, most hideously painful ways possible. All the while, Simon would have been screaming, fighting to get out. The one person who was supposed to love him had nearly destroyed him.

She straightened, only to find she was crying. Tears filled her eyes and spilled down her cheeks. Tears for the boy who had been brutally disfigured and tears for the man who insisted on living in emotional solitary confinement.

As she brushed her face with her fingers, she drew in a breath. Mayor Marsha had known all this when she'd first approached Montana about helping convince Simon to stay in Fool's Gold. She'd wisely kept the truth quiet until Montana was ready to handle it.

Whatever her personal feelings for Simon, there was more at stake than her fragile heart. Simon needed to see there were good people in the world, people who cared about each other. She had to find a way to make him want to stay in Fool's Gold. No matter what.

"Tell me what you love about this," Nevada said as she pulled weeds from between the roses. "It's hot and sweaty. You're digging in the dirt and the roses are attack plants." She sat back on her heels and studied a new scratch on the side of her arm.

Denise laughed. "You make it sound so unpleasant. I happen to like gardening."

"I get that. What isn't clear is why."

"It relaxes me. And I have something to show for my labor. I can stand back and look at what I've accomplished. I don't get the same satisfaction from things like doing laundry. There will just be more tomorrow."

"There'll be more weeds tomorrow, too."

"You're missing the spirit of the work," Denise scolded her.

Denise had been surprised when Nevada had shown up a few minutes ago, claiming to want to spend a little time with her. While she had close relationships with all her children, they seldom stopped by just to catch up. Usually they invited her out to lunch and dinner for that. When one of her children came home, it usually meant there was a problem.

What Denise didn't know was what Nevada wanted to talk about, but many years of being a mother had taught her patience. Her daughter would tell her when she was ready. Which turned out to be sooner than she had expected.

"I've been thinking about my job," Nevada said a few minutes later. "Ethan's doing more with his windmills and less construction."

Ethan had inherited the family business when his father had died. Although the company had focused entirely on home construction and renovation, he'd branched out into wind energy, building windmills in a facility outside of town.

"Are you interested in taking over the building part of the company?" Denise asked. Nevada had studied engineering in college and, when she'd finished her degree, she'd gone to work for her brother.

"Not exactly." Nevada shifted until she was sitting on the grass. "I need to tell you something, Mom, and I don't want you to get upset."

Not words designed to make her relax, Denise thought, also sitting on the grass and taking off her gardening gloves.

"I can't promise what I'll feel, but I will do my best not to shriek so loud the neighbors hear."

Nevada smiled. "I'll take that." She drew in a breath. "I'm thinking of changing jobs."

"You want to do something else at the company?"

Her daughter stared at the grass, then back at her. "No. I want to go work somewhere else."

"Why?"

"There are a lot of reasons."

Denise didn't know what to think. Nevada had worked for her brother for six years. As far as she knew, they got along fine. Ethan always talked about what a great job his sister did. But instead of asking, Denise once again waited.

"I never had to do anything to get the job," Nevada told her. "It was understood I would join the company when I graduated, and I did. I didn't have to think about what I wanted to do or where I was going to work. Mom, except for summer jobs, I've never been on an interview. I want to figure out how good I am."

"Doesn't that come from within, rather than from an external source?"

"I'm not talking about self-respect or self-esteem. I mean I want to know how good I am at my job."

"Your brother thinks you're great."

"Does he have a choice? Could Ethan actually fire me?"

"Do you want him to?"

"No. But I do want the chance to prove myself."

Denise studied her beautiful daughter and thought about how different their lives were. Denise had been nineteen when she'd met Ralph. While she'd been taking classes at Fool's Gold Community College, she hadn't had any serious plans for getting a degree.

Within six months, Ralph had proposed and she'd accepted. Her sole work experience had been a series of part-time jobs. Three months later, they'd been married and a couple of months after that, she'd gotten pregnant. She'd had the three boys in just over three years, had waited a couple of years, then gotten pregnant with the triplets. By the time she was Nevada's age, she had six kids. Working had never been an issue.

The family business had provided enough money for them to live relatively comfortably. They'd bought this house just before the triplets were born and had paid for it in fifteen years. Saving for college for six kids had been a real challenge, but they'd managed.

When Ralph died, she discovered he'd left her a generous life insurance policy that would take care of her for the rest of her life. Ethan had taken over the family business and was bringing it to new heights. Each of the other children got a quarterly check from their share of the business.

Denise's biggest problem was how to fill her day. After a lifetime of taking care of others, her house seemed empty and sometimes her days did, too. Maybe it was time to explore other options. She could always go back to school — start some kind of career. Whatever she chose would sure be a lot less work than being a stay-at-home mom.

But that was for another day. Right now, Nevada needed advice.

"Have you talked to your brother?" she asked.

"Not yet. I want to make up my mind first. I don't want to leave him dangling."

"Do you have another job in mind?" A horrifying thought occurred to Denise, although she was careful not to let her worry show. "Do you think you need to leave Fool's Gold to prove yourself?"

"For a while I did, but maybe not. There's a big job starting nearby. You've probably read about it in the paper. Janack Construction is building a casino-resort complex northeast of town. I thought I would see what I could do there."

"Janack. Why is that name familiar?"

"Ethan was friends with Tucker Janack years ago. They were at cycling camp together."

"Oh, right." She remembered a skinny, dark-haired boy. His family had been extremely wealthy. Tucker's father had picked up his son in a private jet. "They do big projects all over the world, don't they?"

Nevada nodded. "They just finished that huge theme park in Rio. The land here has been held in trust for descendants of the Máa-zib tribe. His mother had Máa-zib blood in her."

"You've done your homework," Denise said, realizing this wasn't an idle conversation. Nevada had already made up her mind.

"I think it's important to know as much as I can about the company. This is going to be a good deal for Fool's Gold. Part of the construction plans include widening the road into town. We'll get the benefit of more tourists now that they'll have an easier way to get here. Despite being on Máa-zib land, the facility will have to pay some local taxes."

"Mayor Marsha is probably doing the happy dance as we speak."

Nevada laughed. "I'm sure she is."

"So you're going to go to work for them, aren't you?"

"I'm going to apply. If you're okay with that."

Denise took her hand and squeezed. "I've only ever wanted you to be happy. You know that, right?"

"I do, Mom."

"Then be happy. You're right — Ethan

isn't growing the construction side of the business very much. If you were interested in taking it on, he would be happy to let you. It would be a chance to put your mark on things. But if that isn't what you want to do, better to get out now. What was it you said? Test yourself."

Nevada could always go back, Denise thought. Not that she would suggest that. Hinting at failure rarely helped anyone.

"I need to know what I can do," her daughter told her.

"Then go find out."

Nevada pulled her hand free, then leaned in and hugged her mother. "You're the best."

Denise hugged her back. She'd been blessed with wonderful children. "I know. You six were very lucky that I'm your mother."

Her daughter laughed. "It's your modesty we admire most."

"As you should."

"There you are!"

They both turned to see Dakota walking around the side of the house, Hannah in her arms.

"I've been wandering through the house. I saw your car, Nevada, and couldn't figure out why neither of you were anywhere. I actually went to the thought of alien abductions. Then I realized you must be in back."

Denise rose and crossed to her. "Nevada came to help me weed." She turned her gaze to the baby. Hannah grinned broadly and waved her arms, wanting to get to her grandmother.

"Look at you," she said, taking the baby and cuddling her. "All pretty and happy. How's my girl?"

Her granddaughter snuggled close, obviously loving the attention.

Dakota had adopted the six-month-old girl in early June. While the adoption itself wouldn't be final for a bit longer, the whole family had bonded with Hannah. She was affectionate, curious and growing like crazy.

Dakota plopped on the grass next to her sister. "This grandmother thing is pretty fabulous. I get free advice and a built-in babysitter."

"It seems to work for Grandma, as well."

"It does," Denise said happily, then nuzzled Hannah's neck. "Let's go inside. It's getting warm out here and I don't want her getting too much sun."

"Of course you don't," Nevada teased. "Meanwhile, *we* could fall over from heatstroke and that would be fine."

"Probably not fine," Denise told her. "I'd

be worried. I'd probably turn the hose on you at the very least."

They went into the kitchen. Nevada got out glasses and plates. Dakota collected the pitcher of iced tea, and cookies from the jar on the counter. In a matter of a minute or so, they were in their familiar places at the big kitchen table.

"How is it having Kent and Reese in the house?" Nevada asked before biting into a homemade chocolate chip cookie.

"Wonderful. This is too much house for me. I like having family around."

Dakota looked at her. "You're not thinking of selling, are you?"

"No. All of you live in town, except for Ford. We need the space for our celebrations." With luck, her youngest son would also move back when he finally left the military.

They talked about what was going on with Ethan and Liz and how Kent had been offered the job teaching math at Fool's Gold High School.

"Is Montana still seeing that doctor guy?" Nevada asked. "She hasn't said anything to me when we talk and I don't want to bring it up."

"I think so," Denise answered. "Although I'm not sure what's going on there. She

245

mentioned she was showing Simon around town as a favor for Mayor Marsha. Do you think it's more than that?"

Her daughters exchanged a look. "He's pretty appealing," Nevada said. "Handsome *and* scarred. Which I guess makes him both beauty and the beast. Montana seems to be spending a lot of time with him."

"I suppose the best plan would be to simply ask her," Denise murmured. "Any volunteers?"

"I'll do it," Dakota said. "Finn is up in Alaska, finalizing his sale of his business, so Hannah and I are on our own. We're going to the Summer Festival tonight. I'm sure Montana will be there. We can talk then."

"Be sure to tell her we're not prying. We're concerned."

Her daughters laughed.

"It's a thin line, Mom," Nevada reminded her.

"But an important one."

Montana loved the quirkiness of her town. Most places held Summer Festivals during the day. Not Fool's Gold. While the celebration would continue all weekend, it started Friday evening, with live music, dozens of stands selling food, and a fireworks display when it was dark.

She moved through the growing crowd, greeting people she knew. There were a lot of tourists who came every year for the Summer Festival, filling local hotels and motels. Always a good thing. The restaurants would be crowded and there would be too many bikes on the path around the lake, but the residents were used to that. As the various festivals drew mostly families, there were rarely any problems.

She bought a carnitas taco from a stand and ate it standing up, then tasted a couple of types of wine at a different booth. Searching for dessert, she found herself in front of the place that sold elephant ears. Although she usually enjoyed the treat, tonight it made her think of Simon.

Silliness, she told herself. The man was a complication she didn't need in her life. Not that telling herself that helped.

Even as she ordered an elephant ear, she found herself glancing back toward the main part of town. It would be easy to go to his hotel room on the pretext of inviting him to the festival.

She didn't for two reasons. First, she wasn't sure she could act normally around him. Knowing about his past made her even more curious about him. She wanted to talk about it, hear what he'd gone through, learn how he'd figured out how to be so strong. The second reason she didn't go to his room was because she wasn't that interested in bringing him to the festival. And she'd never once gone uninvited to a man's bed.

Wanting to be with him that way wasn't new, but the feeling was more intense. She knew she was reacting emotionally to new information. But from his perspective, nothing had changed. That made her vulnerable. She wasn't sure that was particularly safe for her.

After finishing her elephant ear, she walked around, looking at the different booths. There were people selling everything from handmade jewelry to CDs. A guy offered samples of local wild honey. A woman in a turban told fortunes. One band replaced another and the music continued.

Around eight, she ran into her sister. Dakota had Hannah in a stroller. The little girl grinned with excitement and waved at everyone she saw.

"Having fun?" Montana asked.

"Sure. This is one of my favorite festivals."

"Is Finn still in Alaska?"

"Yes. He comes back tomorrow. I can't wait to see him."

"I'm sure he's thinking the same thing."

Dakota grinned. "That's what he tells me.

I have to say, I really like that quality in a man."

"I would, too."

They started walking together. Their progress was slow, as most of the residents of the town knew them and Hannah, and wanted to stop and talk about how the little girl was doing.

"Do you think we got this much attention when we were her age?" Montana asked as Eddie Carberry, Josh Golden's seventy-something assistant, paused to play "where's the baby" with Hannah.

"We were triplets in a small town," Dakota said with a laugh. "We probably got a parade."

"I wish I could remember it."

"You could try past regression therapy."

Montana shook her head. "I'm not that interested, but thanks."

"Anytime. So what's new?"

One of the advantages of being a triplet was understanding how the others thought. To anyone else, the question would have been casual. Practically a throwaway. But Montana knew better.

"What's up?"

Dakota widened her eyes. "Nothing. Why do you ask?"

Montana moved her off the path and onto

the grass where there were less people. "You want to talk about something specific. I can tell. What is it?"

Dakota drew in a breath. "There is some concern about what's happening with Simon."

Montana wasn't even surprised. "Did you volunteer or lose the bet?"

"I offered to talk to you."

Which was just like her family. Love came with worry and snooping. "There's not much to say. I'm trying to convince him to stay because Mayor Marsha asked me to."

"We know that part. But what about the rest of it?" Dakota studied her. "He's an intriguing man."

"Don't let Finn hear you say that."

"I'm not the one in love with Simon."

"I'm not either."

"Are you sure?"

Montana thought about the question. There was no point in lying — Dakota would be able to tell. "He's a really good guy who's overcome some scary stuff. I've seen him with his patients. He cares. He gives them all he has, but still manages to hold back, emotionally. He's unreachable."

"A handsome, scarred stranger who heals children and can't be touched emotionally," Dakota said lightly. "He's like catnip."

Something she'd thought herself. Great minds and all that. "I've never been a fan of catnip."

"You know what I mean."

"I'm doing okay. I'm not in love with him."

"Could you be?"

Montana didn't want to think about that. "He needs me."

"He doesn't sound like he needs anyone. You can't save him."

"Someone has to."

Dakota's expression turned serious. "No. They don't. Montana, you give your whole self in relationships. That's not always the best way to keep yourself from getting hurt."

"He's lonely."

"He's leaving."

"I know that." Simon had been completely honest about that. She knew that getting involved was dangerous, that given her history, falling for a guy like him could be a disaster.

"Do you?"

"Of course. He's made that very clear. He's going to Peru when he leaves here. I'm fine. You don't have to worry about me."

"It comes with the job," Dakota reminded her. "We want you to protect yourself. Just a little."

Because the reality was, Simon could break her heart. She could fall in love with him, only to watch him walk away.

"I want to help him. But you're right — I have to be smart about it. And I am. I know how this is going to end."

Dakota looked like she was going to say more, then sighed. "That's all we can ask."

"There's my precious baby girl." Bella Gionni, a local hairdresser in town, walked toward them. She crouched down to smile at Hannah.

"You're ignoring us," Montana pointed out, grateful for the interruption.

"I'll get to you next," Bella promised, cooing over Hannah. "She's growing so fast. Is that a tooth?"

"She has a couple now," Dakota said. "But even though she's teething, she's hardly ever fussy."

"I'm going to go walk around," Montana murmured.

"Are we okay?"

She smiled. "Of course. I know you love me. Sometimes it's annoying, but mostly it's nice."

"Gee, thanks."

Montana walked away. As she got lost in the crowd, she thought about Simon. Her need to see him had only increased. Now, what was she willing to do about it?

Simon hadn't intended to come to the Summer Festival. He'd seen it on his way back to the hotel, where he'd planned to order room service and then read. But instead he'd found himself changing his clothes and heading out.

The night was warm and the sounds of live music drifted to him. The sidewalks were crowded and he could see where the streets had been blocked to car traffic so those attending could spread out.

He'd lived in cities where people walked or used public transportation, but he'd never been anywhere like Fool's Gold. The small town feel appealed to him, which he never would have expected.

Despite the short time he'd been there, he recognized several people. When they greeted him, he responded. It was almost as if he'd lived there forever. An illusion, but a nice one.

He ate ribs and a corn dog, washing both down with a beer, then walked around some more. He told himself he was simply exploring, but he knew the truth. Montana would be here and he wanted to find her.

"Hello, Dr. Bradley."

He turned and recognized one of the

nurses from the hospital. She was with a man and two small children. Her family, she confirmed, as she made introductions.

"Are you enjoying the festival?" she asked.

"Very much."

"In the early fall we have an artist series. I haven't heard who all is coming, but it's fun to guess. A few years ago we had Wyland come. He's the one who does those huge murals of undersea life? So beautiful. I love his work."

"Sounds impressive." A more polite response than the reality — which was that he wouldn't be in town come fall.

"I'm sure you'll like whoever comes."

They chatted a few more minutes, then he excused himself. He walked purposefully now, searching for the one face he most wanted to see.

He heard laughter by the carousel and turned. He caught a flash of blond hair, but it was only one of her sisters. The one with the baby.

He took two more steps, then stopped. She was close — he could sense it. And then she was walking toward him. She smiled as she spotted him.

He stayed where he was, letting her come to him, letting it be her choice. When she was in front of him, she took his hand, as if

254

this had been their plan.

"Let's go home," she said and led the way.

CHAPTER TWELVE

They went to her house. Simon noticed very little about the short walk through a quiet residential neighborhood. He could see the houses were small but well maintained. Montana's was a single story, set back from the sidewalk. They climbed the two steps to the tiny porch, then she used her key to let them in.

The living room was about half the size of his hotel room. She'd left a single lamp on to illuminate the space, but didn't stop there. He saw a dining room, a kitchen, then they were in a short hallway. The door on the left led to a bedroom that had been converted into an office. Next was a bathroom. The door at the end of the hall led to her bedroom.

There was no moon and they'd long left the light of the living room behind. As they walked through the doorway, Montana reached for a switch on the wall. Two nightstand lamps went on.

Simon glanced around, positioning the dresser and the bed in his mind before turning off the lights. He sensed more than saw her turn toward him.

Desire held him in an uncomfortably tight grip. He was aware of his blood pounding in his ears, the rush of need that made him hard to the point of pain. He wanted her more than he'd ever wanted any woman, but having her would come at a price. The point was driven home further when she turned the light back on.

"I thought men liked to see as well as do," she said lightly, her brown eyes searching his.

"It's better in the dark."

She pressed her hands lightly on his chest. "I'm not like them."

"Like who?"

"The ones who didn't want to see your scars. I'm not intimidated by them."

"You should be."

She was determined, he realized. She thought that her ability to see what had been done to him would change things. She was right in that, but wrong in the outcome. The scars would horrify her. She might try to get through it, but she would be stiff and unable to respond. He should know.

Most of the women he'd spent time with had agreed that it would be best if he left on his T-shirt. Easier for both of them. But he already knew that Montana wasn't like other women.

"I want you," she said, her expression earnest. "I want to be with you. Now. Here. I want all of you."

For reasons he couldn't explain he had trouble telling her no. As if the act of refusing might hurt her and he couldn't risk that. But to show her the scars . . .

Montana wore a summer dress in some floral fabric. The top outlined her curves while the skirt was full and fell to her knees.

As he watched, she unfastened the buttons down the front, then shrugged out of her dress. Underneath she wore a lace bra and bikini panties. Both were a soft pink.

Every part of her was beautiful. Her full breasts, the curve of her hips, the slight roundness of her belly. His erection throbbed. Need nearly suffocated him. But before he could reach for her, she stepped back.

"My last serious boyfriend was also a doctor. I was in Los Angeles, thinking I needed to see something beyond Fool's Gold. While he wasn't a plastic surgeon, he was very into perfection. One night, after we'd made love, he put his hands on my body and showed me everything that was wrong."

She raised her chin as she faced him, but he heard the hurt in her voice.

"He said he could 'fix' my breasts," she began. "That there were laser treatments to get rid of my freckles. He said I would be really pretty, if I lost 15 pounds on top of all that. The best part was that he seemed to think he was helping me in some way. . . . I know it's not the same, but it's not unusual to be judged by your appearance."

Her eyes were overly bright, as if she were holding back tears.

"He was an asshole," Simon growled, beyond furious. The need to lash out, to find the man who had tried to break Montana's spirit burned as hot as his passion. She was everything a man could want. What kind of low-life bastard did that to anyone, let alone a woman like her?

"You intimidated him in some way," he continued. "He didn't think he was enough so he had to make you less."

She smiled, but her lips trembled. "I didn't intimidate him, believe me. He wanted perfection and I could never be perfect. Worse, I wasn't that interested in being perfect. Perfect is boring. At least that's what I tell myself. Most of the time, I even believe it."

He moved toward her and cupped her face in his hands. "You are so beautiful that sometimes it hurts just to look at you. Your eyes are a thousand shades of brown and gold with hints of blue and green." He touched her cheekbones with his thumbs. "Your freckles are like the girl-next-door fantasy brought to life. Your mouth is sexy and soft and when you smile, the world seems like a better place. Swear you'll never change anything. Swear it."

More tears filled her eyes. "Wow. That was really good. I wish you'd been there back then. I was pretty heartbroken. I'm better now. I figured out he was a jerk and not for me, and I came home.

"I can't begin to know what it was like for you," she continued. "But please, Simon. I want to make love with you. With all of you. Not just some parts of you."

His desire disappeared as if it were a fire suddenly crushed by snow. Giving in to the inevitable, he nodded once and stepped back.

He worked quickly, knowing there was no point in drawing out the moment. He pulled his shirt free of his jeans and unbuttoned it. After shrugging out of it, he tossed it onto a chair in the corner of the room. Then he grabbed the bottom of his plain white T-shirt.

"Whatever you're imagining," he said flatly, "it's worse."

She nodded once. There were no visible signs of her bracing herself, but he suspected that she did so. That the voice in her head warned her not to show any emotion.

He ripped off the shirt and stood there, exposed. He bunched up the fabric in his hand, squeezing it tight, as if by sheer will he could make this all go away.

He told himself to close his eyes, that watching would only make it worse. But he found it impossible to turn away from Montana's face.

He had to give her credit. Nothing much changed. Her mouth tightened a little — although not, he would guess, in revulsion. She looked more thoughtful, a little sad. Then she moved closer and raised her hands.

He knew what she was seeing. The burns on his face and neck weren't that bad, but those on his torso were angry, ugly scars. Burns on burns, he thought, remembering his frantic scramble from the flames and how his mother had pushed him back a second time.

Montana would see the different colors,

261

the places where red faded to an unnatural gray. What she wouldn't know and what he wouldn't tell her was that some days they still ached. That if he moved wrong, he felt pain and limitation in his range of movement. That his hands had been spared but not his psyche, and when he least expected them, the nightmares returned.

She moved her fingers slowly, lightly, feeling every part of the scars on his chest. When she leaned in closer, he had no idea what she was going to do and was startled by the feel of her mouth on the scars.

His body stiffened, locked immobile by a single brush of her lips. She kissed him again and again, then moved slowly to his back, where he felt her gentle touch and the sweet caress of her mouth.

It was a form of acceptance he'd never imagined. An instinctive desire to heal. The task was impossible but the intent was so pure, the last of his reserve, his fear, disappeared like smoke in the wind. In that moment, there was only the night and the woman he wanted with a desperation he'd never experienced before.

He continued to hold himself still, mostly to be sure, but also to give her time to complete her journey. When she faced him again, there were more tears.

"The scars are a part of you," she said simply, then wrapped her arms around his neck, raised herself on tiptoe and kissed him.

Her willingness to see him for himself was something he hadn't expected. He pulled her close and hung on, wanting her but perhaps also needing her as well.

Montana felt the surprise in Simon's kiss. He held back a little, at first, as if her reaction was unexpected. The scars were worse than she'd imagined, but she only had to look at them. He had to live with them and the memories of what had caused them.

She drew back and stared into his gorgeous eyes. "Are you thinking I'm a bad person because here you are, showing me your burns, but I'm too distracted by your body to notice? Should I be more sympathetic?"

Instead of getting mad or telling her she was an idiot, he started to laugh. A deep sound that rose from his chest and filled the room. There was relief in his laughter and something that sounded very much like sheer happiness. She found herself smiling along, then he scooped her up in his arms.

She shrieked and hung on to him.

"What are you doing?" she demanded, not at all comfortable to be in the air.

"Having my way with you."

He lowered her to the bed. He stepped back and quickly removed the rest of his clothes. In that second before he joined her, she had a quick glimpse of the rest of him. He was, as she'd guessed, the non-boring form of perfect. Long legs with well-defined muscles. A flat belly, narrow hips and an erection that made her insides get even more squishy in anticipation.

Then he was beside her, pulling her close and kissing her.

His mouth claimed hers with a passion that would have made it impossible to stay standing. She felt his need and it fueled her own. She parted her lips and he thrust his tongue inside. That dance was no less exciting for being familiar. If anything, knowing what he could do to her mouth only made her want more.

He shifted and slipped his hand beneath her, easily unfastening her bra. He removed it and tossed it over her shoulder. She probably should have heard it hit the floor, but her senses were otherwise distracted by the feel of his warm, wet mouth on her bare breasts.

She needed to find a word that was better

than *exquisite*. Some way to describe the combination of lips and tongue swirling and sucking and teasing and caressing. Deep, slow tugs sent liquid desire seeping to all parts of her body. She was already wet and swollen, beyond ready. When he moved his attention to her other breast, she squirmed wanting to feel him inside her.

She'd never been big on the intercourse thing. Sure, it was okay, but she'd never felt an overwhelming desire to be claimed in that way. It was just something you did.

This time was different. This time she wanted Simon inside her, taking her.

That was it, she realized. She wanted to be claimed. If there was some way for him to mark her, she wanted that as well. She wanted to carry the very brand of him forever.

Unable to stand it any longer, she stretched out her arm and blindly felt for her nightstand drawer. When she found the knob, she pulled it open. She'd made a recent purchase of condoms. She pushed him back and pulled off her panties. Then she urged him between her legs and reached for him.

He filled her hand, thick and hard. She tried to draw him closer but he put his hand on her breast, holding her in place.

One eyebrow rose. "What are you doing?"

She felt frantic and hungry. Desperate. "I want you inside me."

"Not yet."

He sounded more amused than irritated, which was probably good.

"I'm taking charge. Okay, I'm not very good at it, but you should just go with it. I need to practice."

"I want you to come first."

"I will." Which probably wasn't true, but he didn't need to know that. "Simon." His name came out as a plea. "Just be inside me."

"I promise we'll get to that. But I have a few fantasies of my own I need fulfilled."

She dropped her hand. "About me?"

"You are the only one I fantasize about. Sometimes when I'm walking in the hospital I imagine doing things to you."

Her body went limp and she didn't even know the details. "What kind of things?"

"Do you want to know the legal ones? Or the illegal ones?"

Her breath caught. "Both."

"That's a lot to show you."

He rolled onto his side so they were next to each other on the bed. He propped his head on one hand and moved the other between her still open thighs.

"Sometimes I think about doing this," he said, parting her sensitive folds of skin and easing his fingers into the swollen wetness. "I wonder what you'll feel like, how you'll respond. I think about exploring you."

As he spoke, he moved slowly, as if discovering every part of her. He brushed over her most sensitive spot, making her muscles tighten, then moved on to slip a finger inside her.

"I thought I knew how good it would be, but I was wrong," he murmured, still watching her. "This is better."

"Great," she managed, knowing she wouldn't be able to talk much longer. Not when he moved his fingers back to that yummy spot.

"I've thought about touching you here." He ran his fingers over and around. "What it would feel like. How you liked it. Slow?" He reduced his pace until he was barely moving. "Fast?" He sped up.

Her breath caught. "Either."

He shifted his hand so his thumb rubbed her center while he pushed a finger inside her. "I wanted to do this."

The combination of sensations was incredible. The steady pressure of his thumb circling around and around, made her draw up her knees and dig her heels into the mattress.

Her breathing was getting fast as her body responded to everything he was doing. Just as erotic was the way they looked at each other. She kept telling herself to close her eyes, to lose herself in the sensations, but she couldn't. She needed to watch him watching her.

"There's a spot inside," he said quietly, his finger pushing in deeper. "Right about here."

She groaned. It was as if he were rubbing her clitoris from the inside as well. No, that wasn't right. It was different but exquisitely delicious. She pressed down, wanting more, needing more.

"Yes," he breathed. "Just like that." He swallowed and swore softly. "Watching you like this is killing me."

She wanted to say something, but couldn't speak. Her body wasn't her own anymore — it was a vessel of pleasure, driven by Simon's touch. She was unable to do anything but feel the waves, the building pressure.

Her climax was inevitable. She could practically see it in the distance. But there was no hurry, not when the journey felt this good.

He moved a little faster, pressed a little harder. Her breathing quickened even more as her muscles began to tremble. She pulsed her hips in time with his movements and then, without warning, lost herself in her release.

The crash caught her unawares. One second she was straining for more, the next bliss surrounded her, claimed her. The waves came one after the other, going on and on and still he touched her, drawing it out, and still her gaze locked with his. She let him see this most intimate thing, wanting him to feel it, experience it with her. She rode him until the waves subsided and her breathing returned to normal.

When she was done, he withdrew slowly, then bent over and kissed her. As she wrapped her arms around him, she felt he was trembling as well.

"Simon?"

Without answering, he shifted so he was between her legs. He grabbed the condom box without being asked and quickly put one on. Then he was slowly pushing inside her.

He filled her even more than she'd thought he would. As her body stretched to accommodate him, she wrapped her legs around his hips and put her hands on his back.

He stilled.

She didn't understand at first, then realized she was touching his scars.

"This is where I remind you that you find me irresistible."

He stared at her.

"Simon, you saw my soul."

She could see the battle raging inside him. Would he trust her enough? Then he pressed his mouth against hers before pushing in her deeply.

She ran her hands up and down his back, urging him on, even as he thrust inside her over and over again. She lost herself in the way his muscles tightened, the way his pupils dilated. She could feel him getting closer, could see it in his face. The combination aroused her and she found herself traveling down that path again.

Deeper and deeper. Faster and faster. Rushing toward the inevitable.

The contractions began again, starting deeper this time. Deep inside, pulsing outward. She could barely breathe, but forced herself to keep her eyes open, to let him see what he had done to her again. He pushed in one last time, impossibly deep. Their bodies trembled in unison. She gasped, he groaned. And then they were still.

■ ■ ■ ■

After, with Simon, was easy. If Montana had thought about it she might have assumed it would be awkward. Instead they slid under the covers as if they'd made love in this bed a thousand times before. They wrapped their arms around each other, still needing to be close.

He touched her hair, stroking the length of it, brushing it back from her face. His expression was relaxed in a way she'd never seen before. He looked almost boyish. Unguarded. She was aware that they were lying such that his facial scars were pressed into the pillow, but that was okay with her. She understood that his need to keep them hidden wasn't even conscious anymore. It was simply something he did.

"Thank you," he said.

She smiled. "Given what you did to my body, that should be my line."

He didn't smile in return. If anything, he looked more serious. "I can't stay."

"After sex or in general?"

"When my time is up, I'll be leaving Fool's Gold."

Oh, that. "Yes, Peru. I know. Not the most

romantic postcoital declaration I've ever heard."

"Montana, I'm not playing a game. You need to understand. . . ."

"That you'll leave." She rolled onto her back. "It would be good for you to stay."

"I can't."

"You won't."

"I won't."

She turned her head to look at him. "Because there are people who need you?"

"Yes."

"They could come to you here."

"Not all of them."

"You can't heal all of them."

"I can try."

"That's a lot of pressure."

"Yes, but that doesn't matter. You don't know what it's like. There are places where people die because they don't have access to clean water. I do what I can. It's my job."

It was more than his job, but he already knew that. Telling him that saving the world wouldn't save *him* was dramatic, and true, but also wouldn't help. He used his job as a way to heal, not just others, but himself as well.

"It's not a gift if you have to keep paying for it," she whispered.

"I know."

272

He kissed her then, probably because he wanted to shut her up. She didn't complain. Whatever the outcome, being in Simon's arms right now was the best place in the world.

Simon made his way back to the hotel late Saturday morning. He needed to go into the hospital to check on a few patients and clear his head. Then he would return to Montana's house.

He reluctantly went to shower. The scent of her lingered on his skin. As the hot water hit his muscles, he told himself he would see her later. He would lose himself in her again and for those few hours he could forget about everything.

After he'd dried off, he dressed and was about to leave when someone knocked on his door. He opened it and found Montana's mother standing in the hotel hallway.

"Bobby down at the front desk said you'd come up a little while ago," she said with a smile.

"Ah, yes. I was out this morning."

He rarely felt guilty about the women in his life, but staring at Denise Hendrix, he felt as small as a sixteen-year-old caught making out in the backseat of the family car.

Remembering his manners, he stepped back. "Please, come in."

She stepped inside the hotel room and raised the cloth bag she carried. "Montana mentioned your suite came with a refrigerator and a microwave. I thought you might be getting tired of eating out all the time, so I made you a couple of casseroles. It's sort of a Fool's Gold thing."

He'd slept with her daughter and she'd brought him food? He would guess she didn't know about last night, but still. He could feel himself flushing.

"Thank you," he said, taking the bag from her. "That was very nice of you."

"One is a Mexican dish. It's a little spicy. The other is Italian — plenty of meat and pasta. It was my late husband's favorite."

Simon told himself that the fact that he was slime was something he would deal with later. Right now he only had to get through the next five or ten minutes.

She gave him the heating instructions, then waited until he'd loaded the dishes into his small refrigerator and took back her cloth bag.

"Are you enjoying yourself while you're here?" she asked.

He nearly choked. "Yes. The people around here are friendly. My patients are always a pleasure. Even the difficult ones."

"What you do is amazing."

"Sometimes. Not often enough." He thought of Kalinda and the years of surgery ahead of her. He wanted to make her journey easier, but didn't know another way.

He waited to see if Denise would ask him about Montana or perhaps warn him away. Instead she talked about the festival, the weather and suggested a few places for him to visit. Then she excused herself and left.

Simon stood in the center of the room, confused by her visit. The food was the obvious reason, but why had she done that? And then he remembered. There were people who were simply nice. The majority of children grew up in stable homes, feeling loved and cared for. What he knew, what he and the Freddies of the world had experienced, was the exception.

"It's open," Montana called when he knocked on her door, later that afternoon.

He walked in to find her carrying a tray with a bottle of wine and cut up sandwiches.

"If I'm going to have my way with you again later, you'll need to keep your strength up."

She was smiling as she spoke. Her face was bare of makeup, her hair long and loose. She'd dressed in jeans and a blue T-shirt and her feet were bare.

He stopped where he was just to look at her, to take in her radiance, to feel the life pulsing through her. Then he crossed the room, took the tray from her, put it on the coffee table and pulled her into his arms.

When they surfaced from the kiss, she continued to hang on to him. "You do have a way with greeting people. Not that I would encourage you to do that with the other women in the hospital. They would be throwing themselves at you constantly and that would make it hard to work."

"Yes, it would."

She laughed.

His cell phone rang.

He didn't want to answer it. For once, he didn't want to be called to the hospital for an emergency, didn't want to help or heal or . . . He swore and pushed the talk button.

"Bradley."

"You sound grumpy," a cheerful Alistair said.

Simon relaxed. "I'm busy. Go away."

Alistair chuckled. "Ah, yes, the ever present American overexuberance. Who is she?"

He glanced at Montana, who wasn't

bothering to pretend she wasn't listening. "Someone special."

"A girl?"

"A woman."

"Better and better," Alistair told him. "Would I like her?"

"Yes, but you can't have her. I'm hanging up now."

"Give her a kiss for me."

"Not a chance."

"A friend of yours?" Montana asked when he'd hung up.

"Yes. Alistair. I've known him for years. He's a surgeon, as well. We'll be in Peru together."

He drew her close and kissed her. "He's handsome, witty and British. You'd like him."

"I like you better."

He kissed her again, released her and reached for the wine. "Your mother came to see me earlier."

Montana froze, her eyes wide. "Why?"

"She brought me food."

"Oh. Good. She's like that. You didn't tell her, did you?"

"No."

"Not that I mind her knowing. Sort of. I don't know. The whole sex-parent-child situation confuses me. I don't want to know if she's doing it, and I suspect she feels the same way about me."

"I didn't tell your mother what we'd done." He poured red wine into two glasses, then handed her one.

"I don't usually drink wine at three in the afternoon."

"I wish I could say the same," he joked.

"Ha. I knew you were the bad boy type."

"Not until I met you. I was pretty boring and studious as a kid."

She sank onto the sofa. "I guess I need to tell you something."

She sounded worried. That should have concerned him, but this was Montana. Nothing she could say would shock him.

He sat across from her and leaned forward. "Go ahead."

"I know what happened to you. The scars, I mean. Someone told me."

He'd been expecting some sort of confession, not this. His first reaction was embarrassment. No one liked admitting they had been so unlovable as a child that their own mother had set them on fire. Only there wasn't a "them." There was him.

"I was a smart kid. Scary smart. I never fit in. Skipping a lot of grades meant I was always the youngest in the class. That didn't help either."

He leaned back on the sofa. "My mother wasn't one who enjoyed working for a living. She preferred to find a man to support her. Something that wasn't so easy with a freaky kid around. When I was eleven, her boyfriend was kind of a weasel. I don't know exactly what he did for a living, but I'm sure it was illegal."

He took a sip of the wine, more as something to do than because he wanted to taste it. "He complained that I was always staring at him, which wasn't true. When I was home I knew to keep my head down. One day they had a big fight and he walked out. On the way he said I was the main reason he was leaving. My mother was already drunk and she started screaming at me. Crying and screaming."

He kept telling the story as if it belonged to someone else, as if relating a movie premise. He didn't want to remember that this had happened to him.

"She threw a couple of things across the room. My schoolbooks, I think. I went to leave but she grabbed me by the front of my shirt and shoved me hard. She told the police that she didn't mean for me to fall in the fire, but she did. There was no screen, nothing but burning logs."

Despite his best intentions, the memories

returned. The split second of disbelief followed by searing pain. Pain that exploded, pain that was unendurable. He remembered screaming and scrambling, trying to get away, begging her to make it stop. And when he managed to crawl out, she pushed him in again.

The rest of it was a blur. It was a cold day and when he managed to get outside, still screaming, he threw himself into a snowbank. But the cold didn't help. Nothing helped. He screamed and screamed until the sirens came. He remembered men surrounding him, telling him he would be all right. Even then, he'd known they were lying.

"I was in the hospital for a long time," he continued, sparing her the worst of the details.

"Did you ever see her again?"

"No, she went to prison. She died there." He shrugged. "By then it didn't matter. I lived at the hospital. The doctors and nurses were my family. I had a lot of surgeries. For reasons I can't explain, my hands were untouched. Within the first year I realized I wanted to be a doctor. A surgeon. I wanted to help kids like me."

Montana set down her wine and crossed to him. She knelt on the floor in front of him and put her hands on his thighs. "Didn't the doctors and nurses always leave?"

"Don't make it more than it was."

He knew where she was going. That because the people he cared about left, he left as well.

She stared into his eyes, as if searching for answers. He thought about telling her he wasn't as deep as she imagined, but he doubted she would believe him. There had been plenty of people looking into his head while he'd been in the hospital. Therapists and psychiatrists. He knew the jargon, understood the theories.

"So somehow that all got twisted into the idea that if you sacrifice your personal needs, you can heal everyone?" she asked.

"You don't understand. I love what I do. This is all I want to do."

"What about belonging? What about loving and being loved?"

He put down his wine and stood. He should've seen this coming, he told himself. Montana was that kind of girl.

"Love doesn't matter. I won't say it doesn't exist, because I've seen it on occasion."

She rose to her feet and faced him. "Love is the only thing that matters."

He knew that wasn't true. He'd gone his whole life without feeling love and he was fine. It was easier to stay distant, to be an observer. Cleaner.

"Everyone wants to belong," she insisted.

"No. You want to belong. I have to leave and take care of other people."

"Want to or have to?"

"Does it matter?" he asked.

He saw the sadness in her eyes and knew she understood now. He hadn't been kidding when he'd said he was leaving. In some ways he'd never really been here at all.

"I don't want to hurt you," he said.

"Too late."

CHAPTER THIRTEEN

Visiting the Fool's Gold nursing home was usually the highlight of Montana's day. She loved bringing a vanload of happy dogs to the residents, enjoyed taking them around, watching them work their magic. By now she knew nearly every person at the facility by name, remembered who preferred a small dog to cuddle and who wanted to throw a ball for a bigger dog. She'd seen those who barely responded to their environment at all smile when nudged by a grinning service dog.

But today, as she parked and got out of Max's van, she felt as if she were moving through water. She hurt all over, but not in a physical way. She hurt on the inside.

Simon wasn't staying. Yes, he'd always said that and, yes, she'd understood the words, but this was different. This was her realizing that she was falling for a man who had no intention of sticking around even if he'd

found something here he'd never find anywhere else. Whatever she felt for him, they
would have no future. Even if he was willing to travel back and forth to Fool's Gold,
or if she was willing to travel to visit him
every now and then, that wouldn't be much
of a relationship.

Deep inside, she'd always wanted a happy
ending. True love, like her parents had. A
long, successful marriage, kids. Sure, she
wasn't perfect, but the guy didn't have to
be, either. Unfortunately, the man she was
very close to falling in love with would never
be that guy. He wasn't interested in marriage or kids or forever. He wanted to keep
moving.

Telling herself he had the right to his own
dreams wasn't helping. She couldn't seem
to be rational about the situation, which
meant she had to be extra careful when she
was around him. Protect herself. While not
seeing him at all was probably the most
intelligent course, she couldn't bring herself
to simply walk away. So, for now, she would
do her best to make sure she didn't get hurt
more than she already was.

She walked around to the back of the van
and opened the door. The dogs were all staring at her, anticipation bright in their doggie eyes, but not one of them made a run

for it. They waited until she'd snapped on their leashes, then one by one they politely jumped down. She had to help two of the smaller dogs, including Cece.

After closing the van's rear door, she started toward the nursing home. The dogs led the way, passing through the automatic door. At the main desk, she greeted the receptionist and signed in.

"Everyone is looking forward to your visit," the woman said with a laugh. "Just for the dogs' entertainment, they're going to be dancing."

"I can't wait."

She went by the nurses' station, to let them know she was here, then began the process of spreading around the dogs. Buddy and two others were given to the attendants in the main recreation room. The three medium-size dogs went to physical therapy. Cece and an equally small Yorkie named Samson would go bed to bed, visiting those who couldn't get up.

"There's my girl," the first of the bed-ridden residents called as Montana walked into the room.

"Hello, Mrs. Lee. Cece's very excited to see you."

"And I'm excited to see her."

Montana set the poodle on the bed. Cece

immediately raced up to Mrs. Lee and put her tiny paws on the woman's shoulders, then gently licked her cheek.

"I've missed you, too, sweet, sweet girl."

"There you are."

Montana turned and saw Bella Gionni, one of the salon owners in town. Mondays, when her business was closed, she volunteered at the nursing home.

"Hey, Bella. How are things?"

"Good. I've been hearing rumors about you and a certain doctor."

Bella was a forty-something woman with dark hair and gorgeous eyes. She and her sister Julia owned competing salons in town. The sisters had been feuding for more than twenty years and no one knew why. To be loyal to one was to make an enemy of the other. Most people got around the problem by alternating between them. It was generally considered a much safer policy.

"I'm showing Simon around town because Mayor Marsha asked me to," she said firmly.

"That's a good story and I would encourage you to stick to it. Maybe someone will believe you."

Montana laughed. "You're impossible."

"But in a good way, right?" She approached the bed. "Hey, Mrs. Lee, I see your favorite visitor is back."

"She is."

Bella petted the poodle, then glanced at Montana. "I have the list. Go deliver Samson to his fans."

"I will. Thanks."

Cece would spend about fifteen minutes with each of her "regular" residents. Bella would take care of delivering her where she was supposed to go, and kept track of time. Samson visited in the men's wing. Another volunteer would meet Bella there and take charge of Samson. Having the help left Montana free to make sure the bigger dogs circulated evenly in the main recreation room.

Her visits usually lasted about three hours. She knew that by the time she left, close to noon, she would be feeling much better about herself and her life. It was impossible to watch the dogs in action and not be reminded how much good there was in the world.

She made a quick stop by physical therapy to check on her charges, then walked back to the front of the facility. As she approached the recreation room, she heard the sound of music and knew the dancing had begun.

Some of the residents simply swayed in their chairs. A few sang along with the music. But what Montana liked best were the old couples who still danced.

She made sure her dogs were behaving and paying attention to each resident individually, then let her awareness return to those in the center of the room. As always, her gaze settled on the Spangles.

They'd been married seventy-one years. She knew — there'd been a cake for their anniversary last month. Despite the lines on their faces and the frailness of their bones, they were as much in love today as they had been all those years ago.

The facility had allowed them to room together, twin hospital beds pushed together. One of the nurses had told Montana that they fell asleep holding hands.

Watching them, the way they held each other, made Montana smile. This was how it was supposed to be, she thought. People could love each other until death parted them. Sometimes, at the end, love was all that was left.

Rather than being hurt or feeling rejected, she should feel sorry for Simon. He didn't believe in couples like the Spangles. He believed in being alone.

As not seeing him again didn't seem to be an option, she would simply have to remember that she wanted different things than he did. While being with him was fun and making love with him was extraordinary, at the end of the day, he wasn't anyone she could depend on. Recognizing that now would allow her to protect herself.

She hoped.

"I don't understand," Fay said, from the other side of Kalinda's bed. The girl's mother was frantic, practically wringing her hands as she stood guard, desperate to do something. Anything.

"She has a fever and it's climbing," Simon told her.

Worse, Kalinda was barely conscious.

"I know that part. I sit with her every minute of every day. What I want to know is why now? What is happening to her?"

He closed the chart. "I don't know," he admitted, leading Fay into the hallway. "There are several possible causes. She could have an infection, she could have caught a virus or her body could be reacting to the burns."

"But it's been nearly a month since the accident."

Fay Riley had no idea what her daughter had been through, he thought grimly. No matter that she'd stayed faithfully, had watched her suffer, had done her best to make things better. She couldn't understand the depth of the damage, the incredible strain the injury put on the rest of the body.

He thought about explaining. There were technical words he could use, pictures he could show. But to what end? She would still be a frightened mother, dealing with a very sick child.

"I think it's unlikely she has a virus. We'll check for infection, but I don't think it's that, either. The healing process for what Kalinda is going through is massive. If we use the example of having to climb Mount Everest, then Kalinda has barely started on the plane trip taking her to Nepal."

The woman stared at him. Her color drained as her eyes widened. "Are you saying she could still die?"

The truth was, she could die, he thought, but he wasn't going to say that. Still, Fay must have guessed. Tears filled her eyes as she covered her mouth. Then she bent slightly and gave in to the sobs.

"I can't lose her," she gasped. "Not after all this. You have to save her."

"We're keeping her comfortable, helping as best we can. It's up to her."

Fay straightened and glared at him. "She's only a little girl."

"I know."

He knew more than she gave him credit for. He'd been where Kalinda was now — suffering, close to death.

Fay continued to cry. He shifted uncomfortably, wanting to excuse himself.

"Maybe we should speak later," he began.

She nodded and turned away.

He took a few steps toward the nurses' station, then glanced back. Fay stood in front of the door to her daughter's room, her arms wrapped around herself, her body still shaking from the sobs.

He'd faced situations like this before and usually found it easier on everyone if he simply walked away. Getting involved only complicated an already difficult process. Still, he found himself walking toward her, then pulling her around to face him.

"I'm sorry," he told her.

She nodded once, then went into his arms.

He held her while she cried, knowing he had very little else to offer.

After a few minutes, the tears stopped.

"I'm sorry," she whispered, stepping back and wiping her face.

"Don't be. You're dealing with a lot." He hesitated. "I really am doing my best to save her."

"I know." She swallowed. "I should get back to her."

"I'll be by in a few hours. If anything changes, have me paged."

"I will. Thank you."

He watched her go, then started down the hallway.

Kalinda needed more surgeries. The problem was he couldn't do anything until she was stronger. The fever would leave her even more weak.

His time in town was limited. The way things were going, he would be lucky to operate on her twice before he had to go. She was facing dozens more procedures. Which meant someone else would be seeing her through the next few years.

Usually he didn't mind if other physicians finished what he'd started, but something about Kalinda made the situation different. Maybe it was because she talked about wanting to be a doctor, like him. He could tell that her injury had already had a profound effect on the way she viewed herself and her future.

"Let it go," he told himself as he checked his messages.

An hour later he was back in his office. There was no Cece to greet him. Montana had left a note saying she was taking the dog to a nursing home that day.

He found himself missing the small crate

in the corner and the wildly excited greeting whenever the dog saw him. He'd never been much of a dog person, but Cece was changing his mind.

He buried himself in paperwork, catching up on his charting and scanning a couple of journal articles. Just before lunch, he heard a knock on his door.

"Come in."

He knew better than to expect Montana, but he was still disappointed when a tall, well dressed woman entered his office.

"Dr. Bradley," she said with a smile.

"Dr. Duval."

The hospital administrator was one of those frighteningly efficient women who managed to get her point across with a single lift of her eyebrow.

"How are you enjoying your time here in Fool's Gold?" she asked, taking the chair across from his.

"Everyone has been very friendly and cooperative."

"That's the kind of town we are." She glanced toward the corner where the dog crate was kept. "I see Cece isn't with us today."

"No. Montana wanted to take her to a local nursing home."

"Interesting young woman, our Montana,"

Dr. Duval said. "It took her some time to decide what she wanted to do with her life. Working with the therapy dogs seems to be her calling. She's done some extraordinary work."

In his experience, hospital administrators focused on the logistics of running a hospital. There were a thousand details to be managed — personnel, patients, supplies. Usually those in charge were not familiar with things like therapy-dog programs and how well those running the programs were doing in their personal lives. But very little about Fool's Gold was like any place he'd ever lived before.

"I heard Kalinda is having some trouble," she continued. "Such a small child to endure such a horrible accident. If the dog helps, I'm grateful you've allowed the dog to be here."

He knew there was more to the conversation. Dr. Duval hadn't stopped by just to chat. So he leaned back in his chair and waited.

The wait wasn't long.

"As we discussed when you first came here," she began, "we're having a fundraiser in a couple of weeks. I wanted to confirm that you'll be attending."

He doubted that *confirm* was the right

word. She was here to make sure he planned on attending, and if he put up a fuss she would find some way to force him. He knew the type. Dr. Duval was the kind of woman who got things done, which made her someone he respected.

He didn't want to go to the fundraiser. Being the focus of attention in a room with two or three hundred people was his personal idea of hell. But it was one of the costs of doing business.

"I'll be there."

She looked both surprised and relieved. "I'm glad to hear that. Having you here is an incredible gift, but you don't come cheap."

He smiled. "I'm confident the cost is worth it."

"It is." She leaned toward him. "You could have charged us more. Your fee is the least of it."

"I get more than enough out of what you pay me."

What he did had made him relatively well-off. He didn't need to gouge local hospitals for sport. Most of the costs of having him came from the fact that he required the hospital to allow uninsured patients free of charge. If someone needed his help, they got it, regardless of their ability to pay.

This forced the hospitals to raise money both before and after his visit. But it meant children like Kalinda had a chance.

She rose. "I look forward to seeing you at the fundraiser. Will you be bringing anyone?"

There was Montana. While a part of him wanted to see her dressed up, wanted to spend the evening with her, maybe even dance with her, he had his doubts about this kind of event.

"I haven't decided."

Dr. Duval's gaze was steady. "Let me know either way, so we can accommodate your guest at the table."

She left.

Simon drew in a breath. What he should do for Montana was at odds with what he wanted to do for himself. He didn't usually indulge in moral dilemmas. But then he didn't usually indulge himself with women like Montana.

Denise was getting a little concerned that the people at the winery tasting room were going to start charging her rent. She supposed she should find a second place for her string of hideous first dates, but the tasting room was so convenient. They served "small bites" of food, the wine was excellent and she doubted there was a better view in a fifty-mile radius. All of which were very helpful when one was meeting strange men.

Her latest first date was with a man named Art. They'd met online, something she didn't usually do, but . . . desperate times and all that. He'd been in the "over fifty" section. No more younger men for her.

As she walked into the tasting room, she searched for a man who looked like the picture she'd seen on her computer. He'd had nice eyes and slightly graying hair that was a little curly.

"Denise? I'm Art. Nice to meet you."

It was all she could do to keep her mouth from falling open. The man standing in front of her was barely her height, nearly as wide as he was tall, with a few wisps of white hair. She saw some resemblance to the man in the picture she'd been sent, but the man in front of her was more his father than anything else. She'd been looking for a guy in his fifties. Her date had to be pushing seventy.

"Art?"

"Yep. Nice to meet you. I'm a little surprised."

He was surprised? If they had a contest about that, she was pretty sure she would be the winner.

"You look just like your picture," he told her. "That almost never happens. Lucky me."

"Yes, lucky you," she murmured.

They got a table on the patio. It was barely four in the afternoon, but an awning protected them from the sun. The server came around and they each ordered a glass of wine. Red for her, white for him. Art asked for a couple of cubes of ice in his. When the server flinched, Denise did her best not to cringe.

"So tell me about yourself," Denise said, knowing she was stuck for at least half an hour. Then she told herself she shouldn't be so quick to judge Art. He was probably a very nice man. If she gave him a chance, maybe they would hit it off.

"I'm retired," he began. "I live east of Sacramento, in a nice little mobile-home park. Got me a double-wide. But I'm thinking of moving to Florida. Love Florida. There's lots of fishing. You fish?"

"Not so much."

"You should try it. It's great fun. I've been looking at some real estate online. I can't decide between a condo or a patio home. I don't want to worry about a yard." He grinned. "At my age, you always got to be concerned about a heart attack."

The server returned with their wine and a mini quesadilla.

Art swirled his glass, clinking the ice cubes together, then took a sip. He smacked his lips together. "That's a fine wine." He looked over the quesadilla. "I'm really not supposed to have a lot of cheese," he said, then grinned. "What the hey. You only live once, right?"

He picked up the whole quesadilla and swallowed it in two bites. Then he looked at Denise. "Did you want some of that?"

"I guess not."

Art seemed unfazed by her response. "We can order another one."

"That's okay. I'm not hungry."

They spent the next ten or fifteen minutes discussing the ins and outs of retirement financial planning. Art was very proud of his 401(k). He also told her in great detail what she should look for when she had to pick a Medicare supplement.

"I'm a few years from Medicare," she said faintly.

"It's never too early to start getting prepared."

"I suppose."

So far she hadn't touched her wine. As a rule, she didn't like to have a glass without having something to eat, but she wasn't going to order more food. That would not only be awkward, it would mean she would have to stay longer.

She checked her watch. It had only been twenty minutes. Was there something wrong with the earth's rotation? It felt like an hour had passed. She sighed.

"What else do you like to do?" she asked. So far they had only talked about Art, but she was okay with that. It wasn't as if they were going to have a relationship.

He set down his glass and leaned toward her. If she didn't know better, she would swear he was leering at her.

"I still enjoy those bedroom games," he said with a wink. "I wouldn't mind doing a round or two of the escaped prisoner and the warden's wife, if you're interested."

Denise opened her mouth, then closed it. She felt herself blushing and hoped no one had heard him.

She stood. "I don't think so. It was very nice to meet you, Art, but it's time for me to go."

He grabbed her hand. "You've been widowed ten years now. You've got to be hurting. I'm willing to help, offer what I can." He wiggled his eyebrows suggestively.

She didn't know whether to laugh or scream. Frankly, the best idea seemed to be throwing his ice cubes with white wine in his lap. But that would cause a scene and she wasn't that kind of woman. More's the pity.

"Goodbye," she said firmly, as she put her handbag over her shoulder.

She turned and marched purposefully toward the exit. The stone path was a little uneven and as she rounded the corner she nearly lost her balance. Before she began to fall, she felt someone take hold of her arm and steady her. For one horrifying moment, she thought that Art had followed her. That he was the kind of man who didn't understand the word no.

She straightened and looked at the man who had rescued her.

Frying pan, meet fire, she thought, staring into a familiar pair of dark blue eyes.

She might not have seen Max Thurman in nearly forty years, having spent the past year avoiding running into him, but she sure recognized him. He had the same broad shoulders, the same muscled build. And, dammit all to hell, the man still looked like a god in jeans.

"Denise?"

Max stared at her. She thought he looked more pleased than surprised, but she wasn't sure. Just as unsettling, her stomach went all fluttery, and she felt nervous, as she had when she'd first met him. She'd been seventeen and he'd been twenty. A man, while she'd still been on that cusp between girl and woman. The night of her eighteenth birthday he'd helped her cross over.

He grinned. "It *is* you. I've been hoping we would run —"

Into each other? Not likely. She'd done her best to make sure that never happened. She'd wanted to avoid any moment like this one.

"I have to go," she said desperately, interrupting him.

She couldn't talk to him now, not like this. Not after all this time. What if he saw Art and thought they were together? What if he said she looked old or . . .

Her mind was close to exploding with hideous scenarios. So much for the years adding serenity and grace.

Then she did the only thing she could think of. She ran.

Simon stood in front of Montana's door. He'd done his best to avoid her and instead had found himself missing everything about her. Being intelligent didn't seem to play into his decision-making process. The need to see her overwhelmed everything else.

He raised his hand to knock, then heard a strange sound from inside. It was almost a cry, but one he couldn't place. Was he interrupting something?

The thought of her with another man enraged him and he pounded his fist against the door. Who could she be with?

He waited while she called, "Just a minute." Then the door opened.

Montana stood in front of him, wearing shorts, a cropped T-shirt and little else. Desire joined fury as he pushed past her and entered her living room.

"Where is he?"

He glanced around, expecting to see wine and candles. Instead the drapes were open, along with the windows. There was no evidence of a romantic evening. Where he thought he would find a man, he saw three black-and-white puppies fighting over a sock. One of them yipped, replicating the sound he'd heard before.

He turned back to her and saw she held another puppy in her arms.

"Where is who?" she asked, tilting her head as she stared at him.

"I . . . No one." Feeling stupid, he shoved his hands into his jeans pockets. "Hi."

"Hi, yourself. Is everything okay?"

He nodded. "Should I have called first?"

"Probably, but it's okay that you didn't."

"You have puppies."

"Four of them. Both their parents are great service dogs, and part of a breeding program. I'm keeping the puppies with me at night for a couple of weeks to help assess them. Max has them during the day."

"He's giving you the rough duty."

"I'm the junior staff member. It's part of my job."

He tried to figure out what she was thinking. Feeling. When he'd last seen her, they'd argued. No, that wasn't the right word. Whatever it had been, they hadn't been getting along. Although he'd planned to spend the night with her, he'd ended up leaving.

"Are you all right?" he asked.

"Yes. Are you?"

Very few people asked him that. He was the one in charge — the one who made the decisions, changed the lives.

"I thought you were mad at me," he said.

"I was never mad."

She set down the puppy. It raced off to join the others fighting with the sock. Sounds of their happy yips and growls provided surprisingly pleasant background noise.

"I missed you," he admitted.

"So you decided I was seeing someone else?"

"Not until I got here and heard strange sounds."

"You don't date much, do you?" she asked.

"I don't date at all."

"I know there are women. You're too hunky for them to ignore you. So what do you do with them?"

Hunky? No one had every described him that way. The thought was distracting. He was a freak. A monster. How could she see him so differently?

"I sometimes meet women. But it's usually . . . light."

She raised her eyebrows. "Let me guess. Dinner and small talk followed by mutually satisfying sex."

"Something like that."

She stared at him.

"Fine," he ground out. "Exactly that."

"Then, you leave them."

"Then I leave."

"Are you ever sorry? Do you ever miss these interchangeable women?"

"No."

"Are you going to miss me?"

Now it was his turn to stare, to take in her wide eyes, her long blond hair, the shape of her mouth. He would know her taste or scent anywhere. There could be a thousand women in a dark room and he would have no trouble finding her.

He crossed the room and kissed her, doing his best to memorize her touch. She leaned into him, her arms wrapping around him, holding him close.

Her body tempted him and he used his hands to rediscover her curves. It was only an incessant tugging on the bottom of his jeans that caused him to draw back.

He glanced down and saw one of the puppies chewing on the fabric.

"Who are you?" he asked, bending over and scooping up the dog.

The puppy was more white than black, with a happy face and floppy ears. He relaxed as Simon rolled him onto his back and held him against his chest.

"That's Palmer," Montana told him. "There are three boys and one girl. Palmer, Jester, Bentley and Daphne."

"Palmer, huh? That's a big name to live up to." He held the dog in the air as he spoke. Palmer swiped his tongue across Simon's chin.

"You're a natural," she said.

He chuckled. "So, what's the drill?"

"I do my best to tire them out, then we

306

have a potty break before bed. About two in the morning I get them all up for another potty break, then we sleep until about five-thirty."

"Grueling."

"They're worth the trouble."

"Want some company?"

"You mean you want to stay here tonight?" she asked.

"Yes."

"I'm not sure."

Her answer burned down to his soul. He felt as if she'd hit him with the side of a car. "I see."

"No, you don't. You didn't answer the question."

It took him a second to remember, then he took her hand in his and kissed her palm.

"I'm sorry. I thought I had." He looked at her. "I will miss you, Montana. For the first time in my life, I'll regret leaving someone behind."

She squeezed his fingers, then pulled her hand free.

"Okay, then. We're going to play fetch. With nine-week-old puppies, it's kind of an imperfect version, but it's lots of fun."

She walked over to the entertainment center in the corner and took four small balls off the top shelf. When she pushed them, they made a sharp, squeaking sound. All four puppies slid to a halt and turned to face her. Their ears were raised, their tails wagging in anticipation.

"Ready?" she asked, grinning.

The puppies were already running down the hall.

She threw all four balls at once. Barks exploded as the small dogs scrambled for a ball. Montana laughed and raced after them. Simon watched her and the puppies and knew that regret didn't come close to what he would feel when it was time to leave.

CHAPTER FOURTEEN

"One more," Simon said, then pulled out the last stitch. He examined the boy's face under the strong light, then nodded. "You're good."

Kent moved closer and studied his son's cheek. "I can't believe how fast he's healing."

"The advantage of being a healthy kid," Simon said. He put his hand on Reese's shoulder. "Change the bandage the same way you have been. Give it another week, then you're done. I'm leaving you in charge."

The boy grinned at him. "Sweet." He turned to his dad. "Did you hear that?"

"I sure did."

Reese scrambled off the table. "Can I go see Kalinda? I told her I was coming in today to get my stitches out, and she said I should go see her."

While the girl's fever was down, she wasn't

a hundred percent. Not by a long shot. Still, the company might help.

"You'll have to wear a gown and mask," Simon told him. "She can't risk getting sick."

"Sure! Will you come get me when you're ready to leave?" Reese asked his father.

Kent nodded. "I'll stop in and see one of the guys I know who works in the office. Then I'll come get you."

Reese ran off.

"He's a good kid," Simon said.

"Yes, he is. I got lucky with him." They walked out of the examining room together. "How are you liking your time here in town?"

"Tell me you're not part of the conspiracy," Simon said.

"The one to get you to stay?" Kent shook his head. "I was just making conversation. But, given what I know about this town, I'm not surprised you're getting a little pressure."

"I'm flattered by the attention."

They paused in the hallway. It was nearly lunchtime and the area was quiet.

"I have a question," Kent said. "Feel free to tell me to mind my own business."

Simon braced himself. Kent was Montana's older brother. Of course he would be worried about family. "Ask away."

"Why do you keep your scars? When Reese was hurt, I did some research online. Doctors have figured out a lot of ways to treat scars. I would guess you know about all of them."

It wasn't the question Simon had been expecting, nor did most people have the courage to ask it, although he knew they wondered.

"I keep them for my patients. I want them to know it's okay to look different. I want them to believe they can still be happy, even if they have scars or some other kind of disfigurement."

He also kept them as a reminder, but he wasn't going to tell Kent that.

"That makes sense," the other man told him. "I hope the question wasn't too personal."

"Hard to hide these."

"Thanks again for everything."

"You're welcome."

Kent walked toward the elevator. Simon took the stairs up a couple of floors and came out by the burn ward. He walked to Kalinda's room and stopped when he heard the sound of laughter. From where he was standing he could see Reese walking like a zombie, his arms raised, his legs stiff. Both kids were giggling.

She wasn't getting better fast enough. He knew that and didn't know how to change things. The fever bothered him. It drained her and made it harder for her to heal. It meant her body was still adjusting, that there was still danger.

Uncertainty was part of the job, but he'd never accepted it. He always searched for answers, solutions that made sense. But sometimes they weren't there. By now Kalinda should be progressing better. She should be safe and it didn't sit well with him that she wasn't.

"I thought doctors took off work to golf," Montana said, sitting across from Simon in Margaritaville, one of the restaurants in town.

When he'd phoned her to ask if she wanted to have lunch, she'd suggested this place.

"You're more interesting than golf," he told her.

She laughed. "Is that even a compliment?"

"It is if you like golf."

"Do you?"

He shrugged. "It's okay."

She laughed again. "Are you teasing me? Does the stern doctor board know? If they find out, you won't be asked to speak at their conference."

"I can live with the disappointment."

"And here I wanted to see your picture in the newsletter."

Their server appeared and quickly made guacamole tableside. Montana watched intently, giving herself over to the moment.

She did that a lot, he realized. So many parts of her life were fun. She must go from highlight to highlight. It would never be his style, but he could learn from her.

When the guacamole was finished and placed between them, she leaned forward. "You are going to love this. Seriously, it's amazing. Everyone goes on and on about the margaritas they serve here, but I think they're missing the point."

She offered him the chips, then waited while he sampled the dip.

"Well?"

"Very nice."

She rolled her eyes. "You need to work on your superlatives. Nice is a clean toothbrush. This is life changing."

She scooped up some with a chip and popped it in her mouth. "Mmm. Perfection."

He wanted to tease that she should get out more, but didn't. Nothing about Montana needed changing.

"How are the puppies?"

"Growing. If you look at them long enough, you can see it happening. Oh, and last night there were no accidents."

He'd learned in his lone overnight stay at her house that getting the puppies up at two in the morning for a potty break didn't mean they weren't going to pee on the floor.

"Progress."

"I know. Now I'm waiting for them to get through the night. The 2:00 a.m. thing is getting really old. How are things at the hospital?"

"Good."

He was tired, Montana thought, watching him as he told her about a difficult surgery. Working too hard. But that was probably always the case. He did as much work as he could in the short time he was around. Not that she was going to think about him leaving. Better to enjoy him while he was here.

"Montana! So nice to see you and your young man out in town."

Montana looked up and winced. "Hello, Gladys."

Gladys had been a fixture in Fool's Gold for a lot longer than Montana had been alive. She was a good-hearted sort of person but often spoke her mind, and in a scary

314

kind of way. She was the sort of person who made everyone around her cringe and then couldn't see what she had said that was the least bit awkward.

She patted Montana on the shoulder and leaned down to speak in her ear. "Too bad about his face, but I bet the rest of him is working just fine."

Montana didn't know whether to scream, hide under the table or run for the mountains just outside of town. She hoped that Simon hadn't heard the comment, but when she glanced at him one eyebrow was raised.

"Sorry," she mouthed silently, then turned to Gladys. "You make me crazy, you know that, right?"

An unrepentant Gladys grinned. "Then my work here is complete."

She straightened, waved at Simon and walked away. Montana covered her face with her hands.

"This is when I think I should've stayed in L.A. I never ran into anyone I knew there. Maybe it was better." She dropped her hands to her lap and looked at him. "How mad are you?"

"I'm a little offended that you didn't defend my honor."

She frowned. "What are you talking about?"

"You didn't tell her how great I am in bed."

"Is that what you wanted? I'm sure I'll be invited back to the city council in the next week or so. I can put it on the agenda."

He picked up his glass of iced tea. "I would appreciate that."

"If I really did that, you wouldn't know what to say."

"I'm not so sure." His gray-green eyes sparkled with humor. "The first few weeks I was here, everyone was very polite. Now I'm getting not-so-subtle hints that I should live in Fool's Gold permanently. Oh, and yesterday, some old lady in a tracksuit told me I should make an honest woman of you."

Montana winced. "My guess is you ran into Eddie and, yes, that does sound like her. Sorry."

"Don't be. This is a good place. I like it here."

"I have a PowerPoint presentation illustrating all the reasons you should consider relocating here." She kept her tone light and made sure she was smiling as she spoke. She wanted him to think she was kidding, and she was, sort of.

"Color graphs?"

"What is a PowerPoint presentation without color graphs?" She reached for another chip. "Doesn't this happen everywhere you go? Don't they always want you to stay?"

"Mostly."

"Does that surprise you? You're a very gifted surgeon. Having you around would mean a lot to any community. And you're good-looking."

His expression tightened. She did a mental rewind, trying to figure out what she'd said wrong. Nothing came to her.

"What?" she demanded. "You have scrunchy face."

"What the hell is scrunchy face?"

"When your face gets all scrunchy. Like you're mad. What did I say?"

"You talk about my face as if it's normal."

He was choosing his words carefully. She could tell from the cadence of his speech and how he paused between the words. But why?

"Yes, I said you were . . ."

She got it then — what she'd said. Not knowing if it was good or bad, she admitted the truth.

She leaned toward him and lowered her voice. "Simon, I don't see the scars. I haven't for a long time."

Something flashed in his eyes. She would have given a lot to know what he was thinking, but he'd always been incredibly good at keeping his thoughts from her.

"How can you not?"

She shrugged. "You're just you. That's who I see." They were getting into dangerous territory. "If we're going to have this conversation, I think it's about time you returned my never ending compliment. I mean, hello, I'm the girl here."

She spoke confidently, which was a complete crock, but he didn't have to know that.

One corner of his mouth turned out. "You're right. We don't talk about you enough." He stared into her eyes with an intensity that made her squirm. "Have I told you how beautiful you are today?"

She tilted her head. "Are you asking me if you said it today, or are you asking me if you've told me I look beautiful today? They *are* very different."

He surprised her by leaning back in his chair and laughing. The sound was loud and came from his belly and made her feel good all over.

When he straightened, he looked more relaxed. Younger. "You are very beautiful all the time and I don't think I've told you that yet today. While we're on the subject, I am lucky to be with you. You're extraordinary, Montana."

She felt herself blushing. "I was just playing."

"I was telling the truth."

She felt awkward and flustered, and didn't know what to do with her hands. Fortunately their server arrived with their meals.

By the time the food had been placed and their drinks refilled, the topic of conversation had been forgotten. Or at least not brought up again.

"Reese came by to visit Kalinda," he said.

"I'm glad he's still doing that. How did it go?"

"I think it helped to have the distraction of company."

Montana wanted to ask how the girl was healing but knew Simon wouldn't discuss that with her. The last few times she'd been there with Cece, one of the nurses had been in the room. She'd only been able to drop off the dog and then excuse herself. Next time she would try to speak with Fay.

"I know you think I'm counting the minutes until I leave," he said, "but that's not true. Kalinda is an example of a patient I will regret leaving behind. She needs so many surgeries."

"The implication being another doctor won't get it right?"

"That makes me sound arrogant."

"You kind of are."

He gave her a reluctant smile.

She was such a liar, she thought sadly. Pretending this was about Kalinda, when in truth his words had made her want to ask if he'd meant it when he'd said he would miss her. If he would have regrets about ending their relationship. When he left, would he remember her at all?

"Enjoying your lunch?" Mayor Marsha asked as she walked up to their table.

"Yes," Montana said. "How are you?"

"Very well." The mayor turned to Simon. "I see you're enjoying yourself in our lovely town."

"Yes, I am."

Marsha laughed. "Don't worry. I'm not going to start on all the reasons why you should stay. But I was pleased to hear you're coming to the hospital fundraiser." She glanced back at Montana. "I can't wait to see what you'll be wearing, my dear. Remember, it's cocktail-dressy, rather than formal." She smiled at them both. "You'll be a very handsome couple. Have a nice lunch."

"Thank you," Montana murmured, staring intently at her plate.

Fundraiser? Now that she thought about it, she remembered seeing posters about it around town. It was to raise money to support the work Simon was doing. Obviously it was something Simon had to attend — he would probably be the guest of honor. Usually people brought a date to an event like that. The mayor had assumed Simon's date would be Montana.

But he hadn't asked her.

Simon wasn't the kind of man who forgot things. Even when he was busy, he knew exactly what was going on around him. Which meant he hadn't planned on asking her.

She wasn't sure why. Whether it was the public nature of the evening, or him not wanting to lead her on about their relationship. All of which was logical. She supposed she should be able to understand and accept.

But the truth was a voice was screaming in her head. A voice that demanded he explain how she could be good enough to sleep with, but not good enough to take to a stupid fundraiser.

"I didn't ask you because . . ." His voice trailed off.

She raised her head and looked at him. He seemed more uncomfortable than embarrassed. And then she got it.

For all her claims that she *knew* he was

leaving, that all this was temporary, she'd assumed what they had together was still some kind of relationship. That they were together. A couple.

That wasn't the way it was for Simon. She was a convenience, someone he wanted and maybe liked a little, but no one significant. She'd been worried about whether or not he would miss her when he left. That was the least of it. What she should be more worried about was whether or not he gave a damn about being with her while he was here.

Her chest tightened and her throat began to close. She recognized the symptoms and knew she didn't have much time.

She looked up and gave him what she hoped was a startled expression. "Oh, no. I just realized I'm supposed to be meeting Max. I can't believe it. I need to hurry or I'll be late."

She fumbled in her purse and threw a twenty on the table. "Sorry."

"Montana." He rose when she did.

She waved him back in place. "No. Please. Eat your lunch. This is my fault. I'm so scattered."

She offered a frantic little wave, then dashed out of the restaurant.

Terrified he would follow her and demand

to talk, she ducked into the closest store, then out the back, so she was standing alone in the alley. It was only then that she allowed herself to begin to cry.

"I know it's not much," Nevada was saying as she paced back and forth in Montana's living room, a puppy in each arm, dodging the other two as she walked. "But I swear it was a *moment.*"

Montana was still dealing with her luncheon revelation, so she was having a little trouble following Nevada's story.

"You saw Mom at the tasting room place outside of town, and she ran off when she saw Max? Are you sure those two events are linked? Maybe she was late for something or the date had been really bad."

"I thought of that." Nevada sank into the chair opposite the sofa. "But there was that second when they saw each other. Mom went completely white. I was afraid she would pass out or something. And Max froze. I'm telling you, he's *the* Max. Your Max is her Max."

Her mother and Max Thurman? "No. I can't believe that. I've worked for Max for a year and she's never said a word about him. It's not like I don't talk about my job or my boss."

"Hasn't Max lived here before?"

"Sure, but not for years. He left before we were born."

Nevada gave her a "See!" look.

"You're inventing drama where it doesn't exist," Montana told her.

"I don't think so. Look at the facts. Mom has the name Max tattooed on her hip. We don't know much about him, except he used to live in the area, but not in town. He left before Mom and Dad got married. Max Thurman moves back to Fool's Gold after being gone over thirty years. He's mysterious."

"He's not mysterious," Montana said, interrupting. "He's a nice guy."

"Where does he get his money? Doesn't he finance all the work the therapy dogs do?"

"We get some donations, but yes, Max pays for most of it. So, he's rich."

"From what? Did he inherit? Rob a bank? Make great investments?"

"We don't talk about that."

"But he did live here before. Seriously, Montana, how many guys around Mom's age who once lived in town are named Max? I'm telling you, he's the one."

"I'm not sure I want him to be," she admitted. "It's weird to think at one time she loved a man enough to get his name tattooed on her body and then she met Dad."

Bentley scrambled into her lap. She patted him absently.

"But you said Max was nice," Nevada pressed.

"He is. I like him a lot. I wouldn't mind if he and Mom got together. I just hate thinking she loved someone else. You know, before."

"Because Dad should be her one true love?"

"Yes."

"Why would knowing who Max is change that?"

"Maybe it doesn't." Her mother was allowed to have a past. Everyone did. "You know what — if they're the same Max, then this could be really interesting, right?"

Nevada sighed. "Sorry. Why didn't I see it before?"

"What are you talking about?"

"You. There's something wrong. Is it Simon? Did something happen?"

"No. Nothing happened. That's the problem."

"I thought you'd slept together."

She rolled her eyes. "Sex doesn't solve problems, it starts them."

"Which means something happened."

"I knew he was leaving. I've known from the beginning. Despite Mayor Marsha's request that I convince him to stay, we all know that's not going to happen." She cuddled a sleepy Bentley. "But I was okay with that. I haven't been attracted to someone in a while. I liked being with him and how I felt around him. So the leaving part was simply something I had to deal with."

"What changed?"

Montana looked at her sister. "I thought he cared about me, too. I thought I was important to him. It turns out I was just a convenience. A way to get laid."

"Are you sure?"

"That big fundraiser for the hospital? He's the guest of honor or something like that. He didn't ask me."

Nevada didn't look as shocked as Montana would have liked.

"And you're sure that's about you?" her sister asked.

"Who else could it be about?"

"Him. From everything you've said, Simon isn't interested in being the center of attention. So why would he bring you to an event like that, where everyone will notice? Maybe this is more about protecting you than avoiding you."

"You can't know that," Montana snapped, annoyed Nevada wasn't taking her side.

"You can't be sure you're right, either. Not until you ask." Her sister drew in a breath. "You tend to blame yourself when things go wrong."

"This time I'm blaming Simon."

"I don't think so. Your description of the relationship is all about how you assumed things and you were wrong. What if you're not wrong? What if instead of being a jerk, he's trying to be nice? It's not wrong to want to be with someone. It's not wrong to think the regular rules of love, or like, or whatever apply."

"I hate it when you're rational," Montana grumbled, even as she thought maybe Nevada was right.

"I'm just saying talk to him. Find out why he didn't invite you to go with him. If he says it's because he doesn't care about you or wouldn't be caught dead with you in public, then kick him in the balls and leave."

"He's been seen in public with me before."

"Ask."

"Fine."

Nevada rubbed the puppies she held. "You know you're falling in love with him, right? That's the real problem."

Words Montana really, really didn't want

to hear. "I'm not in love with him yet."

Her identical-triplet sister shook her head. "Yes, Montana. You are."

CHAPTER FIFTEEN

"This is stupid," Daniel told Montana as he stood with his hands on his hips, glaring at her. "I don't want to be here. I want to be out with my friends."

Montana put down the book she'd been holding and glared right back.

"Wow. Talk about a news flash, because it's the same thing you said last week and the week before that and the week before that. If you're really sick of it, why do you keep showing up? What's the point? Why don't you forget it? After all, it's just reading. You don't need to go to high school and maybe play football. You could drop out and get a job. Oh, wait. You need to read to get a job."

She reached down to pet Buddy, who'd come over to check on her.

"I'm tired of people not trying and then complaining when things are too hard. I'm tired of people not making an effort. Did it ever occur to you that Buddy here would rather be outside playing with his friends? But he's not. He's here to help. Because that's just the kind of dog he is. And I'm here, too. Do you appreciate that? Do you thank us? Of course not. Because it's hard. You know what? Sometimes life is hard. You have to learn to shoot a basketball in the hoop before you can be any good at the sport. At first you don't get it through the basket very often, or even at all. But one day you do and then it gets easier. But only because you put in the work."

She grabbed the book again. "Here's the thing, Daniel. I'm not giving up and Buddy's not giving up and there's no way you're giving up, either."

By the time she wound down, the kid was wide-eyed and looking a little nervous. But he didn't bolt or call for help, which she took as a good sign.

She sighed. "I'm sorry. I know I'm ranting. It's just, reading is so important. That's why we have this program. A friend of mine was burned really bad when he was about your age. He spent nearly five years in a hospital after that, working hard to get better. Now he's a brilliant doctor and he saves people. My nephew was in a car accident and his face got cut up. That doctor was able to help him. But what if he'd given up? What if he'd decided it was all just too hard?"

"I'm not going to be a doctor," Daniel mumbled.

"How do you know?"

He stared at her for a long time. "You're really serious about this."

"Yes, I am. Are you?"

"I guess I am now."

He took the book from her and walked over to the beanbag chair. Buddy followed and settled next to him.

Montana slipped out of the room, but stayed within earshot.

Things were pretty bad when she was going off on children, she thought with a sigh. All of a sudden her life seemed complicated and she wasn't sure how to fix that. She needed a plan or a massage or maybe just a cupcake.

Leaning against the wall, she listened to Daniel's slow reading. As always, he sounded out each word. The pace was painful and had to be discouraging him, she thought. Maybe she should talk to someone about helping him in a different way. Maybe the dog thing wasn't working.

"There . . . are . . . fif . . . fif . . . teen . . . shoes . . . un . . . under —" Daniel stopped for a second. "There are fifteen shoes under the bed."

He read clearly and without hesitating.

Montana straightened but told herself not to get too excited. He might have accidentally memorized the sentence. But even as she tried to be calm, she knew that reading happened like that. One minute there was a collection of individual sounds, the next the sounds became words.

"Fifteen shoes for fifteen boys," he continued. "Mr. Smith knew everyone would be happy when he told him about the shoes."

Montana stared at the open door, wondering if she was hearing this right.

Daniel kept on reading. Excitement filled his voice as he continued through the book. Then there was a slam and he came running out of the room.

"I can read!" he yelled. "I'm reading this book. Listen."

With that, he opened it from the beginning and started the story over. He read through without hesitating, Buddy standing anxiously at his side, as if not sure this was a good or bad development.

Montana grinned. "You did it!"

"It's like you said about shooting baskets. At first I couldn't do it at all, but now it's easier." He ran down the hall to the cartful of books to be put back on the shelves. He shuffled through them and pulled out a story about a lonely bunny.

"Lonely bunny was all alone," he read, standing in the middle of the hallway. "All lonely bunny wanted was a friend. But when he hopped down to the pond, the ducks there wouldn't talk to him. They turned their backs on him and walked into the water, leaving him behind."

Daniel looked up, his eyes glowing. "I can read."

Montana grinned. "You sure can. You've been practicing and getting better, but you couldn't see it until now."

The boy crossed to her and wrapped his arms around her waist. "Thanks for yelling at me. It really helped."

"I'll remember that for next time."

He laughed and released her, then hurried back to the cart. "Help me find more books, please. I want to take them home and practice. I can read to our cat, right? He'll just fall asleep, but that's okay. Then I can surprise my mom."

Before Montana could get to him, he ran off, yelling for Mrs. Elder, announcing to all who could listen that he could read.

Montana crouched down in front of Buddy and rubbed his face.

"You did good," she told the worried dog. "You're a good boy. This is why we do it, right? To help a child learn to read, or to make someone in a nursing home smile. You make a difference in people's lives and so do I. Butthead men may come and go but we will always have the work we do."

Buddy regarded her with his solemn stare, then licked her nose.

"Thanks," she told him. "I love you, too."

"If you can't do the job correctly, then get assigned to another department," Simon said with a growl.

The nurse, obviously fresh out of college, flushed. "Dr. Bradley, I —"

"Have an excuse? I'm sure you do. This is a burn ward. There's no room for excuses. Mr. Carver had his arm burned by a blowtorch. Until you know what that is like, until you've lived through that kind of pain, you're not allowed to offer excuses. Get off this floor and don't come back. Do I make myself clear?"

The nurse burst into tears and ran away.

He saw the other nurses watching him, then quietly returning to their work. No doubt he would have to endure all kinds of scurrying and whimpering for the next few days. It always happened when he kicked someone out of his department. But dammit, was it too much to expect people to get their jobs right?

He walked toward his office, aware of people ducking into rooms to avoid him. In this corner of the world, he was a god, and a vengeful one. He was required to give his all and expected the same from those around him. Maybe they hadn't made the identical deal with the devil, but when they were working with him, they were required to act like it.

He walked into his office and closed the door. As he crossed to his desk he admitted to himself that one of the problems was Montana. He missed her. No, it wasn't just that he missed her. He'd hurt her.

That damned fundraiser. He didn't want to go and he didn't want to take her. Not that he wouldn't enjoy spending the evening with her, but those kinds of events were so uncomfortable, so awkward. He'd never considered subjecting her to that. But she wouldn't see it that way. She would come up with some other explanation, because his was too twisted for someone like her to imagine.

He didn't allow himself a lot of regrets. There was no point. He always regretted losing a patient, even if there was nothing he could have done. But he didn't regret the choices he made, how he lived, that he was alone. All that was part of the bargain he had accepted years ago. But hurting Montana? He shook his head. That he regretted.

Someone knocked on his door. Before Simon could answer, it opened, and Reese Hendrix stuck his head inside.

"Hey, Dr. B," he said with a grin. "I'm here to see Kalinda. My grandmother brought me and she said I should ask you first. So is it okay?"

"I'm sure she would be happy to see you." He motioned for the boy to step into the room, then studied him in the overhead light. "Whoever your doctor was, he did great work."

Reese laughed. "You know you were the doctor."

Simon patted him on the shoulder. "Come on," he said. "I'll go with you. Cece, Kalinda's service dog, has been up there for a while. I'll take her outside for a walk while you two keep each other company."

Fay was just coming out of her daughter's room as they approached. For once she didn't look close to tears. "Hello, Reese. Dr. Bradley, I think she's doing better. Kalinda wants some ice cream from the cafeteria. I'm going to get it for her. Do you want me get you something, Reese?"

"No, thanks," he said, ducking around her and entering the room.

"Ice cream is good, isn't it?" Fay asked. "She hasn't been hungry in a while."

"Hunger tells us the body is healing."

"Her fever is down, too. I'm so relieved." She smiled and patted him on the arm. "We're getting through this, thanks to you. I don't know what we would have done without you."

They would have had someone else, he thought, wondering if that doctor would have cared as much, done as much. In his head he knew whoever had taken care of her would have been just as dedicated, but in his gut, he was less sure. For him, there were no distractions. Only his patients.

At least that's how it had always been until Montana.

Pushing her from his mind, he entered the hospital room. Reese had already set up the computer game and Kalinda had raised her bed so she could sit up.

"Hey, guys," he said.

"Dr. B, we're going to play," Kalinda told him. "Can we take care of whatever you want later?"

"I'm here to give Cece a bathroom break."

He turned to the little dog, who was already standing. Cece gazed at him adoringly, her brown poodle eyes bright with affection. As he reached for her, she angled toward him, butt first, in what Montana had explained was her "You can pick me up" position.

He reached under her chest and supported her rear as he lifted. She gave a little push against the bed, as if offering help.

"You weigh six pounds, kid," he muttered. "I don't need the help."

Kalinda giggled. "She does that. She's very polite."

Polite or not, what he felt was her quivering excitement as she squirmed to get closer and bathe his face in dog kisses. Her tail thudded against his chest in a frantic, happy rhythm.

Reese glanced up. "She really likes you."

"So I've been told. I'll be back shortly."

"Okay."

Neither kid was paying attention to him anymore, which was how it should be.

He made a quick stop in his office to put Cece into her harness and leash, then carried her outside. He walked to an unused bit of lawn and set her down. She immediately began sniffing around, then peed.

Although he could probably take her back

inside, he thought she might like to stretch her legs a little. Montana had brought her by relatively early that morning.

"Are you up to walking around the complex?" he asked.

Cece stared at him, her head tilted as if she were trying to understand. Her tail wagged.

They started down the sidewalk. His plan was to walk the perimeter, including the parking lots and garages. It would probably be close to a mile.

During his early-morning workouts he was careful to watch the news. Current events served as a distraction. But now, with the little dog prancing at his side, there was nothing to keep him from his thoughts.

Despite Fay's excitement over her daughter's improvement, he was cautious. She could still take a turn for the worse and there was nothing he could do to prevent it. This was not anything he would share with the emotionally fragile mother. Kalinda might truly be recovering and everything would be fine. Statistically that was the case, although his experience made him wary.

Cece stopped by a tree and sniffed intently. She squatted, peed a couple of drops, then looked at him with an expression that could only be described as satisfied.

"Telling them you were here?" he asked her.

She wagged her tail, then began walking again.

The late-morning air was warm, promising a hot afternoon. Summer in Fool's Gold was beautiful with plenty of blue skies, and the mountains looming to the east were green.

They continued on their walk, Cece prancing beside him. His thoughts drifted to Montana.

There was no way to avoid what had happened between them. No way to gloss over the fact that he'd hurt her. He'd been stupid to think she wouldn't notice the fundraiser. Given how much time they were spending together, of course she expected him to ask her.

He hadn't meant to hurt her. He'd never had to worry much about a woman's feelings before, he realized. The brief, temporary connections he usually made excluded emotions on both sides. There was mild interest, some conversation and sexual release. Little more.

Montana was different. He finally understood what it meant when people said someone had gotten under their skin. It was more than a cliché — it was a sensation. An ache, a need, an inability to forget or ignore.

He kept seeing her wounded expression, the pain in her eyes. Remembering that made him feel guilty, because he made it a point not to get close enough to wound anyone. He didn't get involved for a reason. Some of it was because he was always moving on, and some of it was because he didn't want to feel guilty.

He supposed the logical solution was to simply end things with her. To walk away, complete his time and leave. Simple. Clean. Honest.

But every time he thought about doing that, everything within him rebelled. How could he not spend time with her? Not only because she haunted him, but because of what she'd said while they were having lunch. She no longer saw his scars.

No one had ever done that before. People got used to them, considered them a part of him, but no one had been able to transcend them.

He'd always known she was special, but that simple statement had made him see she was more than that. More than he deserved. And to hurt her without reason, to cause her even a second's worth of pain would be to violate some of the newfound good in his life.

"Complications," he muttered.

Cece looked up at him and wagged her tail.

They made their way back to the side entrance, where they'd come down. As they approached the stairs, Cece stopped and assumed the "You can pick me up" position, then gave a little jump as he reached for her.

"You're a smart little girl," he said, holding her close.

She gave him a quick lick on the chin, then snuggled against his chest, her paws tucked against his arm, as if it would never occur to her that she would be dropped.

"Such trust."

He took Cece to Kalinda's room, thinking he would remove her harness there. As he walked toward the half-open door, he heard soft crying.

"Don't," Reese pleaded. "Don't cry."

"I don't want to be like this."

"They're just burns."

Simon stopped, still out of sight but able to hear.

"They're horrible and they hurt and I'm ugly. I'll be ugly forever." The cries got louder and harder. "No one will ever like me. No boy will ask me out. I'll never get married."

Simon couldn't begin to imagine how uncomfortable Reese must feel. He was just about to walk into the room to see if he could help when the boy spoke.

"You're not ugly and you'll have lots of friends. Tell you what. If nobody asks you to marry him and you still want to get married, I'll do it. We can get married."

"You mean that?"

"Sure. Pinkie promise."

There was a shuffling sound.

Simon stepped in and saw Kalinda smiling through her tears.

As easily as that, he thought. Because she was just like Cece. She believed and trusted that no one would deliberately hurt her.

He found himself wanting to make sure that trust wasn't broken. That she would grow up the way Montana had — safe in a world that took care of her.

Montana sat on the lawn at Max's. The dogs and the new puppies were busy with a complicated game of play that involved jumping over Montana. Or in the case of the puppies, scrambling.

She lay on the warm grass, staring up at the sky, trying to figure out her life. In the past few weeks, a lot of things had disrupted her simple plans.

Max came out of the house and started toward her.

She sat up and studied her boss, taking in his long, easy stride and rugged good looks. He must have been irresistible when he was younger, she thought. Tall and lean and probably more than a little dangerous. Had he really swept her mother off her feet? And if he had, why had Denise chosen to stay in Fool's Gold and marry Ralph Hendrix?

Not that she was sorry. If her mother had made different choices, none of her children would have been born.

Montana still hadn't found a way to bring up the issue of her mother. Somehow starting a conversation with her boss by saying, "So, my mom has 'Max' tattooed on her hip. Is that you?" didn't seem to be the shortest road to employee of the month. There was also the not-so-insignificant detail of not being sure she wanted to know any more details.

Max stepped into the fenced enclosure. All the dogs ran toward him, begging for attention. The puppies scrambled after, not sure what the excitement was about, but wanting to be in the middle of it.

Max crouched down and petted as many as he could reach. "You have a delivery."

"A package? I didn't order anything."

"It's not a package, it's flowers. Based on the size of them, he must have really screwed up."

Flowers? She felt herself getting all gooey inside, which was dumb. Yes, the flowers were probably from Simon. He was the only man in her life. But as she had recently learned, theirs was a one-way relationship. While sending flowers was a lovely gesture, it didn't change reality.

She scrambled to her feet. "What are you talking about? What does size have to do with it?"

Her boss laughed. "Honey, if we're talking about a guy, size always matters. The bigger the screw up, the bigger the arrangement. Based on the size of these, I would guess he seriously injured a family member."

"Of course he didn't," she said, even as she went through the gate and carefully closed it behind her. She hurried toward the house, which also doubled as Max's office.

She let herself in the back door. The flowers were in the kitchen. The display was as big as Max had indicated. The vase was at least eighteen inches high with a spray of exotic blossoms reaching toward the ceiling.

She recognized a couple of different kinds of orchids, but after that got completely lost.

Her mother would probably know what everything was. The flowers were bright and fresh, with a delicate fragrance that drew her closer. When she spotted the card, she reached for it.

She hesitated before opening the envelope, telling herself there was nothing he could say that would change anything. But she opened it anyway and read the note.

"I'm not very good at this. I'm sorry."

She frowned at the card, not sure what he meant. He was sorry he wasn't very good at whatever he was talking about. Or maybe he was saying, "I'm not very good at this and I'm sorry, but it's over."

"I would have thought the flowers would've made you happy," Max said.

She held out the card. "You're a guy, tell me what this means."

"I don't have my reading glasses. Tell me what it says and I'll tell you what it means."

She read the short message. "And?"

"I haven't a clue. What did you two fight about?"

"We didn't fight. It wasn't like that. I just . . ." She sighed. "I know he's leaving. I know this is temporary. I made the mistake of thinking that while he was here, we had an actual relationship. He doesn't think that."

"How do you know?"

She told him about the fundraiser and how it had been apparent that Simon had no intention of asking her to accompany him.

"Events like that are exactly what couples go to together. It's a date thing. If he cared about me at all, he would've asked me. I'm an idiot."

"You're a lot of things, Montana, but idiot isn't one of them. From what you've told me about this guy, I'd say he has it bad. If he didn't care about you, why would he apologize? Maybe not asking you to the fundraiser is about him."

Which was sort of what Nevada had said, she thought, getting irritated at the people around her.

"Why are you taking his side?"

Max walked over to her and put his arm around her, then he kissed the top of her head. "We have officially exceeded my ability to give advice on your love life. I'm not taking his side. I'm suggesting that before you assume he's a jerk, find out why he didn't ask you."

Her boss walked out of the kitchen, leaving her alone with a huge arrangement of flowers and a small, cryptic card. Neither of which offered any answers.

■ ■ ■ ■

Montana was forced to put the vase of flowers on the floor of her backseat. Even then the very tips of the stems brushed against the ceiling. The flowers dominated her tiny dining alcove as the scent drifted through her small house.

She couldn't seem to eat much at dinner and spent a restless hour trying to rearrange her closet. A foolish attempt when her mind was elsewhere, wrestling with the problem of Simon.

At seven-thirty, she heard a knock on the door.

She didn't have to answer it to know who was there. As she approached the door, she still wasn't sure what she was going to say or how she was going to act.

Simon stood on her porch, dark circles under his eyes. He looked tired. No, that wasn't right, he looked weary. She found herself wanting to pull him inside and hold him, as if she could somehow pass her strength on to him and heal him.

"I hate events like this," he began. "They all do it, hold a fundraiser, and I'm the guest of honor. Everyone wants to talk to me. But I'm not the kind of guy who has funny stories appropriate for a cocktail party, and it's not the kind of place where it's appropriate for me to discuss the details of my work. I didn't ask you, because I hate going, not because I wanted to hurt you."

She stepped back to let him in. He moved past her into the living room, then turned to face her.

"I don't do this," he continued. "I don't get involved. But I've never wanted anyone as much as I want you. It started out as chemistry, pure sexual attraction. I don't even know what to call it. But it's different now. It's bigger and I can't control it and I can't not be with you."

She stared at him, trying to take in all that he had said. For a powerful man who changed lives with the magic of his hands, he looked surprisingly vulnerable. Exposed. As if she could see all of him and he knew and he worried.

With every romantic relationship she'd ever had, she'd worried about not being enough. Had been told she wasn't enough, time after time. Here was Simon — wonderful and kind and everything a woman could want — and he worried about the same thing. Not being enough. How was she supposed to keep from loving him?

She crossed to him and put her hands on

the lapel of his jacket, before pushing it off his shoulders. Catching it as it fell, she draped the garment on the back of her sofa.

He grabbed her arms. "Say something."

"Thank you for the flowers."

She raised herself on tiptoe to kiss him. He bent his head and pressed his mouth to hers.

At the first touch, at the first whisper of his breath, she felt herself relax. She would think about his words later, let them heal her, but for now, all she needed was him.

He reached for her, then drew back.

"Don't you want to talk about what happened?" he asked.

"No."

She didn't need to. Not anymore.

He drew her to him again, this time holding on as if he would never let go. His mouth claimed hers in a deep kiss that stirred her very soul. His hands were everywhere — up and down her back, along her arms, cupping her face. She felt his arousal, but more important, she felt his need and responded in kind.

She touched him, fumbling with the buttons of his shirt. Underneath was a T-shirt and she groaned in impatience as she pushed it up so she could touch bare skin. He undid the zipper at the back of her dress, unfastened her bra with a flick of his fingers, then cupped her breasts.

Heat engulfed them. The wanting grew until it was more powerful than the need to breathe. She was already wet and desperate, her legs shaking.

"Take me," she whispered against his mouth, her fingers tugging at his belt.

He froze, his body stiff, his eyes locked on hers.

"Take me," she said again, rubbing her hand against his erection.

For a second, he did nothing. Then he grabbed her hand and pulled her into the bedroom. He jerked open the nightstand drawer so hard, it crashed to the floor. Everything in it went flying, but he found the box of condoms in seconds.

While he opened the box, she pulled off her thong and slid onto the bed. He kicked off his shoes, unfastened his slacks, shoved them down, then joined her.

"Montana, I should —"

"No."

She reached between them, guiding him to her. The tip of him brushed against her opening and she pulsed forward, pushing up as he slid inside.

He filled her spectacularly, stretching, rubbing, exciting. She wrapped her legs around his hips, drawing him in more. His mouth settled on hers, his tongue teasing her to a new level of arousal while his erection did the same to the rest of her body.

Deeper and deeper, faster and faster. She lost herself in the desperate race to her release. She touched him everywhere she could reach, clung to him, pumping her hips as her muscles tightened. He filled her over and over again. With every thrust, her tension rose.

He drew back a little so he could stare into her eyes. She looked back, knowing he saw the pleasure on her face as she saw it on his.

Still watching her, he straightened a little more. Continuing to thrust in and out, he reached a hand between them and rubbed her swollen center. One circle, two, and on the third, she lost herself in her climax, the waves rippling through her, making her shudder and cry out and hang on.

The pleasure went on for what felt like forever, then he gasped and went still, his muscles jerking as he gave himself to her.

Later, when they were both naked and in her bed rather than on it, he stroked her face.

"I don't understand you," he said. "You're not still mad."

"That's true."

"But it's not the flowers."

"No. It's what you said." Nevada and Max had been right. Simon's actions had been about him, not her. He hadn't been making a statement, he'd been trying to protect her.

"I don't understand."

She grinned. "You don't have to."

"I guess not." He brushed his fingers across her lips. "It occurs to me that you might not have the same feelings about the fundraiser as I do."

"That's true."

"So you might like to go with me."

"I might."

"Will you?"

She would, she realized, go with him anywhere. But that wasn't the question he'd asked and this wasn't the time to tell him that.

"I would be delighted to come with you. I'll do my best to protect you from the worst of it."

"Even you are not that good."

She laughed. "We'll see."

CHAPTER SIXTEEN

"Explain that to me," Max said as he walked Cupcake, one of the newer service dog candidates, on the sidewalk by the park.

Montana looked where he pointed and saw several of the Fool's Gold cheerleaders practicing.

"What's to explain? I know you watch football. You've seen cheerleaders before."

"There's a lot of them."

"We encourage participation here in town. You should see them at Christmas."

Max glanced at her. "Christmas?"

"They do holiday cheers as a fundraiser so they can go to cheerleader camp in the summer. You hire them to go cheer at someone's house. They appear at business events, as well. The tourists love them."

"Fool's Gold has gotten weirder in the past few years."

"It's wonderful. Don't be such a cynic."

They walked next to each other, each with

a service dog. Buddy walked next to Montana. This time his primary function was to show Cupcake how it was done. Along with her unfortunate name, Cupcake had a bit of Border collie in her. She was one of the smartest dogs they had, but a bit prone to getting into trouble. Max wasn't sure if she would make it through the program.

"You're happier today," he said. "Win the fight?"

"There wasn't a fight and there wasn't a win. You were right — he didn't ask me to the fundraiser for reasons that had nothing to do with me. He was being nice. In a weird, twisted guy way."

"Gotta take the good with the bad. But you still won."

She groaned. "No. If you want to win, then someone inevitably loses. That's not the way to have a good relationship. Both parties have to feel good at the end of the day, or what's the point?"

"Very wise, little grasshopper."

She laughed. "Not yet, but I'm getting there."

For once the streets were quiet. Hardly any tourists and only a few residents were out. They'd passed the cheerleaders, and stillness filled the air.

"Max, did you used to know my mom?"

He kept his attention on Cupcake. "Why do you ask?"

"She has the name Max tattooed on her hip and I wondered if that was you."

He was quiet for a long time, then came to a stop and faced her. "You should ask your mother."

She felt her mouth drop open. "That means yes."

Montana knew what Nevada had told her, what her sister believed, but she'd dismissed the possibility. There was no way her mother had ever dated Max Thurman. But it looked like Montana was wrong.

"You guys went out. You were involved! What happened? Why did you leave town? Was it because of my dad? Were you there first or was he?"

Her mind swirled with possibilities. "Were you in love with her?"

"Kid, I'm not answering any of your questions. Like I said, if you want to know more, ask your mother. It's her business."

"And yours?"

He raised his eyebrows as if asking her if she really thought he was that stupid, then continued walking Cupcake. Montana moved with him.

"You're not going to say anything else?" she asked.

"On that topic? No."

"So I should change the subject?"

"That would be my suggestion."

Montana sprawled in a chair in Dakota's living room while Hannah played on a quilt on the floor. Nevada and Kent were digging chips into salsa. Dakota sat on the sofa, her feet propped up.

"Ethan said we're making too much out of nothing," Nevada announced after she'd chewed and swallowed. "Sometimes he's really a pain in the —" She glanced at Hannah. "A-s-s," she spelled, then rolled her eyes. "I think he's too happy with Liz and all their kids. It's making him sanctimonious."

"I know," Montana said. "He was all about us leaving this alone. I can't. It's too weird."

"Mom didn't just fall to earth, fully formed, the day she married Dad," Dakota said reasonably, then she leaned her head against the back of the sofa. "Who am I kidding? I'm totally freaked by this. I don't want her to have had a life before Dad. It's not right. I always knew about the tattoo, but tried to tell myself it was a very strange birthmark."

Kent sat on the floor with Hannah and

pulled the baby onto his lap. "I remember years ago, when I was Reese's age, seeing one of my teachers on a date, at the movies. It was the strangest thing. Until then, I'd never thought about teachers having lives outside of school. I guess I thought they were shut down and put in a box until it was time for class."

"This is bigger than seeing a teacher eating buttered popcorn," Nevada told them. "This is Mom and Max Thurman. The tattoo is a big deal. Back when she was what, nineteen or twenty, nice girls didn't get tattoos. It's not like it is now. So there was something going on between them."

Montana had a feeling that something was a lot of hot monkey sex. "Whatever it is, it ended and she married Dad. Isn't that what's important?"

"Why did it end?" Dakota asked.

Montana completely understood the significance of the question. It was one thing if their mother had met Ralph, fallen madly in love, then dumped Max. The story had a very different flavor if Max had been the one to end things, or if somehow he had stolen her away from their dad. But that wasn't right, because she'd married Ralph and not Max.

"We could ask her," Nevada said tentatively.

"*You* could ask her," Montana said. She drew in a breath. "I'm trying to tell myself I'm making too big a deal out of this. So she had a boyfriend." Except she couldn't reconcile the word *boyfriend* with the reality of her middle-aged mother with a tattoo.

"You don't suppose . . ." Dakota's voice trailed off.

They all looked at her.

"What?" Nevada demanded, then shook her head. "No. No way. I don't accept that."

"Accept what?" Kent asked.

Montana was about to ask the same question, when she realized where Dakota's mind had gone.

If Max had come first, was it possible their mother had been pregnant when she married Ralph? Pregnant with Max's baby?

"I don't believe that," Montana said.

"Believe what?" Kent demanded. "I hate it when you guys do this."

"What if Mom was pregnant with Max's baby when she married Dad?" Montana asked. "That would make Ethan our half brother."

"You three are crazy." Kent continued to play with Hannah. The baby grinned happily as she bounced on his lap. "Ethan is

359

not our half brother. Have you seen him? He looks exactly like Dad. Whatever was going on with Max, it has nothing to do with the six of us. You're searching for trouble where it doesn't exist."

The sisters looked at each other. "He has a point," Dakota said. "It's just Max is kind of dangerous and sexy, even now. Imagine what he was like thirty-five years ago."

"Do I have to?" Kent asked.

"She's right." Nevada shifted in her seat. "Max is the kind of guy who sweeps a woman off her feet. They have to have been together first. I can't believe Mom was dating Dad, left him for Max, got a tattoo and then went back with Dad."

"We have to figure out what happened between them," Dakota said.

"Not necessarily. We don't consider Dad a sexy guy, but we weren't dating him," Montana pointed out. "They were always crazy about each other. Maybe it was love at first sight. Maybe Dad came between Max and Mom."

"One of you should talk to her," Kent said.

Nevada raised her eyebrows. "One of us? Why one of us? Why not you? Or is this a girl thing?"

"It's exactly a girl thing. The only thing Mom and I talk about is how much she hates Lorraine." He sighed. "Okay, that's not fair, but I can see it's on her mind. I am not asking our mother about her love life when she was a teenager."

"Coward," Dakota said with a grin. "You men are so emotionally delicate."

"I'll do it," Montana said. "I haven't been to see her in a while. I'll talk to her about Simon and then ease the conversation into past loves and Max."

"Do you really think she'll be fooled? Nevada asked.

"No, but I can pretend she will be. I'll ask and report back."

Simon found himself at a large table at the Fox and Hound, surrounded by women. Some were younger, like Charity Golden, the town's city planner. Others were well past the age of consent, as one of his favorite nurses used to say. Women able to get a senior discount without showing ID. Mayor Marsha fell into that category, as did several other city council members and a rather stern-looking seventyish woman in a bright yellow tracksuit. Her name was Eddie something and she was the one who had told him he needed to make an honest woman of Montana.

So far the conversation had been pleasant.

The women had chatted about various things happening around town. He'd been brought up to date on Pia's twins, Dakota Hendrix's pregnancy, the upcoming groundbreaking for a new casino resort north of town, and the fact that the Castle Ranch had finally been purchased by a family who seemed as if they were going to stay.

On the ranch front, someone had said something about a woman named Heidi who raised goats and lived with her grandfather, but he figured they had to be making that up.

Lunch had been ordered and delivered, food mostly eaten and still no one mentioned the actual reason for the meeting. That they were going to do their best to convince him to stay.

He was used to the pressure. It happened everywhere he went. He'd had village chieftains offer him everything from chickens to virgin daughters. In more westernized areas, the enticements included money, positions on boards, stock options and the occasional daughter, with no promise of virginity made.

Their server came and cleared the plates. Simon glanced toward the door and wondered if he could simply make a run for it. Glancing at the women seated around him, he doubted he could make it to the door before them. Senior citizens or not, they were determined.

"I'm sure you've guessed why we asked you to join us for lunch," Mayor Marsha said.

"I have an idea."

"You've brought so much to this community," she continued. "Your work is extraordinary, but it's more than that. You have a dedication to your patients that touches us all. You care and we respect that."

Care? He saw himself as brilliant, gifted and, at times, a complete tyrant. But caring? Had they met him?

"One of the things that makes Fool's Gold a unique community is that we are so much more than a group of people who happen to live in the same place. We have an emotional bond that makes us more like a family. Many of us can trace our roots back several generations."

"The Hendrixes are one of our founding families," Eddie said helpfully. "You like Montana, right?"

One of the other women shushed her.

"What?" Eddie demanded. "We've all seen it. Are we going to pretend we don't know they're having sex?"

Charity winced, then turned to him. "Sorry. Eddie is . . . er, unique."

"Don't talk about me like I'm not here."

Simon held up a hand. "It's fine. I get her point." At least Montana wasn't here to witness all this, he thought, not sure if she would laugh or be embarrassed. Probably both.

"As I was saying," Marsha continued, shaking her head slightly, "you bring a lot to the hospital and we think we have a lot to give in return. Which leads me to my question. What is your dream offer?"

"Excuse me?"

"Tell me what it would take to get you to stay. We're building a new hospital. You could help with the design — create your dream facility."

He wasn't used to that, he realized. All the other places had simply thrown things at him, hoping to convince him with volume. No community had ever thought to ask what he wanted.

He looked at their hopeful faces and knew they would try to fulfill any request. If he wanted to run the hospital board, they would make it happen. It he wanted a fifty-foot picture of himself on the mountain, it would appear.

If only it were that simple.

"What I want," he said slowly, "is for people to be more careful around fire, because this one life is all we get. What I want is for parents to stop hurting their kids." He drew in a breath. "That's not what you meant."

Marsha smiled gently. "No, that's not what we meant."

What did he want? He knew there was no answer to the question because staying wasn't an option. Selling him on the town wasn't necessary — he already liked it here. If he could stay . . .

"I appreciate the offer," he told them. "Fool's Gold is great. I've enjoyed my time here. My decision to leave isn't about the town. It's about me."

"How can we change that?" the mayor asked.

"You can't."

"I appreciate that you stopped by," Montana said, "but you look weird lying on the grass in a suit."

Simon kissed her palm. "I took off my jacket."

"Well, then, that makes it okay."

After his lunch with the mayor and her friends, he'd come by the kennel to see Montana. She had been outside with the puppies, enjoying the warm afternoon. He'd joined them, stretching out on the grass, letting the puppies crawl all over him.

He glanced at his watch.

"How long do you have?" she asked.

"An hour."

She bent over and kissed him. "Slacker."

He laughed. "Occasionally."

"So, tell me about this lunch you had with all those sexy women."

He stared up at her beautiful face. "Not that I don't admire Mayor Marsha, but the woman is in her seventies."

"We should all look so good at her age."

He sat up and studied Montana. He traced her cheekbones, the line of her jaw. "Speaking as a professional, you have nothing to worry about. You'll always be beautiful."

He watched color stain her cheeks as she looked down. "Simon, don't."

"What? Tell you what I know will happen?"

"I'm not that special."

"You are to me."

Daphne wiggled between them and started licking him.

"Your other girlfriend wants your attention."

He picked up a delighted Daphne and cradled her in his arms. "You're shameless."

Daphne gave him a doggie grin and closed

her eyes as he rubbed her belly.

"The lunch?" Montana prompted.

"They want me to stay in town."

"Did that surprise you?"

"I knew it was coming. They asked me to tell them what I wanted, rather than simply offering one thing after another. To be honest, I'm surprised it took them this long to get around to making their pitch. Usually I get it from the beginning, either directly or indirectly. Sometimes one person will be sent in to convince me, sometimes it's a committee. Either way —"

He stopped talking as Montana went white, then pressed her lips together.

"What?" he asked.

Guilt flashed through her eyes. "Oh, God. I forgot. No, it's not that I forgot, it's just . . ." She squeezed her eyes together, then opened them. "You're going to take this wrong. I know you are. Don't be mad, okay? Just let me explain."

He had no idea what she was talking about. "All right."

"It's me. They sent me. Right after you got here, Mayor Marsha asked me to get to know you and find a way to convince you to stay in town. I was supposed to be that person. And we've been together and now you're thinking I lied to you, but I didn't.

Most of the time I forgot. I mean, I had a couple of conversations with people about where to take you and stuff and . . ." She swallowed. "You hate me now, don't you?"

He carefully put Daphne down on the grass, leaned toward Montana and kissed her.

"I don't hate you."

"I don't understand. You should be furious. I betrayed you."

He chuckled. "Hardly." He cupped her cheek. "Don't take this wrong, but you didn't do a very good job. We rarely talked about the town."

"I know. Like I said, I forgot."

"You'd be a lousy spy."

She sighed. "I wouldn't want to be a good one. All that lying."

She kissed him back, her mouth soft and hungry against his.

When they parted, he asked, "Did the mayor ask you to sleep with me?"

Montana stared at him. "Of course not. She would never do that."

He held in a laugh. "Just checking."

"Simon! How could you even think that?"

"I didn't. I was curious as to how far the good people of Fool's Gold would go." He stretched out on the grass again. "I've been offered virgins before, after all. And a cow."

"I know someone who has goats if you want to check into those."

"No, thanks."

"Okay, but it's your loss. I think they're French goats. Very sophisticated."

"Well, if they're French . . ."

She tilted her head. "You're not going to suggest the sister thing as a way to entice you?"

"What sister thing?"

"Guys get this idea that because we're identical it would be really cool to have all of us in bed at once. We think it's icky, but trust me, we've had more than one request."

He sat up. "No. You're the only one I'm interested in."

"Really?"

"You're completely different from your sisters." He took her hand. "Not to hurt anyone's feelings, but you're much prettier and more fun to be with."

She laughed. "Thank you, but I think you're biased."

He knew he wasn't, but she wouldn't believe him. "Your names are interesting. A family tradition?"

"No. A quirk of fate. Mom had some trouble during delivery. For a while there was a question as to whether or not she would make it. There was my dad with three newborns in the hospital and three young boys at home. My brothers missed their mother and resented their yet unseen sisters for taking her away. To help smooth things over, my dad said they could pick out our names."

She grinned. "Over the years, we've heard some of the alternatives. Oceania was tossed around, apparently, so we figure we got lucky. At least people can spell the states."

"Multiple births are hard on the mother."

"Is this the doctor speaking?"

"Sorry. I get carried away."

"It's okay. I like that about you."

"When's your birthday?"

"We're Christmas babies. So Dad was dealing with the possibility of losing his wife and the mother of his children on Christmas Day."

"Poor guy."

Palmer and Jester raced toward her. She caught them both in her arms and kissed their heads.

"How are my best boys?" she asked, her voice full of affection. "You, too, Bentley. You're one of my best boys."

As if Bentley spoke English and would be hurt if he were left out.

Simon had never met anyone like Montana and doubted he ever would. While

Fool's Gold had gotten to him more than any other place he'd lived, what he would miss the most was Montana. Her laugh, her smile, the way she led with her heart.

Come with me.

The words formed in his mind and he almost spoke them. Because for the first time in his life, he was willing to consider the possibility of something more than a temporary relationship.

Then he looked around at the kennel and the grounds, at the other service dogs, lying in the sun. He thought about her family and her home.

This was where she belonged. Besides, to ask her to leave would imply a promise on his part. A promise he could never make.

If she were different . . . he began to imagine, then realized the foolishness of that line of thought. If she were different, he wouldn't want her.

CHAPTER SEVENTEEN

"Mom, I want to ask you something," Montana said as she sat in her mother's kitchen, a glass of iced tea in front of her.

"Of course. What is it?"

Her mother set a plate of chocolate chip cookies on the table.

They were fresh and the scent of chocolate reminded Montana of all the times she and her sisters had made cookies in this kitchen. Denise had set up three stations, so each of them could measure and stir, then carefully place the raw cookie dough on the cookie sheet.

"You did a good job with all of us," she said impulsively.

Her mother laughed and sat across from her. "Thank you for that endorsement."

"It can't have been easy, raising six kids. Plus, Josh came to live with us."

"After the first couple, it's not that much harder. I had a lot of help from your father and not one of you was especially difficult."

"Still."

Montana wanted a family, but she'd never thought of having six kids. Talk about overwhelming.

"How are things going with you?" her mother asked.

Montana told her about the puppies and the fundraiser she would be going to with Simon. "Work is busy," she said. "All my standing appointments. The library reading program is working out really well. Max has brought in some new dogs for training."

She watched her mother as she spoke, but Denise didn't respond to the name. Obviously, being subtle wasn't going to work.

"Mom, I want to talk about my boss."

"Sure, honey. Is there a problem?"

"Not a problem. Just . . ." She shook her head. "Is Max Thurman the same Max you used to date? Is he the guy from your tattoo?"

Her mother rose and crossed to the sink. "What an odd question. Why do you ask?"

"Because I work for him. If you two have a past, I don't want to say something I shouldn't."

"How could you possibly do that?"

"You're not answering the question."

"I'm not sure I'm going to." Denise turned

to face her. "Yes, I had a life before I met your father. But that was a long time ago. I married your father and I loved him with all my heart. He was a wonderful father and an amazing husband. I would give anything to have him back."

Her mother sounded emotional and maybe even angry.

"I'm not questioning your commitment to Dad."

"I should hope not. I've been a widow over ten years. I'm just barely starting to date, even though I don't like it." Her gaze narrowed. "Have you girls been talking about this?"

"A little. We're just wondering what happened."

"Nothing that concerns any of you. I won't discuss this and I don't want you three talking about it, either."

"Mom, why are you mad?"

"I'm not mad. I'm pointing out I don't need my adult children butting into my private life."

Montana felt as if she'd been slapped. "All right," she murmured, standing. "We won't discuss it again. I'm sorry."

She grabbed her purse and ran to her car.

■ ■ ■ ■

Simon reached for his cell phone. "Bradley."

"It's Erica. How are things in Fool's Gold?"

"Good."

Erica worked for the company that coordinated his assignments. As his time in Fool's Gold would soon be ending, it made sense she was calling.

He glanced at the calendar on the wall. The months had gone by quickly.

"I have dozens of requests, as per usual," she said. "After Peru, I think the two that look the best are either helping out at a clinic in Appalachia or joining a humanitarian aid group in Pakistan. I suppose it depends on where you want to spend those months. Both teams would be delighted to have you. Should I email the information?"

He felt a light scratching on his leg and glanced down. Cece gazed at him adoringly, obviously wanting to be in his lap. He scooped her up.

"Sure. Send the files and I'll look them over. I can travel to either place."

"If you're going to Pakistan, you'll need a couple more booster vaccines. One of the thrills of international travel."

He petted the little dog as she stared at him. Love burned in her little brown eyes. When he shifted his hand so he was scratching her chest, she licked his wrist.

"Send me that information, as well," he told her.

Erica agreed she would and they hung up.

Montana tapped on his partially open door, then entered. "Hi. I was waiting in the hall. I didn't want to interrupt your call."

"You wouldn't have."

She stopped in front of his desk. "I'm here to take Cece for a walk."

The little dog had been spending most of her days at the hospital. When she couldn't be in Kalinda's room during a treatment or for meals, Fay dropped her off in his office.

"What's wrong?" he asked, taking in the troubled expression.

"I had a fight with my mom. Except it wasn't exactly a fight. I don't know. I asked her about Max."

"Your boss?"

She told him about the tattoo on her mom's hip, how she'd had it for years, probably since before she'd gotten married.

"We never knew who the guy was. Even when Max moved here and hired me, I didn't put it together. He never said anything and Mom never talked about him. But Nevada saw them together. Or rather, not together. They just stared at each other. It was intense."

"But if they had a relationship, it was years ago."

She sank into the chair on the other side of his desk. "I know, so it shouldn't matter, right? She loved Dad. We all know that. But when I asked her about Max, she got angry and told me it wasn't my business. That she didn't want me and my sisters talking about her. She seemed really angry. We have a good relationship. I'm not used to being on the outs with her."

"So talk to her again."

"Maybe. I'm giving it a couple of days. I would apologize, only I didn't do anything wrong. We've always been a family who talks about things. She and Dad encouraged that. No secrets. But here we are, ignoring a very tall man."

He'd never had a close family, so he couldn't relate to what she was feeling. What he did know was that Montana was hurt and he had to help.

"Maybe she's embarrassed and doesn't want you to know."

"Embarrassed about what? An old boyfriend? Max is a great guy. I guess what scares me is that I always thought Dad was the great love of her life. But what if she loved Max, too?"

"People can love more than one person."

"Other people. Not my mother."

He relaxed back in his chair and petted Cece. "That's rational."

"I know." She sighed. "As I said, I don't usually fight with my mom and I don't like it. All right, enough about me. Who were you talking to before? Is it okay to ask that? It sounded like you were talking about a trip."

"My assignment after the next one."

"Oh."

She glanced at her lap, then back at him. "Where are you thinking of going?"

"Appalachia or Pakistan."

"That's a big difference."

"There's poverty in both places, and people who need my help."

"How do you decide?"

"I have someone send me background information. I look over the cases and see which seems like the place I can do the most good."

"So why did you come to Fool's Gold?"

"The hospital set up a program that brought dozens of patients from several states here. Also children from Mexico. I don't have to be in a Third World country to make a difference. I go where I think I can get the most accomplished."

"I'm glad you chose us."

He waited for more, for some hint that he should stay, or an attempt to make him feel guilty. Instead she smiled.

"You and Cece are becoming quite the item."

"She's my kind of girl."

"Adoring?"

"It helps."

"You are just such a typical guy."

He knew that wasn't true but liked hearing the words.

He rose, supporting the dog in his arms. "You okay?"

She stood as well. "I guess. I'll talk to my mom and everything will be fine again."

"Can I do anything to help?"

"You already did. Talking about it was good." She reached for Cece. "I'll take her for a walk and bring her back."

He glanced at the clock. "I have to prep for surgery."

"Okay, then I'll go to Kalinda's room and see if Cece can stay there. If not, I'll take her back to Max's."

Simon waited for her to ask more questions about where he would be going, or to suggest he should stay. Instead she kissed him lightly, then walked out of his office, leaving him very much alone.

"Hold still," Dakota grumbled, checking the hot curlers clinging to Montana's head. "These have to stay in longer."

"How much longer? They hurt." Montana did her best to ignore the sense of heat burning perilously close to her right ear. She was more a curling iron kind of girl, but hot rollers made the curls last longer.

"You're such a baby," Nevada told her, lounging on the bed, flipping through a magazine.

"So says the woman in jeans and a T-shirt."

"I'm not the one going to a fancy fundraiser. I don't have to dress up." Nevada sounded smug.

Montana stood in the bathroom off her bedroom and checked her makeup. Dakota hovered behind her, worried about Montana's hair.

She'd asked her sisters over to help her get ready so she wouldn't be too much in her own head before her date with Simon. Wanting to be perfect for him was a whole lot more work than she'd thought, and she didn't need the added stress of making herself crazy.

"You look amazing," Dakota said. "Leave your makeup alone. Give your hair five more minutes, then I'll take out the rollers and we'll fluff."

"And spray," Nevada called. "Her hair is pretty long. Those curls are going to need help staying in."

Montana studied her face. She'd done a decent job creating a smoky eye and had even applied her lipstick with an annoyingly tiny brush. Once her hair was done, she would put on the onyx and diamond earrings her grandmother had left her, and she'd be ready.

Her dress was simple — a sleeveless, black tank style with two-inch-wide straps. The whole thing was fitted and short, dipping just low enough in front to be intriguing. She'd smoothed on a lotion with a faint shimmer, giving her tanned legs a glow. Fancy, high-heeled black sandals waited by the front door, and Dakota had lent her a black satin clutch.

"I'll give you this," Nevada said, looking up from her magazine, "the curves are impressive."

Montana laughed. "You have the same ones."

"They look better on you."

"Thanks. You should see what I have on underneath."

"Shapewear?" Dakota asked.

"It's practically bulletproof. I can't breathe, but it makes a big difference."

She walked barefoot into the bedroom. "Anybody talk to Mom in the past day or so?"

Her sisters exchanged a glance, then looked at her and shook their heads. She'd already told them what had happened when she'd brought up the subject of Max.

"We shouldn't have let you do that yourself," Dakota told her. "We should have spoken to her together. Strength in numbers, and all that. She couldn't be mad at all of us."

"I'm not so sure," Montana told her. "She was pretty upset. The thing is, I don't know why. We're talking about something that happened over thirty-five years ago. No one cares about that."

Nevada sat up. "She does. What we don't know is why. Want us to all go talk to her?"

"No. I'm going to wait a little longer, then go see her myself. One of the things she told me was that she doesn't want us talking about her and Max. So having us bring it up might make things worse."

Dakota motioned for Montana to return

to the bathroom. After the now-cool rollers were removed, Montana bent at the waist and finger-combed her hair. When it was fluffed sufficiently, Dakota sprayed.

Montana straightened, smoothed her hair in place, then covered her face with her hands for the second spraying.

"You look amazing," Nevada said, sounding impressed. "Maybe I should grow my hair out."

Montana fingered the long, curly hair that tumbled well past her shoulders. Going back to her natural blond color last year had been the right decision. "Thanks," she said, hoping Simon would be blown away.

Dakota leaned against the counter. "You're crazy about him, aren't you?"

"I am. I should have been more careful, but I wasn't and now every time we're together, I wonder how much longer we'll have before he leaves."

"You're sure he's going?" Nevada asked.

"Yes. He'd already made plans to go to Peru. That's next. He's working on the assignment after that. It could be anywhere from Appalachia to Pakistan."

"Have you talked to him about it?" Dakota asked.

"More than once."

She wasn't comfortable telling them that

Simon believed that one of the prices of his gift was that he had to always be on the move. Especially since she didn't think that came close to the heart of the matter. His wound went deeper. How could he trust — truly trust — after what he'd been through as a child? Distance was safe.

"I know he's lonely and that he wants to belong. He just won't let himself."

"Given what happened to him when he was a kid, I'm not surprised," Nevada said. "Rules help. They create boundaries. The last thing this guy wants is something out of his control. His mother got out of control and look what happened. Caring is messy and unpredictable. His way keeps him safe. Sure, he misses out on a lot, but even that discomfort doesn't surprise him. He knows what to expect."

Both Montana and Dakota turned to stare at her.

"What?" Nevada demanded.

"That was very insightful," Dakota told her.

"I may not have a Ph.D. in psychology, but I'm not a complete idiot when it comes to relationships."

"Apparently not," Dakota said with a grin.

There was a knock on the door.

Montana's stomach tightened. She walked

to the front of the house, and pulled open the door.

She took in the well-tailored, dark suit, the blinding white shirt and the red power tie. But what really caught her attention was the look of admiration and lust on Simon's face.

"Hi," she said, stepping back to let him in. "I'm ready. I just have to get my bag."

He grabbed her arm. "Montana," he said, his voice husky. "You look amazing."

"Thank you."

She returned to the bedroom and found her sisters standing in the doorway, listening.

"I was hoping for more," Nevada said. "That he would be overwhelmed and have sex with you right there on the sofa."

"Not with you two listening."

"We would have let ourselves out the back."

Montana pushed between them and grabbed her small clutch. "You still can." She grinned. "Besides, you didn't see the look on his face."

Dakota laughed. "Point taken. Have fun. Call and tell us all the details."

"I will," Montana promised, and returned to the living room. "I'm ready."

"Me, too," Simon said with a sigh. "I'd

prefer to stay here for a while, but if we're too late, they'll get suspicious."

She thought about mentioning the fact that her sisters were standing in her bedroom, but then decided he didn't need to know that. Besides, there was always later.

"Rain check?"

"Absolutely."

Simon usually hated these kinds of events. He wasn't a party guy and had always preferred quiet conversation over loud music. However, this fund-raiser seemed to be better than most. For one thing, he knew a surprising number of people attending.

The mayor had greeted him at the door. Most of the ladies from his recent lunch were there, along with much of the hospital staff. His recent return to good temper meant that the nurses were now speaking to him. But the biggest difference was Montana.

He'd never attended something like this with a date before. Not only was she the most beautiful woman in the room, she had a social ease that made him feel more comfortable. She knew everyone, knew their children or their parents. She asked the right questions, smiled and laughed in the right places.

"You must be finding a lot to enjoy in our city," an older woman said, looking more than a little determined. "Fool's Gold has so much to offer."

Before Simon could sidestep the implication, Montana spoke. "I've been showing him all over town," she said easily. "Have you been out to the vineyards lately? I think this is going to be our biggest harvest ever." She turned to Simon. "Grape harvesting is always a huge event in town."

She returned her attention to the woman. "Now, which of the festivals is closest to the grape harvest?"

And as easily as that, they were talking about wine and grapes and tourists. The pressure to get Simon to stay, forgotten.

"You're very good," he told her, when they escaped yet another determined citizen.

"The art of distraction. I've been practicing."

"I appreciate it."

"I'm a full-service girlfriend. You might have noticed."

Girlfriend. It wasn't a word he used in the context of any relationship he'd ever had, but she was right.

He picked up her hand and kissed her palm.

A waiter passed carrying a tray of champagne. Simon collected a glass for each of them.

They were in the ballroom of the hotel up on the mountain. It was an elegant resort designed with comfort in mind. Chandeliers glittered overhead. A small band played in a corner and the sound of conversation competed with the music. French doors led out onto a patio. Beyond that was an acre or so of grass before the mountains rose toward the sky.

He returned his attention to Montana. As always, he wanted her. He couldn't be in the same room with her and not desire her. But more than that, he enjoyed her company. She was both arousing and comforting. A delicious contradiction.

The music shifted to something slow and sexy.

"Dance with me?" he asked.

She raised her eyebrows. "You don't strike me as the dancing type."

"I'm not. But I'd like to dance with you." He took the glass from her hand and set it on a small table, then led the way to the dance floor at the far end of the ballroom.

"Do you know what you're doing?" she asked. "Do you want me to lead?"

He took her in his arms and led her through a series of complicated steps. She followed easily.

"Wow," she said.

"When I was in the hospital, several of the nurses would dance with me. It was an easy way to get exercise. They swore one day I would find the girl I wanted to dance with. I didn't think it was ever going to happen."

He'd never told anyone about that before, had never had any reason to use his waltzing skills.

"You're pretty good yourself," he said. "What's your excuse?"

"Mom made us take lessons. Just the girls. It was very sexist of her."

"I think it's sweet."

"You didn't have three brothers making fun of you."

"I'm confident you and your sisters were able to handle them."

"We were, but that's not the point."

He bent his head and kissed her cheek then kissed her jaw. He moved his mouth against the side of her neck, across her shoulder. Her skin was warm and smelled like some exotic flower. He felt her body pressing against his and knew there was something to be said for dancing, after all.

"What *is* the point?" he asked, referring to her previous statement.

She blinked at him. "I have no idea what

we were talking about."

He laughed. "I like that you're easy."

"I'm actually not. Or I guess I am, but only around you."

He stopped dancing and looked into her eyes. "It's the same for me, too."

Someone bumped into them. Simon pulled her against him and began dancing again.

They danced to several more songs, drank champagne and tasted the hors d'oeuvres. He debated bond measures for local schools with the town treasurer and discussed jail versus community service with the police chief. When Montana excused herself to use the restroom, he was deep in conversation with the mayor.

"Kent and I were wondering if we could borrow the good doctor."

Simon found himself between Kent and Ethan Hendrix.

"Of course," Mayor Marsha said and walked away.

"Having a good time?" Ethan asked, leading Simon out the French doors and onto the lawn.

There were fewer people here. The sun had set and the stars had come out, but he didn't think they had left the ballroom to look at the view.

"How can I help you?"

Ethan and Kent exchanged a look.

"We want to talk about Montana. At the risk of sounding like a cowboy in an old Western, what are your intentions?"

Montana was in her late twenties, had lived on her own for years and would probably shriek if she knew what her brothers were asking. But Simon got the point. These men cared about her and wanted to make sure she was taken care of.

"I'm not discussing my personal life with you."

"Sure you are. Montana says you're one of the good guys. Don't make her a liar." The dramatic statement was tempered by Ethan's obvious sincerity.

But there were no bad guys here. He was leaving. Simon's stay had always been temporary. He was no threat, nor was he a permanent fixture in their sister's life.

He'd made it clear that he was leaving, hadn't he? Still, when she called herself his girlfriend, he'd let her. And he'd been pleased. He'd mentioned he might come back to visit. Was she thinking he meant more than that?

He'd screwed up, he realized. He'd misled her in the most fundamental of ways and never realized it until now.

"Excuse me," he said, pushing past them and returning to the ballroom.

He wove his way through the crowd, searching for the gorgeous blonde in a short black dress. The woman he planned on making love with later that night. The woman who haunted his dreams and drove him crazy every time he saw her.

He found her talking to Charity Golden.

"Hello, Charity. Do you mind if I talk to Montana for a moment?"

"Of course not."

"Thanks."

He took Montana's hand and led her out of the ballroom. Not outside where her brothers might still be waiting, but back toward the entrance. He found a quiet alcove and faced her.

"Is everything all right?" she asked.

He stared into her dark eyes, searching for the truth. "Do you love me?"

Her mouth parted slightly and she flushed. For a second she said nothing, then she raised her chin and spoke. "Yes, Simon, I love you."

The words were like a kick to his gut. His muscles tensed and he found it hard to breathe.

He should've seen this coming, he thought as he turned his back on her. He swore under his breath. What the hell had he been thinking? She wasn't anything like the women he was used to. Not cold, not calculating, not familiar with a man like him. He'd been nothing but selfish, thinking only of himself, of what he wanted.

He turned back to her. Her mouth curved up into a shaky smile.

"Your reaction tells me this isn't the best of news."

"Montana," he began, then stopped. What was he supposed to say? How could he make this right?

His phone vibrated in his jacket pocket.

He pulled it out and flipped it open. There was a text message. Even as he began to read it, his phone rang.

"It's Kalinda," he said.

She gave him a push. "Go."

He was already running, heading back to the hospital.

CHAPTER EIGHTEEN

Kalinda's body was shutting down. Simon knew it before he walked into her room and saw Fay and her husband in each other's arms, weeping. He scanned her chart, then walked over to examine her, determined to figure out what was wrong.

Even though he already knew.

Fay saw him and lunged toward him. "Dr. Bradley, it's bad. It's really bad. You have to do something."

"I know."

He touched Kalinda's face and felt the heat from her fever. The results of her latest blood work told the same story the nurse on duty had repeated when he'd arrived on the floor. The girl wasn't responding to her treatments, her organs were failing and there was no miracle left to save her.

The burns didn't just destroy in the moment. The damage continued long after the flames were gone. Healing exhausted the body, and the shock from what had occurred lasted far longer than anyone knew. She'd already used up her precious reserves hanging on this long.

Kalinda opened her eyes. "Hi, Dr. B. I don't feel so good."

He took her hand in his. "I know."

On the other side of the bed, her parents moved next to her.

"Hey, baby," her mother murmured. "You have to hang on. You know that, right?"

Kalinda continued to stare at him. "I hurt."

"Can't you give her something?" Fay demanded.

He glanced at the IV, taking in the already high dose. "She's getting as much as she can take."

"You have to do something."

"It's okay, Mom," Kalinda whispered. "I'm okay. It doesn't hurt that bad."

Pain ripped through him as he watched the brave little girl trying to comfort her parents.

"We still have work to do," Simon told her, doing his best to sound upbeat and positive.

"The surgeries don't matter. It's not like I can be pretty again."

"Yes, you can. I can make you pretty." Or

at least normal, he thought grimly. Eventually that would be enough.

"No, you can't." Her blue eyes saw into his soul. "You're leaving."

He felt as if she'd shot him.

She was right, of course. How could she trust him? He'd never said he would stay. Someone else would finish what he'd started. Someone else would see her through.

He didn't know what to say to her. There had been other children who had begged him not to go, but he'd never listened. He'd always known he was needed somewhere else. He'd left his patients, just as his doctors had left him.

The difference was his doctors had left because they had lives of their own to live. Families, commitments. He left because . . .

In that moment he couldn't remember why, only that it was important.

"I'll get better if you stay," Kalinda whispered and held out her hand. "Pinkie promise."

Just like Reese had pinkie promised to marry her if no one else would. For this little girl, a pinkie promise meant something.

He didn't want to lie to her but he also wanted to save her. Staying? Impossible.

Still, he moved his hand toward hers, pinkie extended.

Before they touched, the monitors began to scream. Red lights flashed and the sound of buzzing and sirens filled the small room. Kalinda's hand dropped to the bed, her eyes rolled back in her head and she lost consciousness.

Simon took in all the data, then tossed the chart on the chair.

"Get back," he demanded. There was no need to call for help. As soon as the alarms started, the team would be on their way.

He bent over Kalinda and tilted her head back. Even as the heart monitor flatlined, he began CPR, breathing deeply and rhythmically into her mouth.

His mind went blank as he focused on what he was doing, on the mechanics that could save her. Less than a minute after the first alarm, a swarm of people burst into the room, as the crash team responded to the alert.

He was pushed aside. He stepped back and made his way around them, then drew her parents out of the crowded room.

Fay shook with sobs. "No!" she screamed. "No! Don't let her die. My baby. Kalinda!" She shook off his hands and threw herself at her husband. "Not now. Not like this."

Simon stood next to them, not watching the medical team at work. He knew what they were doing from the sounds. He heard the call for medicine, the hum of the defib machine. He knew they were already too late.

He thought about telling her parents he was sorry. That sometimes this happened. But he wasn't sorry, he was angry. Worse, he felt as if he were somehow responsible. As if he should have been able to save her.

He turned away and walked toward his office. He felt sick inside, helpless. It wasn't supposed to be like this. He was supposed to save these kids.

He turned the corner and came to a stop when he saw Montana standing in front of his closed and locked office door.

She still wore the black dress she'd had on at the cocktail party, but in her arms she held Cece. The tiny poodle quivered at the sight of Simon and strained to leap into his arms.

"I didn't know what else to do," Montana told him. "I called Max and he brought Cece to me. I thought she might help."

"Kalinda's gone," he said flatly, knowing in the next minute or so he would get a call telling him what had happened.

Montana's eyes filled with tears. "No. She

was doing better. I saw her yesterday. She was laughing."

He didn't want to talk about this, didn't want to be with anyone. Especially not with someone who claimed to love him. He didn't want her to carry ugly images in her head.

"I have to go."

He knew he should say something else, but there weren't any words. Just the pressing need to be anywhere but here.

He turned and walked toward the stairs. He opened the door and raced down. When he found himself outside, he drew in deep breaths, but they didn't help. Nothing helped.

Without thinking he pulled out his cell phone and pushed the speed dial. Seconds later a familiar voice said, "You're up late."

"Alistair."

His friend's voice changed from joking to serious. "What's wrong?"

"I lost a patient. A child."

Alistair swore. "I'm sorry. It wasn't your fault."

"You don't know that."

"Yes, I do. Simon, you're the best."

Maybe, but tonight, it wasn't enough. "Do you ever want . . ."

"To walk away?" His friend paused.

"Sometimes it gets to me. The pain, the suffering. But someone has to help and, frankly, who better?"

"Do you ever want something more? A life?"

"I had one."

Simon winced. Alistair's beautiful wife and baby girl had been killed in a car accident three years ago. A month later, Alistair had joined Simon in Africa. As far as Simon knew, the other man had never been back to London.

"Sorry," he said. "I shouldn't have asked that."

"It was a long time ago."

"Not long enough." Simon knew he would remember gentle Kalinda forever. What would it be like to lose his own child? Or to have one in the first place?

"You go on," Alistair told him. "Keep putting one foot in front of the other. You asked me once if it was worth it. Loving them and losing them. Was it worth it to help your patient?"

"Of course."

"Then that's your answer."

Montana brushed away the tears. In her arms, Cece looked at her, as if aware something was wrong.

"She's gone," she repeated, knowing the words wouldn't make any sense to the little dog. Not that they made any sense to her, either. Kalinda's death seemed unnecessary and arbitrary. What had gone wrong?

She stared at the door to the stairs, wondering if she should follow Simon. After a couple of seconds, she turned the other way. Telling him she loved him wouldn't have helped him feel any better. If she went after him, he might think she was pressuring him or trying to prove herself. He'd found her before — if he needed her, he would find her again.

For a second she wondered if she'd been wrong to tell him the truth. If knowing she loved him would make things more difficult. Then she shook her head. No. She wouldn't go there. Loving someone was a gift. It's not like she'd asked for anything or tried to manipulate him. Simon could be freaked out or not — that was his decision. For her part, she was proud that she had put herself out there. What he did with the information was up to him.

She walked toward Kalinda's room. She wanted to see Fay, to say how wonderful her daughter had been. Whatever they needed, the town would provide. Montana would help as best she could, even if that meant simply getting them a room for the night.

But as she approached the girl's room, she didn't hear crying. Instead there were voices — happy voices. Not just from Kalinda's parents, but from the staff.

Montana hurried forward.

The door was open and she saw Fay and her husband standing on either side of Kalinda's bed, smiling, wiping away tears and holding hands across their daughter. Fay looked up and saw her.

"She's okay," she whispered, smiling broadly. "She's okay. Her heartbeat is getting stronger. The crisis passed."

Montana felt weak with relief. Her own eyes filled with happy tears.

"I'm so glad. This has been difficult for all of you."

"We'll get through it," Kalinda's father said, never taking his gaze from his little girl.

Fay's eyes moved over her. "Look how you're dressed. Were you at a party?"

Montana nodded. "I was with Simon when he got the message. He came right here. I didn't know what to do, so I got Cece. Has someone told Simon she's all right?"

"One of the nurses is taking care of that."

Fay walked across the room and hugged her, squeezing the dog between them. Cece wagged her tail and licked them both on the chin.

"Thank you for all you've done for her."

"I want to help. Do you think a little poodle company would help right now?"

"I think it would be perfect," Fay told her.

Montana set Cece on the foot of the bed. The dog carefully picked her way over the covers until she was level with Kalinda's hip. She bent over and gently licked Kalinda's hand, then curled up and closed her eyes.

All three adults watched intently. The girl barely stirred then slowly, very slowly, her fingers shifted so she could gently pat the little dog. Her lips curved up in a smile and she mouthed, "Thank you."

Montana checked her phone before leaving the hospital and was surprised to see a message from her mother. Although it was nearly ten, she decided to call her back.

"Hello?"

"Hi."

"Oh, Montana." Her mother sighed. "Thank you for calling me back. I thought you might be at the fundraiser with Simon."

"I was, but he got called away for a medical emergency." She thought of Kalinda, resting comfortably with Cece curled up next to her. "Everything is fine now."

"I'm glad to hear that." Her mother paused. "Montana, I'm sorry about what happened before. How angry and unreasonable I was. I'm sure you thought I was crazy."

Montana walked to her car and leaned against the door. "Not crazy. I wasn't sure why you were so upset. We weren't trying to butt in, not exactly. Of course you had a life before. You weren't born the day before you married Dad. It's just Max is my boss and . . ." She sighed. "I'm glad you're not mad."

"I'm not. The Max thing is complicated. Not because there's any big secret, but because I really didn't expect my past to show up now. We did date. I knew him before I knew your dad. But Max wasn't the kind of guy who looked much past the moment. I wanted more than that. Then I met your father and I knew he was the one."

Montana smiled. "Sounds like an exciting time."

"It was, but being married to your dad was better."

"Thanks for telling me this."

"You're welcome. And I really am sorry. I

404

love you, sweetie."

"I love you, too, Mom."

They promised to speak again soon and hung up. As Montana climbed into her car, she wondered about the rest of the Max story. There were things her mother wasn't sharing. Then she told herself to let it go. Whatever had happened was in the distant past. It wasn't as if her mother and Max were going to get back together.

Simon walked around Fool's Gold until his body ached. It was late — after midnight, at least — although he didn't bother glancing at his watch to find out the exact time. It didn't matter.

Restlessness drove him to keep moving, even without a destination. He'd received several calls updating him on Kalinda's condition. The fever was gone and she was stable. She would make it.

Good news, he told himself. The best news.

His footsteps echoed in the quiet of the night. He hadn't seen another person in a long time. He knew he should return to his hotel and try to get some sleep, but he couldn't imagine relaxing enough to lie down.

Instead he turned at the next intersection

and walked down dark residential streets until he reached a familiar one. He stood by a tree, watching the house.

The lights were still on, but he couldn't be sure she was awake. Finally he saw the shadow of someone crossing in front of the window.

His heart quickened as he recognized Montana. He knew in his gut she was waiting for him. She already knew he would need her, would seek her out. Because she wanted to be there for him.

He distinctly remembered his mother telling him she loved him. Sure, she was usually drunk when she said it, but it was only when she drank that he got any affection from her at all. She would hug him and tell him he was everything to her. That they were going to go away forever. She swore she was giving up men, that it would be the two of them and that she would be the best mother ever.

For years he'd believed her, had waited for her to start packing. He'd looked at maps and thought about all the places they could go. He'd imagined a perfect life.

By the time he'd turned ten, he'd stopped waiting. When she hugged him and told him she loved him, he didn't believe her. When her boyfriends had started hitting him, he instead pictured himself in another place. A better place. He vowed he would figure out how to survive on his own and simply disappear.

Then she'd pushed him into the fire.

There were no words to describe the excruciating pain, the primal response as he struggled to escape the agony, only to have her push him back again. The screams he'd heard, his own screams, hadn't even been human. He hadn't known such torture existed.

Once he'd escaped and run outside, he'd been unable to stop vomiting and shaking.

He'd learned later that though she'd claimed it was an accident, she'd been overheard privately telling her court appointed attorney that she'd done it on purpose. Years later, he'd read the transcripts of her interview with the police. She hadn't said she was sorry. She'd said he'd always been a burden and she'd always regretted having him.

She'd never loved him. It had all been a lie.

Since then, he'd never bothered to see if love could exist for him. He'd gone to high school from a hospital bed and had been a scarred freak in college, too young and too smart. The same in medical school. By the time his age matched that of the people around him, it was too late. He was never in one place long enough to make connections, and he preferred it that way.

Then there was Montana. A woman who had grown up in an idyllic setting, with a loving family. She'd never known suffering or pain, beyond the usual bumps and bruises, either emotional or physical. She couldn't begin to understand what he'd experienced.

But she didn't let that stop her. She accepted his scars. She believed in the best of him. She loved him.

He'd seen love before, in the parents who begged God to save their child or offered to die in their child's place. He'd seen a wife or a husband never leave a bedside. He'd been caught up in the vortex of grief when a patient was lost. But he'd never truly felt it himself.

During his years in the hospital as a teenage patient, he'd spoken with several psychologists and psychiatrists. They had explained his mother's inability to emotionally bond and talked about how he had to heal mentally as well as physically.

He'd heard the words and pretended to agree with them. Inside, he'd shut down and known it would always be like that.

He crossed the street and walked toward Montana's front door. When he reached it, he knocked softly.

She opened it at once.

"I've been worried about you," she said, pulling him into the house. "You heard about Kalinda, right? Isn't it wonderful?" She smiled. "Her parents are so happy. I left Cece with her for the night. I'll pick her up in the morning. I can't imagine how you go through this with all your patients. But this time it all worked out."

She was so beautiful, he thought, touching her face. She would do anything for him, including pretending the void that was his heart wouldn't hurt her. But she would be wrong. Eventually she would feel as if he were some kind of emotional vampire — sucking out her lifeblood and giving nothing in return. Eventually she would see that, and when she changed her mind about him, the devastation would be worse than anything he'd ever known.

He dropped his hand to his side.

"I don't want to see you anymore."

He spoke the words flatly, without emotion, his voice cold.

She stared at him, confused. "I don't —"

"I'll be leaving town in a few weeks so there's no point in us continuing to be together."

She surprised him by standing straight and tall, her chin raised.

"All right," she murmured.

He wanted to call the words back, to tell her he was wrong. She was so much more than he'd ever expected. So much more than he deserved. But he couldn't say anything. It was as if everything inside that had ever been good or kind or decent was frozen.

She walked to the door and held it open.

"I won't keep you," she said, tears filling her eyes. "Goodbye, Simon."

He walked past her and out into the night. For a second, he drew in the scent of her perfume. Then it was gone, the door closed, and he was alone.

Exactly how he'd wanted it, he told himself as he walked away. Exactly what was best for both of them.

Chapter Nineteen

Montana held the tiny baby in her arms and felt the warmth of her body, wrapped so tightly in a soft blanket.

"Such a good girl," she cooed softly to Rosabel. "So precious and beautiful."

Nevada bounced Hannah on her lap, while Dakota held Pia's other daughter, Adelina.

"This is great," Pia said, stretching out in a lounge chair, her feet up on a pillow, an herbal iced tea in her hand. "Seriously, I thought the baby thing would be tough, but so far, I'm loving it."

"Have you even had one second with just you and them?" Nevada asked.

"I think there were at least fifteen minutes last week." She sighed. "Someone is always dropping by to help. I know eventually everyone will return to their own lives, but I'm enjoying the help while it's available. The pediatrician says as long as everyone is healthy, it's good for the babies to be exposed to a lot of people. Socializing and all that."

Montana rocked Rosabel gently. "Are you adjusting to being a mom?"

Pia had worried she wasn't maternal enough and that she would mess up everything.

"It's kind of what they say," Pia admitted. "The second you hold them, you feel the connection. I've explained I'm going to do my best and they're pretty patient with me."

Nevada grinned. "Wish I'd been here for that conversation."

"I did most of the talking," Pia told her.

Montana was aware of Dakota and Nevada exchanging glances. Although she hadn't said anything, she knew her sisters were worried about her. The downside of being a triplet, she thought. It was tough to keep a secret.

They talked about local gossip — how the Fool's Gold cheerleaders were off to their annual camp, and that Ethan and Liz were taking all their kids to Hawaii for a week.

"How are things with Simon?" Dakota asked, sounding casual.

Montana wasn't fooled. "We broke up."

Pia sat up. "Was I supposed to know this?"

"No. It just happened last night."

"Are you okay?" Nevada asked. "Want to get Kent and Ethan to beat him up?"

"No. No one should hurt him. It's fine."

Pia leaned toward her. "Fine? You're wearing about sixteen layers of concealer."

"I didn't sleep well."

She'd also cried a lot, thrown a few pillows and had eaten nearly a pint of Ben & Jerry's.

Not only had he broken up with her, but he'd been mean about it. He'd done his best to wound her, and that was the part she didn't understand. Simon was many things, including distant and emotionally elusive, but he wasn't unkind by nature.

She'd seen him with his patients. She knew how much they meant to him and what he sacrificed for them. Which meant lashing out at her had been about something else.

Fear, maybe. She'd been the one to break the unspoken rules. She'd been the one to fall for him.

"Want to tell us what happened?" Nevada asked.

Montana kissed the sleeping baby's cheek. "We went to the fundraiser. Apparently Ethan and Kent took him aside and basically asked his intentions."

Her brothers had confessed all shortly

after Simon had left. They'd been concerned his abrupt departure had been about them. At the time she'd laughed and reassured them. How wrong she'd been.

All three women groaned.

"I know they were trying to help," Dakota muttered. "Brothers."

"Tell me about it." Nevada sounded disgusted. "Then what happened?"

"Simon walked over and asked me if I was in love with him."

She glanced up at three identical expressions of shock.

"What did you say?" Pia asked.

"I told him the truth. That I did love him. Then he got paged to go back to the hospital."

She explained about Kalinda, how she'd nearly died, and how Simon had taken off.

"That was it. He showed up at my house about three hours later and told me it was over."

She didn't repeat what he'd said — there was no point in having her friends hate him.

"I knew what he was like when I got involved with him."

Dakota glared at her. "Tell me you're not taking responsibility for the breakup. You didn't do anything wrong."

"I know I didn't, and don't worry. I'm not

saying it's my fault. I'm saying I knew what he was when I let him in. To me, this is no different than going out with a guy who warns you at the beginning that he cheats, and then being shocked when you find him in bed with another woman. Simon told me he didn't get involved. I knew he wasn't looking for a commitment or a place to settle. He was always going to move on. I thought I was protecting myself, but I wasn't."

She looked at all three of them. "I don't regret loving him."

"Finn was going to leave, too," Dakota told her. "Maybe Simon will change his mind."

Montana shrugged. She figured that was pretty unlikely. "It's not that I don't hurt, I do. But I can't find anyone to blame. Neither of us did anything wrong."

"Are you pregnant?" Nevada asked. "If you were, he might want to stay."

"There's a happy way to start a relationship," Montana told her. "I'm not pregnant, and I'm not interested in a man who would only stay for the sake of a child."

"You're so calm," Pia told her.

"That's because I'm at the crying-on-the-inside stage." Montana swallowed. "I do love him and I don't want him to go, but there's nothing I can say to change his mind." She glared at them. "I don't want any of you saying anything, either."

"Would we do that?" Nevada asked.

"In a heartbeat. I want you to promise."

They all swore they wouldn't say a word.

"Good."

Montana continued to cuddle the baby. She was pleased she sounded so in control and that she'd managed to fool three people who loved her. The truth was she felt shattered by what had happened. She wanted to say she would do anything to get Simon to return her feelings, even a little.

Except that wasn't true. Her heart might hurt with every beat, but she'd managed to do the right thing. To accept what had happened and believe in her ability to heal.

It had taken her a long time, but she'd finally grown up. Eventually, she would learn to move on. To forget about Simon. To fall in love with someone else.

"There's always hope," she whispered to the baby in her arms. "You need to remember that."

Simon spent the next several days waiting for someone to attack him. He was sure that it was only a matter of time until he was confronted by a mob, all of them demand-

416

ing he do the right thing where Montana was concerned.

Instead, people were just as friendly as they had always been. They smiled, they asked about his patients, they suggested things for him to do on the weekend. As if nothing had changed.

The only thing he could figure out was that Montana hadn't told anybody. But why would she keep that information to herself? She must hate him. A scorned woman and all that.

He finished his rounds early on Saturday and found himself at loose ends. There was yet another festival in town, something to do with crafts. He walked through the crowd, grabbing a quick lunch at one of the food stands, then stood there with nothing to do and no one to see. Finally he decided he would go to the bookstore and get something to read.

As he turned in that direction, he caught sight of a familiar shape. A woman with blond hair. Several people stepped between them and he couldn't see her anymore, so he hurried in her direction. His heart quickened as need filled him.

He raced toward her, only to stop by a woman selling glass bead earrings. What the hell was he doing? He couldn't go after

Montana. He'd ended things. Worse, he'd hurt her.

He reminded himself that this was what he wanted. To be alone. It was the way things were. But still, he ached for her. Not just her body next to his, but her smile, her laugh, the things she said. He'd never wanted anyone as much as he wanted Montana and he'd never missed anyone as much.

The blond woman moved to her left and he saw her then, the shape of her face and her much shorter hair, and knew it wasn't Montana. It was one of her sisters. She'd never been there at all.

He made his way to Morgan's Books. The store was large, with lots of windows and natural light. There was a display of mysteries written by Montana's sister-in-law. He flipped through Liz's latest and decided to pick it up.

With the book tucked under his arm, he wandered the store. Everyone who saw him was friendly and he suddenly realized he'd been waiting to be punished. He wanted someone to tell him he was wrong, that he'd been the lowest form of bastard. Because with the blame and anger might come defensiveness — a gut reaction that might convince him he'd been right to cut off their

418

relationship.

He rounded a corner and nearly ran into Denise Hendrix.

He came to a stop, knowing at last he had found the one person who would want to bring him to his knees. Mothers like Denise protected their children ferociously.

"Simon!" Denise smiled at him. "I haven't seen you in a while. How are you?"

She was too friendly. "Have you talked to Montana recently?"

"Not in a couple of days. Why?"

At last, he thought almost gleefully. She would hate what he had done.

"We broke up."

Denise looked surprised. "Oh. I'm sorry to hear that."

"It wasn't her, in case you're wondering. It was me. I have to leave soon and I didn't think we should pursue a relationship. She didn't agree. She's in love with me."

Denise was carrying a book. Maybe she would hit him with it. Maybe they would all stand around him, yelling at him. Telling him why he was wrong.

Instead she sighed. "That makes you a very lucky man."

He stared at her, unable to believe what she was saying. "Lucky?"

"Having someone love you is an amazing

gift. Especially if it's someone like Montana." She straightened and squared her shoulders, an action that reminded him so much of her daughter. "So, yes, if she loves you, you are very lucky. And if she loves you, you must be a good man."

He didn't know what to say to that.

"It's taken Montana a while to find her way," Denise continued. "She was never quite sure what she wanted to do with her life. But she never stopped searching and now she's found where she belongs. I'm so proud of her."

He didn't understand. Where was the screaming? Where were the accusations?

"I don't love her."

Denise stared at him for a long time, then leaned in and wrapped her arms around him. "I'm so sorry, Simon. I don't know very much about you, but what I've been told is sad. It must be difficult for you to trust in something you've never seen. Being loved must be one of the most terrifying things of all."

She stepped back and gave him a caring smile. "I hope you can have a little faith. If not in Montana, then at least in yourself."

With that, she turned and walked away. He was left staring after her, more confused than ever and still without a chance at redemption.

Simon pointed to the small red X on the illustration. "We're going to start on the right side of your face," he said.

Kalinda nodded. "Because it's the bad side, right?"

"I don't like to think of this in terms of good or bad. The right side has more damage, and will need more attention."

Kalinda rolled her eyes at him. "Now you sound like my mom."

Her mother sat on the other side of the girl's bed. "Why did you say it like that?" she asked, but she was grinning as she spoke.

Ever since the night of Kalinda's crisis, the little girl had been getting better. Simon didn't have to look at her chart to see the truth. She was awake most of the day, energetic, talkative and interested in what was going on around her. At this rate, he could squeeze in two, maybe three surgeries before he left.

Kalinda pointed to the picture. It was a simple drawing of a face. He used it a lot when he was working with children. Showing someone what would be happening often made more sense than trying to talk about it. Plus, he'd been told he could get

421

too technical and graphic. The last thing he wanted to do was to scare her.

"When you do that are you gonna cover my whole face? Will I look like a mummy?"

"Probably half a mummy."

"Then I can walk down the halls at night with my arms straight in front of me and frighten the nurses." Kalinda sounded delighted at the thought. "You need to make sure I'm a full mummy for Halloween."

Fay looked at her daughter. "You know Dr. Bradley won't be here for Halloween."

"Yes, he will." She looked at him. "You promised. You pinkie promised. You have to stay."

He could see the righteous anger in her blue eyes. At last someone was going to yell at him. Unfortunately, it wasn't anyone he wanted to be mad at him.

"Kalinda," he began.

"Uh-uh. You promised. You were promising when my heart stopped. You can't go back on that now."

Fay stood. "I'll walk you out," she told Simon and led him into the hallway.

When they were standing facing each other, she smiled an apology. "I'm sorry about that. Kalinda can be very stubborn. You probably find it annoying, but I'm so happy to see that she's herself again."

"I see the improvement as well."

He wanted to protest that he hadn't promised, but knew the girl was right. He had been promising. But soon he was leaving anyway.

Going back on his word to a kid? How screwed up was that?

Once again he found himself missing Montana — her emotional sanity had become something he depended upon. Without her he was adrift in a world where he didn't belong.

Fay touched his arm. "I want to thank you for all you've done. We wouldn't have gotten through this without you."

He wanted to tell her that of course she would have, but he accepted her words with a smile. That's what Montana would have told him to do.

Back in his office, he updated his charts, then leaned back in his chair. He stared at his cell phone, knowing how easy it would be to call. But then what? Nothing had changed. It was better for both of them if he didn't make promises he couldn't keep.

"I saw the movies a bunch of times, but this is better," Daniel told Montana as he sat in one of the small conference rooms at the library. "My mom already bought me the whole set. They're kind of hard, but it's fun, too." His nose wrinkled. "Don't tell anyone I said that."

Montana held in a smile. "Because reading isn't cool?"

"No. I don't want to be one of those smart kids."

Peer pressure started early, she thought.

"I'm glad you're enjoying the *Harry Potter* books. They're some of my favorites, too." She watched Daniel pet Buddy, who sat patiently at his side.

"Is a million dollars a lot of money?" she asked casually.

Daniel stared at her. "Yeah." His tone made it clear he thought she was an idiot for asking.

"I think so, too. Do you know that according to some studies, people who go to college earn a million dollars more in their lifetime than people who don't?"

There were plenty of exceptions, but she wasn't going to get into that with Daniel.

"A million dollars more?"

"Uh-huh. Sometimes being smart is kind of a good thing." She leaned toward him. "I don't know why you had trouble reading, but that's all gone. You've jumped two grades in your reading ability just in the past few weeks. It's like your brain was getting ready and getting ready and suddenly it *is* ready."

He gave her a shy smile. "I'm sorry I didn't want to try before. It was hard."

"I know, but you tried anyway. Buddy likes that in a guy."

He hugged the dog. "Buddy's really smart, too."

"He is. But here's the thing. They're going to reassess your reading abilities when you go back to school, and you're going to get moved to a different group of students."

"With the really smart kids?" He sounded concerned.

"It depends on how you do. I know you're worried that your friends won't be happy if you change. But that's what growing up is about. Changing. Trying new things. Do you want to play sports in high school?"

He nodded vigorously.

"You need good grades to stay on the team. The same in college."

"I'd love to play college ball. Do you think I could?"

"I've seen how you've worked on your reading, even when it was hard. I think you can do anything."

"That's what my mom says, but I thought it was because she had to." He shrugged. "She loves me."

The words were spoken with perfect certainty. Montana thought of Simon and wished his childhood had been filled with that kind of affection and support.

"I think knowing you can do anything is a little more about you than her."

Daniel rose and walked around the table. He hugged her, squeezing hard. "Thank you." He straightened. "I'm going to college so I can earn that million dollars."

"I'm glad."

He left the room.

She bent over and stroked Buddy. "You did it, big guy. You were exactly what Daniel needed. Everyone is pretty happy. Daniel's mother sent a letter to the school principal and everything. The program is going to be expanded."

His doggie eyebrows drew together, as if he were worried about keeping up with it all.

She laughed and kissed the top of his head. "Relax. You can handle it and I'll be right there with you."

Kalinda's surgery took over ten hours. The work was detailed, every tiny adjustment, every cut, every stitch would determine how she looked for the rest of her life. Simon felt the weight of responsibility — wanting to get everything right.

Perfect was a bitch, but as he pulled off his gloves, he knew he'd gotten damn close.

After checking in with Fay and her husband, telling them that everything had gone well and that their daughter would be in recovery for a couple of hours, he headed back to his office.

His body ached. Standing for that long always took a toll, as did being hunched over and doing such meticulous work. He grabbed a cup of coffee from one of the nurses' stations and took the stairs up two flights. He should eat something, he thought. Before he started on his rounds. Keep his energy up.

He entered his office and was greeted by a soft yip.

He flipped on the light and saw Cece stepping out of her crate and stretching.

"You're a surprise," he told the happy dog. "Did Montana bring you by so you could be with Kalinda later today?"

The dog's fluffy tail wagged. She danced around him, obviously thrilled they were together at last.

He set down his coffee, then picked her up. She gave him happy kisses, then settled into his arms with a contented sigh. He checked that she had food and water, then walked over to his desk and sat down.

"Want to play?" he asked, opening his bottom desk drawer and pulling out a couple of toys he'd bought for her.

There was a tiny cat with a squeaker in the middle and a Ping-Pong-size tennis ball. Cece quivered with excitement, then scrambled to get out of his arms. She raced to the end of his small office and barked expectantly, as if urging him to get on with it.

He threw the cat toy. She caught it in midair, then held it, squeaking happily. The high-pitched noise made him grin.

"You're pretty proud of yourself, aren't you? Have you seen a real cat? I'm not sure you'd win the fight."

Cece dashed toward him and leapt into his lap. It was something she'd done a dozen times before, maybe more. But this time the partially open bottom desk drawer was in the way.

Simon saw what was going to happen a microsecond before it did. He reached for her but couldn't get there fast enough. Her back left leg clipped the drawer, the impact loud enough for him to hear.

She dropped the toy and cried out, then fell to the ground, yipping loudly. He shoved the drawer back in place and dropped to his knees, beside the writhing dog.

"It's okay," he said, feeling stupid. He didn't know what was wrong, so he couldn't commit to an outcome. Still, the words were instinctive, and he murmured them over and over again.

He reached out and gently stroked her. She quieted, her dark gaze locking on his, as if begging him to make it stop hurting.

He touched her leg and she yelped again. He swore. Was it broken?

"Okay, okay. I'm going to get you help," he told Cece, even as he fought against a nearly overwhelming fear. Fear for her, and with it, guilt that he was responsible for this sweet, loving little dog getting hurt.

He reached over his head to the desk and fumbled until his fingers closed around his cell phone. He pulled it to him and hit the number for Montana's cell.

"Hello?"

"It's Simon. Cece hit her leg on a desk drawer while she was jumping into my lap. She's in pain. I think it might be broken. Tell me what to do."

Montana didn't hesitate. "Take her to the vet. His name is Cameron McKenzie. He just took over for Mavis Rivera, who retired. Which you don't need to know. Sorry. Okay, here's the address. It's going to be just as fast to walk."

She gave him quick directions on how to get there from the hospital.

"I'll call and tell them you're coming."

"Thanks."

He hung up and reached for Cece. Although she moaned when he picked her up, she didn't flinch and settled trustingly in his arms.

As he raced through the hospital and out onto the street, she stared at him, her gaze telling him she knew he was going to make it better.

"Stop believing in me," he told her as he hurried toward the vet. "Chances are, I'm going to screw this up, too."

CHAPTER TWENTY

Dr. Mckenzie's veterinary practice was in an old building that had once been a private home. There were big trees, a kennel area in back and the reception desk sat in the middle of what Simon would guess had once been the living room.

"Montana Hendrix called," he said as he rushed in. "I have Cece with me."

Two women sat with a carrier in the waiting area. He ignored them, along with the kid holding a bowl with a fish, and rushed toward the older woman in a blue scrub shirt.

"Yes, Dr. Bradley. We were told you were coming." She picked up the phone. "Cece is here." She put down the phone and smiled. "Carina will be right up to get her."

He nodded, but what he really wanted to do was start yelling. Right up? What did that mean? Why wasn't this Carina person waiting to take Cece immediately? Although the dog continued to stare at him with love, he knew she was in pain. Her breathing came in pants and she moaned softly. He also didn't like the angle of her leg. If it was broken, he would never forgive himself.

A blonde girl who looked like she was twelve came through a swinging door.

"Hi. I'm Carina."

He wanted to growl he didn't give a damn who she was, but held in his annoyance.

"Montana told you what happened?"

"Yes."

She reached for Cece, taking her gently. Even so, the poodle yelped. Simon flinched.

"Be careful."

Carina gave him a patient smile. "We'll take good care of her, Dr. Bradley. Cam . . . I mean, Dr. McKenzie is brilliant. If you want to give us a phone number where we can reach you —"

"I'm not leaving. I want to know exactly what's wrong with her and what you're going to do about it."

Carina took a step back. "Um, okay. Sure. It may be a little bit. We might have to take an X-ray."

"I would say that's more than a *might*. Look at how she's holding her leg. Are you a trained medical professional? Do you have any experience at all?"

Carina stiffened. "Yes, I do and perhaps this would go faster if you would let me do my job. Now, if you'll excuse me, I'll take Cece in back. Someone will be out as soon as possible to let you know what's going on."

"Good."

She turned and went through the swinging door. Cece strained to look around her arm, her eyes begging him not to abandon her.

He swore and ran his hands through his hair, then stalked to the receptionist. "I have to make a couple of calls. I'll be right outside. Come get me if they learn anything."

She nodded, looking completely unimpressed by his agitation. "Carina knows what she's doing and, like she said, Dr. McKenzie is very good. Your little dog is going to be fine."

"You actually can't know that," he growled, then stalked past the other waiting clients and went outside.

Once there he paced the path to the parking lot, then retraced his steps. A glance at his watch told him Cece had been in the back all of forty-five seconds and it was unlikely they would have found anything yet.

He phoned the hospital and talked to one of the nurses in the burn ward. After explaining that he'd been called away, he told them he'd have his cell with him for emergencies. Then he spoke to one of the nurses in recovery, and was relieved to find out Kalinda was doing so well that she was already on her way back to her room.

That taken care of, he shoved his phone into his pocket and continued pacing.

"Knock, knock," Montana called, walking into the back of the vet's office. While Dr. McKenzie was new and she'd only met him once before, she was friendly with all his staff.

"Montana," Carina said, coming up to her and giving her a hug. "What's with Dragon Man?"

"Who?"

"The guy who brought in Cece. He's the worst kind of pet owner. Terrified and angry at the same time. I thought I was going to have to muzzle him." Carina's eyes were bright with laughter as she spoke.

"He's a doctor."

"Oh, sure. I should have guessed that. He seemed like he wanted to be in charge."

"I'm sure he's more comfortable that way. How's Cece?"

434

"Still with Cameron. Sally's assisting. They're doing an X-ray. We'll have the results in a few."

"Great. Thanks."

"Want to stay back here? It's safer."

"No. I can handle Simon. If you'll excuse the pun, his bark is worse than his bite."

"If you say so."

Montana walked toward the front of the building. Before pushing through the swinging door, she drew in a breath and told herself that whatever she felt when she saw Simon, she wouldn't show it. This was a crisis and he'd called her because of Cece. He'd made his feelings about everything else very clear. Wanting him didn't mean he wanted her back. She had to keep telling herself that.

She stepped into the reception area, only to find it empty.

"Looking for the guy who brought in the poodle?" the receptionist asked.

"Yes."

"He's out front. Pacing. Poor guy. He's pretty frantic."

Montana walked out the door and saw Simon at once.

Even though he wore a shirt and tie, he looked mussed. His thick hair was a mess, as if he'd been running his fingers through it.

He was tired, she thought, remembering that Kalinda was supposed to have had a major surgery today. Compassion and worry for him blended with her own pain at seeing the man she loved but couldn't have.

"How is she?" he asked as he jogged toward her. "Have you heard anything?"

"They're doing an X-ray right now. We'll know soon."

He swore. "I can't believe what happened." He told her about the toys and the drawer. "It's my fault. She's jumped like that before. I was irresponsible."

She instinctively touched his arm, then wished she hadn't. Heat flared between them. Heat that mocked her with its intensity.

"You weren't. It was an accident. They happen. It's not like you deliberately hurt her."

"I should have closed the drawer."

"Yes, you should have, but you didn't. If her leg is broken, they'll set it and she'll heal."

He shook his head and started pacing. "Is this what they go through? The good parents? I want to hit something. I want to rush into the examining room and take care of

436

her myself."

"I don't remember you mentioning you went to vet school," she said, keeping her tone deliberately light.

"You're not helping."

"Sure I am. To answer your question, yes, this is what those parents go through. Although they've loved their children for years and you've known Cece a few weeks, so it's worse."

She didn't get into the dog-versus-child debate. That wasn't the point.

If only, Montana thought as she watched him. If only he'd been able to care for her in return. Even a little. They could have been great together.

The front door opened and Cameron stepped out.

Montana had met him once before. He was in his early- to mid-thirties, tall, good-looking with dark wavy hair. Added to that, he loved animals and was raising his daughter by himself, so he was probably being stalked by most of the single women in town.

"Hi, Montana," he said.

"Cameron." She turned to Simon. "This is Dr. Cameron McKenzie. Cameron, Dr. Simon Bradley. The human kind of doctor."

"Nice to meet you," Cameron said, holding out his hand.

"You, too. How's Cece?"

"She's fine. Nothing's broken. She pulled a muscle and scared herself. She needs to take it easy for a few days, which is tough with a dog. She's already been given something for the pain and an anti-inflammatory. We'll send both home with her, as well." He glanced between them, as if not sure who would be responsible for the little dog.

Simon stepped forward. "She's coming home with me."

Cameron gave him the rest of the instructions.

Simon listened intently and nodded. "I'll go back to my office and get her carrier," he said.

"No problem. She's pretty sleepy from the pain medication. Take your time."

Cameron went back inside.

Simon turned to her. "Is it all right that she stays with me?"

"Sure. Let me know when you want me to get her. I can keep an eye on her while you're at the hospital."

He nodded. "Thank you for this. You didn't have to help."

"Of course I did. Not only is Cece my responsibility, I'm still your friend."

His gaze locked with hers. "I hurt you,

Montana. I'm sorry about that, but apologizing doesn't justify what I said."

Nor did it change the outcome. "You felt trapped."

"You're making excuses for me?"

"No, I'm saying I understand why you reacted the way you did. I knew the rules when we started."

"I'm not sure that's true."

Stay, she thought, wishing begging would help. If only he would stay with her, be with her, love her back.

"Call me if you need anything," she said, then turned back to the building.

She thought about offering to help him with Cece, but she knew what would happen if they spent the night together. She knew they would most likely give in to the ever present passion. And then what? Right now she needed to take care of herself and that meant protecting her heart.

So she did what was right rather than what she wanted and slowly, painfully, walked away.

Montana watched as Nevada sat across from their mother in Denise's cheerful kitchen.

"I did it," Nevada said firmly. "I applied at Janack Construction. They have the last of their permits and have put out the word they're hiring. I have an interview next week."

Denise smiled. "You can stop looking worried. I'm not going to tell you this is a bad thing. You have to do what makes you happy."

"But I'm leaving Ethan."

"You're not going to work for him anymore. There's a difference. As you said, he's more interested in his windmills, anyway."

Nevada drew in a breath and smiled. "You're not mad?"

"Of course not." Her mother turned to Montana. "How are you doing?"

There was concern in her tone and sympathy in her gaze.

"You heard."

"That you and Simon aren't seeing each other anymore? Yes. I heard." Her mother reached across the table and took her hand. "Anything I can do?"

"No. If I asked you to change Simon, you probably couldn't. And even if you could, I don't want him to be different. I love him the way he is."

"That's usually best. Women think they can change a man, but they're often wrong." Denise straightened. "Do you want me to talk badly about him or ask one of your brothers to beat him up?"

Despite everything, Montana laughed. "I'm good. He can continue life unscarred." The laughter faded. "You know what I mean."

"I do. I just want you to know I'm here for you."

"Me, too," Nevada told her. "Whatever you want. We can call him a jerk or worse, if you don't want him beaten up."

"Maybe next time."

She couldn't blame Simon for what had happened. As her mother had said, trying to change someone was a losing proposition. People changed because they wanted to, not because someone made them.

"On a more cheerful subject," she said, turning to her sister. "I have someone you should meet."

Nevada rolled her eyes. "You aren't seriously considering setting me up with someone, are you?"

"Yes. You haven't had a date in months."

"Years is more like it," Nevada grumbled. "I can't find anybody I'm interested in. Or if I am interested, they're in love with someone else."

Montana blinked at her. "You're interested in someone who's married?"

"No. Don't be an idiot. Of course not.

I'm just saying that once, maybe, there was a guy . . ." She sighed. "It doesn't matter."

Montana glanced at her mother, who looked equally intrigued. She would have sworn she knew everything about Nevada's personal life. Apparently she was wrong. Her sister had been keeping secrets.

Nevada leaned toward her. "Fine. Tell me about this guy you want me to meet."

"His name is Cameron McKenzie. He's the new vet in town. He's tall, with dark wavy hair. Very cute. He moved here about a month ago. He took over Dr. Rivera's practice. Rumor has it he has a daughter. She's pretty young. Six or seven. Adorable, or so I've been told."

"Where's the wife?" Denise asked. "Kent has taught us all that the ex-wife is important to the equation. You'll want to find out about her before you get involved."

"I'm not involved." Nevada slapped her hands on the table. "Mom, I haven't even met the guy."

"He sounds very nice."

"Montana said he was cute, with a kid. How does that make him nice?"

"He likes animals."

"Kill me now," Nevada moaned. "Just make it quick." She looked at both of them. "I can get my own guy."

"I'm sure you can," her mother said calmly. "The problem is you won't. I want to see you happy."

"I am happy."

"You're changing jobs and you don't have anyone special in your life. Sell it somewhere else."

Nevada turned her gaze on Montana. "Are you in on this?"

"I swear, it wasn't planned. It just happened spontaneously."

"Let's try to keep that from happening again."

Despite Nevada's obvious annoyance, Montana grinned. "I'll do my best."

Over the next week, Simon braced himself for two events that never happened. The first was a final, hard push by the town to convince him to stay. The second was Montana "just happening" to show up in places where he would see her. Because she had to know that every time he looked at her, he wanted her with a desperation that nearly drove him to madness.

Neither occurred.

He ran into Mayor Marsha twice, some women from the city council once and played golf with Josh, Ethan and Raoul Moreno, the former NFL quarterback who was married to Pia. No one mentioned that he was leaving or hinted at one reason why he should stay. Josh even asked about his next assignment, and the four men debated the merits of working in the States versus traveling to Pakistan.

He didn't get it. He knew he would be an asset to the community, that the new hospital would have state-of-the-art facilities that would tempt any medical professional. Arranging to have patients come to him instead of the other way around added a layer of logistics, but was somewhat doable. He knew — he'd seen multiple presentations on the process over the years. Still, they were all silent on the subject.

He also hadn't run into Montana anywhere. Once, leaving the hospital, he thought he caught sight of her turning the corner, but he wasn't sure and by the time he'd reached the corner himself, she was gone. Although Cece showed up regularly in Kalinda's room, Montana remained elusive. The one time he'd hung around until it was time for the dog to be picked up, he'd met her boss instead. Max Thurman had been the one retrieving the dog.

He'd gone so far as to question Reese, a regular visitor, about how his aunt was. The kid had blinked at him. "Which one?"

Simon had said it didn't matter and walked away.

Not seeing her was even more difficult than seeing her all the time, he realized. At least when he was with her, he could lose himself in her presence. He could inhale the scent of her body, listen to whatever she was talking about, argue with her, make her laugh, touch her. When they were alone, he could make love with her, losing himself in her passion and healing himself in the process.

She was a part of him and being without her was as painful as cutting off an arm.

But he knew he had to keep moving, to heal, to push himself and to concentrate on the financial rewards of leaving and the emotional rewards of staying single.

But he wanted more.

He left his hotel Saturday morning, more because he was restless than because he had somewhere he needed to be. A little boy from Guatemala with a malformed face had had his last surgery the previous day and would probably be cleared to go home at the end of next week. Kalinda was getting ready for her next surgery, but in the meantime was happy and healing.

Everyone he treated, the burn victims, those in accidents and those simply born with differences, were managed, fixed or in the process of getting back to normal. He had nothing to do.

He walked toward the center of town, not surprised to find the area by the park set up for yet another festival. Crowds filled the sidewalk and spilled into the closed streets. The smell of barbecue and caramel corn filled the air.

From what he could tell, Fool's Gold had festivals nearly weekly in the summer. Someone had told him about the Fall Festival, which was before the Halloween Festival but after the End of Summer Festival.

He'd been told he couldn't miss the Saturday Day of Giving in December, and that the Live Nativity was always fun because the animals were real and last year one of the goats had eaten Mary's gloves and then thrown up over everyone.

As he wove through tourists, he imagined the mountains covered with snow and then couldn't help picturing Montana's face softened by the glow of candles.

He paused to buy a hot dog from a vendor and overheard two women talking about the new construction project.

"It's going to be huge," one was saying. "A big, fancy hotel and casino. Shops, too."

"I heard there might be an outlet mall. I'd love that."

"My Frank is applying with Janack Construction. We've heard they're a good company to work for."

"That's what Julia told me when I was getting my hair done. That'll be a boost to the economy."

He eavesdropped as he ate, then finished his soda and dropped the can into a blue recycling bin. He was about to head back to the hotel when he heard a whisper of sound. The faintest of laughters, but unmistakable, even in the crowd.

He turned slowly, searching for the source. Then he saw her. Montana was with her sister Dakota. While Dakota sat on a bench, smiling, Montana held her niece in her arms, laughing as she spun her round and round.

The baby grinned and waved her arms, obviously delighted. The sun touched Montana's face, making her more beautiful than usual.

Simon stood rooted in place, staring hungrily, a starving man within sight of a meal. He soaked in the sounds, the way she moved, the vision of her with a child.

His child, he thought fiercely. He wanted Montana holding his child. No. Their child.

Longing washed over him and stole his breath. The need to be with her, not just for a few hours or days, but always. The craving was greater than anything he'd ever known.

He turned slowly, looking at the people at the festival, the families who took their happiness for granted.

Even as he started to walk toward her, he stopped himself. He couldn't. He just couldn't. Would he really sacrifice all he was, all he had, for a fleeting dream of happiness?

While those words had worked in the past, today he rebelled against them, wanting to take on those who determined his fate. Suddenly suffocated by the crowd, he hurried back to the hotel. He needed answers, he thought grimly, and he only knew one way to get them.

Montana knew she'd put off the inevitable for long enough. It was time to confess all and take her punishment.

Finding Mayor Marsha was relatively easy. She was at the festival with Charity and her new great-granddaughter. Montana admired the baby and then asked Marsha if they could talk for a second.

"Of course."

The mayor led the way to a bench, her

sleeping great-granddaughter still in her arms.

When they sat down, Montana angled toward her. "I'm sorry," she began. "I failed. Simon is leaving."

"My dear girl, I'm far more concerned about you. I heard the two of you weren't together anymore. How are you?"

"I'm getting by." If one considered living with a hole the size of Utah in one's heart "getting by." "I miss him."

"You love him."

"Yeah, well, that wasn't part of the plan, was it? You asked me to help convince him to settle in Fool's Gold. Falling in love was my own fault."

"Love is rarely a bad thing. I'm sorry for my part. If I hadn't thrown you two together, none of this would have happened."

"Don't say that," Montana told her. "I'm not sorry. Simon is an amazing man. Maybe I won't get my happy ending, but I have wonderful memories of my time with him. I really liked being with him and who I was around him. He helped me see that all the choices in my life have led me to where I am. To where I belong. I'm hurting, but I'll heal."

"I know you will." The mayor smiled at her. "You come from a long line of strong women. The women of the Máa-zib tribe were warriors."

Montana laughed. "While I would love to claim them as ancestors, my family moved here. I'm not a descendant."

"True, but their strength is all around us. The trees, the leaves, the very air carries their essence. You are one of them, Montana. They are very proud of you."

The words should have frightened her. Instead she felt oddly proud and a little sniffly. "I hope so."

"I know so." Marsha smiled at her. "Now, don't worry. I'm not getting senile or getting weird. I'm speaking the truth."

Reese ran up to them. "Something's wrong with Dr. Bradley," he announced.

Montana was instantly on her feet. "What happened?" An accident? Had he been hurt?

"He's gone crazy. People saw him running back to the hotel. He was talking to himself. Then he got in his fancy car and put the top down. He drove up the mountain and he was yelling at someone, only no one was there."

"That can't be good," Marsha murmured.

Montana was already hurrying toward her house, where her car was parked. "I'll go after him," she called over her shoulder.

She had no idea what had happened, but

if Simon needed her, she would be there.

Simon drove up the winding road easily, his Mercedes convertible hugging the curves. The sun beat down on him, mocking him with light and warmth. Rain would have been better, he thought grimly. A howling wind.

It had taken a few minutes to get out of town, what with all the tourist traffic. Once he got onto the mountain road, there were a few guys on bikes and no one else.

He knew exactly where he was going — to the meadow where Montana had taken him. A quiet place, spiritual, some might say. An excellent location for the final battle.

As he navigated each turn, his mind fought conflicting ideas. Trapped or protected. Stay or escape. He'd never questioned his choices before. Had never wondered.

The groundbreaking ceremony for the new hospital was only a few weeks away. He could be a part of that, if he wanted. Determine the direction, the focus. He could develop a program that was the best in the world, bring in other specialists, make a difference on an ongoing basis.

He could still travel a few weeks a year. Go somewhere remote — heal those without hope. He wouldn't have to completely give that up. Other people would say it made sense.

He could stay here, have a home, a life. He could be a part of something and belong.

He drove higher and higher, finally pulling off onto a dirt road that led to a clearing, where he parked his car and got out. He walked through the dense trees and bushes, not sure where he was going until he broke free and was in a clearing.

He walked to the center and stared up at the sky.

"I won't do this anymore," he yelled. "I won't be held hostage. I've worked hard — harder than most. I deserve this. I deserve to be happy. You hear me? You hear me?"

His words echoed around him, followed by the sound of thrashing in the woods. He half expected to be attacked by a mountain lion or wolf, but eventually the sound faded and Simon was alone.

He closed his eyes.

He couldn't keep doing this, he thought wearily. He couldn't keep walking away. Especially not this time. Not from the town or his patients, and not from Montana.

"I won't give her up," he said, opening his eyes and raising his arms to the heavens.

He stood there waiting, knowing he would

be struck down. Perhaps by lightning, perhaps by something else.

There was only silence. The sky remained clear and blue, the air warm.

He heard more rustling and turned to see Montana breaking through the brush. He dropped his arms to his side.

"What are you doing here?" he asked.

"That's my question. You know, you're frightening the hikers. Try not to do that. We need the tourist revenue."

She crossed to him, her expression concerned. "Want to talk about it?"

"I'm not crazy."

"I have witnesses who would testify otherwise."

Her brown eyes never wavered. He read the love there, and the certainty. He thought about all she'd given him, how she trusted him, believed in him. How she didn't see the scars anymore.

He swore, then ripped off his shirt. The sun beat down on him, illuminating the ugliness that marred his chest and back. He took her hand in his and pressed it to his heart.

"This is who I am. I will never be perfect, never be like everyone else. I'm only as good as the work I do and if I lose that . . ."

She took both his hands in hers. "You're

not defined by what you do. While your work is extraordinary and a gift, it's not who you are. You will always be defined by what is inside of you. Your strength, your determination, your relentless pursuit of the best for your patients. You're a good man with a heart so big, you've been afraid that if you opened it up, even a little, you would be swallowed whole."

She smiled gently. "I have a secret to tell you. Love doesn't make you weak. It makes you strong. Stronger than you've ever imagined. You've spent your whole life in the service of others. Maybe it's time to have a little something for yourself."

Her words were like a swollen river, carrying him along and throwing him up against the rocks. He felt battered and broken, taunted by what he could never have because . . . Because . . .

He remembered his mother and the fire and his fear and the smell of his own flesh burning. He remembered the pain and seeing his face for the first time, knowing he would always be a monster. And he remembered shutting himself off then. Vowing no one would ever hurt him again.

He'd locked himself away because it was safe. He'd built his own prison and he held the key in his hands. Or perhaps in his heart.

He thought of Alistair — the pain his friend had faced — and knew Alistair would do it all again. Face it all, just for a minute in his wife's presence. That was love.

"Montana," he said, dragging her against him. "Montana, I'm sorry. I was wrong. What I said, how I treated you." He drew back so he could see her face. "I love you. I have from the first. You're the best part of me. You are the light to my dark and without you, I'm blind. I'll give you anything, if only you'll stay with me."

Tears filled her eyes. "I've only ever wanted you. I love you."

For the first time in his life, he allowed himself to believe the words, to feel them. They washed over him, healing wounds long forgotten.

"I love you," she whispered again and kissed him. "I love you, Simon."

"I love you, too." He clutched her shoulders. "I'll stay here in Fool's Gold. Is that what you want? I'll ask for a job on the hospital staff and set up a program. I'll still need to travel every now and then, but I can do most of my work here. Is that okay?"

She laughed through her tears. "Yes. It's wonderful. I'm hanging on to you and never letting go. That's going to make it hard for you to work, but you'll figure it out." She hugged him again. "I'm never letting go," she repeated.

He returned her embrace, knowing they belonged together. That he had been given a powerful and unique gift — Montana's love. As her mother had told him, he was a lucky man.

He could see what their future would be like and he knew everything before had brought him to this moment. He'd been given the chance to make the most amazing woman in the world happy. He would spend the rest of his life making sure that happened.

"You want kids, right?" he asked.

"I want your kids."

He kissed her then, putting all his heart into the moment, then picking her up and spinning her around. They both laughed, the sound echoing off the mountains and drifting across the valley.

In the hospital, down in Fool's Gold, Kalinda smiled and held Cece close. Everything was going to be just fine.

ABOUT THE AUTHOR

Susan Mallery is the *New York Times* bestselling author of over one hundred romances and women's fiction novels. Her funny and sexy family stories consistently appear on the *USA Today* bestseller list and have landed as high as #5 on the *New York Times* list. She has won many awards, including the prestigious National Reader's Choice Award. Her books have been named to the Top 10 Romance Novels lists of 2007, 2008, and 2009 by *Booklist,* a publication of the American Library Association, and she was the only author on the list all three years. Because her degree in Accounting wasn't very helpful in the writing department, Susan earned a Masters in Writing Popular Fiction. Susan makes her home in the Pacific Northwest, where she lives with her husband and toy poodle.

We hope you have enjoyed this Large Print book. Other Thorndike, Wheeler, Kennebec, and Chivers Press Large Print books are available at your library or directly from the publishers.

For information about current and upcoming titles, please call or write, without obligation, to:

Publisher
Thorndike Press
10 Water St., Suite 310
Waterville, ME 04901
Tel. (800) 223-1244

or visit our Web site at:

http://gale.cengage.com/thorndike

OR

Chivers Large Print
published by AudioGO Ltd
St James House, The Square
Lower Bristol Road
Bath BA2 3BH
England
Tel. +44(0) 800 136919
info@audiogo.co.uk
www.audiogo.co.uk

All our Large Print titles are designed for easy reading, and all our books are made to last.